THUGS ARE FOR FUN

A Novel

by
J.GAIL

Brought to you by Jazoli Publishing

J

Jazoli Publishing
P.O. Box 1316
Brookhaven PA 19015

Thugs are for Fun
First edition 2004
Jazoli Publishing

Manufactured in the United States of America

ISBN (paperback): 0-9726978-1-0
Library of Congress Number: 2004090247

To Lisa :

For
the good sistas. Stay strong and keep
your mind open.

This is real life.
It ain't no fairytale.

Part One

chapter 1
First Impressions are the Least Important

Jacy was getting ready for her date with the thug.

"Where did I put that damn belt?" she asked as she scoured her closet. "That belt would have gone perfect with this outfit." She sucked her teeth and finally just gave up looking.

Jacy took a look at herself again in the mirror. Her date was with Rich, a construction worker—or so he said—that she met at Flow, one of the hottest clubs in Philly. She was dressed in a sharp new bright white princess blouse with slight bell sleeves, a pair of tight fitting light blue parasuco jeans and matching white stiletto-heeled sandals. Jacy digged designer clothes, but she didn't sweat them too hard. To her, most of the time no-name brand clothes looked ten times better than the big designers and cost ten times less. With the exception of shoes and purses, Jacy left the designer names to the millionaires. Besides, she thought, why would she want to be some filthy rich designer's billboard, displaying *their* name across her chest all the time for free?

Her phone rang just as she was about to apply mascara to her other eye. She finished her eye and then strutted over to her cellphone, picking it up on the fourth ring.

"Hello?"

"Sup, it's Rich. I'm about to go down to the restaurant right now. I'll be there in like… ten minutes, aiight?"

"Alright, I'll see you there then."

"How far you live from City Line? You sure you don't want me to come pick you up?"

"Yea I'm sure. I'm only 15 or 20 minutes away from the restaurant. I'll probably get there a little bit after you so just sit tight."

Jacy had learned her lesson about letting men she just met know where she lived on the first date. They all tried to make themselves out to be such decent guys who would *never* in their life stalk a woman. "Why would I need to?" is what they said, as if they had it going on too much to be bothered with stalking someone. Lies. Jacy had come across her share of crazy, needy men who seemed to be cool enough at first but then showed their true colors in the end. Despite what men said about women being clingy, some of them were overly pressed themselves.

"Alright, so I'll see you in 20 minutes then," he said.

"Cool, see you then," Jacy hung up the phone and went back to the bathroom mirror to take one more good look.

Jacilyn Thomas was 23 years old, and stood at 5'5, 135 lbs. She had a rich chocolate complexion and straight dark brown hair reaching her mid back. She was not fat, but definitely not skinny. She was small in stature, but thick, and kept herself toned by lifting weights and running on the treadmill in the gym down the street from her small apartment in Philly occasionally. Her B-cups were proportionate to her body size, but her behind was large for a woman her size, inherited from a long line of well shaped African women. Jacy was happy with her body and never watched her weight or complained and starved herself when she gained. In fact she welcomed the extra pounds, just as long as she could keep her stomach as flat as it had always been. She admired women who were even thicker than her and still managed to keep their bodies looking tight and fit.

After about ten more minutes of primping in the bathroom mirror she went back into her bedroom and took one more look in her closet for the belt, but didn't look long because she thought to herself that it would probably be too much for that outfit at a restaurant and the movies anyway. She patted Muffy, her big fluffy cat, on the head as she purred loudly.

"You be a good girl OK?" she told Muffy and finally grabbed her denim Gucci bag and walked out the door.

The drive to Friday's was smooth since it was after 8 o' clock and the rush hour traffic on Route 76 and City line was long gone. Jacy searched for about ten minutes for a parking spot in the eternally packed Friday's and finally pulled into one close to the office building at the back of the lot. She strutted to the entrance of Friday's and walked in, already becoming annoyed at the crowd of people there. She immediately recognized Rich sitting at the bar wearing a throwback jersey and a fresh new pair of butter-colored tims. He was brown skinned with a low cut and perfect teeth. He wasn't gorgeous, but he was attractive in his own way. He was definitely a thug.

"Hey, what's up!" she said over the background commotion, walking over to him smiling.

"Hey girl, sup wit you?" Rich said grinning wide, looking her up and down with a lustful stare along with three other guys at the bar while their dates stared at her with unadulterated hate written in their expressions.

"I'm sorry it took me so long, I couldn't find a parking space." Over 40 minutes had passed since their earlier conversation. "So how are you?"

"I'm aiight," he answered, still slightly mesmerized by what he saw sitting beside him. *Damn! This girl is fine*, he thought trying to stay composed as he listened to her comment about how Friday's on City Line was always packed tight, even on the weekdays. He licked his lips as she continued talking. He hadn't noticed how smooth and flawless her brown skin was when they met in the club. The white blouse she was wearing contrasted perfectly with her complexion—she looked like a black angel.

"So what do you do other than construction Rich?" she inquired with an emphasis on the word 'construction.'

But Jacy knew what was up. Brothers like him used generic professions as a front to females for what they were *really* doing for money. Barber, construction, mechanic. But she really couldn't blame them because as far as she was concerned, a lot of women and people in general just didn't know how to keep their mouths shut. The people she knew were always gossiping, bragging to their friends and giving out crucial information over the phone without conscience. Jacy on the other hand was a very private person.

She didn't advocate what went on in the drug game, but in a world where black men like Rich were kept from making decent money any other way, she understood that they were making a living with the limited skills and opportunities they possessed. Of course people might say that was just an excuse, but she thought that those same people should step in a brother like Rich's shoes for a change. From the very beginning. From the hospital to a hovel of a home. Then on to elementary school in the ghetto where kids like him couldn't bring their books home to study. Then to job interviews where they required a degree. They would quickly learn that there are only two real hopes for escape—drugs and music. Jacy learned as a young child listening to her relatives talk, that people loved to judge; especially when they had their own skeletons river-dancing in the closet. Having her own bones to hide, she promised herself she wouldn't dare judge another's life choices.

"Aaah I do a little bit of this, little of that. I try to stay as busy as possible," he said avoiding eye contact, motioning to the bartender.

When the bartender finally came over Jacy ordered an apple martini and Rich got another Corona. They sat, drank and talked until their table was finally ready.

As they slid into the booth Rich concentrated his line of vision on the cross resting above Jacy's cleavage. He definitely wasn't a church going man, but he did need a girl in his life with a little religion.

"You go to church?" he finally asked.

Jacy concentrated on him for a minute. "Every other week or so. I found a nice church in West Philly."

"Oh yea, that's good. Real good," Rich thought for a while about if he had ever even dated a woman that got up and went to church on Sunday morning.

The rest of the night went by well, conversation flowed and the food was tasty. When the check came Rich pulled out a fat stack of bills confirming Jacy's earlier suspicions.

Afterwards, they went to the movies to see a new flick with John Leguizamo in it. Nothing that impressed Jacy, just another wannabe Scarface movie about a Puerto Rican drug triangle in the Bronx. Rich slept through 80 percent of the movie.

After leaving the movie theater, Jacy and Rich hugged to say goodbye. Jacy gave Rich a peck on the cheek, though he wanted more, and then they finally parted ways. Rich smirked and watched as Jacy walked to her car before swinging his body to the left and heading for his.

* * * * *

Jacy enjoyed the date but was only mildy interested, as usual. She liked Rich but could already see that even if they did get together it wouldn't last. Thugs were only short term—they were just good for a little fun as far as Jacy was concerned. She had been there many times before. She quickly got bored of thug types and moved on. Her idea of a real prize was a tall, good looking brown skinned professional man that wore tailored suits to work. Smelling like expensive cologne. Switching effortlessly into professional speak as if it were his first language. Masterful at his chosen skill.

She snapped out of her little daydream as the light turned green and she followed the road up to the expressway. As she was getting off her exit her cellphone rang. She heaved a long deep sigh as she read the caller ID. It was Terrell. Again.

Jacy had met Terrell that past December at a mutual friends get together at a local bar in Philly. They hit it off and went out a few times before getting semi-serious. Jacy liked him because there was something about him that held her interest. He was charismatic, confident and kept her laughing, but she still wasn't so sure she wanted to be in a committed relationship with him. Plus, while Terrell seemed to be slightly cultured and intelligent, he was still a straight up thug. He didn't seem to have much of a goal in life besides running the streets, he was always doing dumb things that irked Jacy's nerves, and he hardly ever kept his promises to her. While Jacy was thinking short-term, Terrell on the other hand was actually thinking "marriage." At 26 he was feeling the pressure from his peers who were getting married and having children all around him and thought that Jacy would make a perfect wife. Their diverting opinions about the relationship, and Terrell's 'niggafied' ways, as Jacy called it, ultimately led Jacy to break it off, only a couple of months prior.

"Yea Terrell," Jacy spoke into the phone.

"What's up baby what you doin'?" Terrell said sounding amped like he had just gotten off a roller coaster.

"I'm on my way home. What do you want?"

"Awww come on. Why it always gotta be like that Jacy."

"Like what?" Jacy asked impatiently.

"I need to see you."

"For what?"

"I wanted to give you something."

"Mail it to me." This was Jacy's standard answer when Terrell claimed to have something for her. She knew it couldn't be too important.

"I ain't mailing you shit. Smart ass. I want to *see* you and give it to you in person."

"Terrell I don't have time for no games tonight alright? You're always trying to make up an excuse to see me. It's tired, I swear you *stay* on that dumb shit," Jacy fumed.

"Dammit Jacy. Why you got to be so fucking mean to me all the time? I'm over here trying to make this thing work and you just want to be nasty all the damn time. You would think you'd at least miss me or something."

"Well maybe if you gave me a chance to miss you Terrell!" Jacy was sensing that Terrell was about to go off on a tangent again. She had no intention of ever getting back with him. Cruelty was the only way to get through to him, and even then he usually didn't respond. She sighed. "We are not *ever* getting back together like that again ok? Get it out of your mind. Seriously. It's OVER Terrell. And I'm seeing someone else now," Jacy told a little white lie. She was only dating but not really seeing anyone seriously. She just wanted to say whatever to get Terrell off her back for good.

"Who??" Terrell asked like a crazed man.

"None of your damned business. Now I gotta go alright??" Jacy said waiting in vain for him to say OK, or to just hang up.

"No it ain't alright. Don't tell me you been lettin' some other nigga hit Jacy?" Terrell said sounding hurt as if he were about to cry or flip out.

"Didn't I just say that's none of your business! Geez! Look, Imma talk to you some other time Terrell," Jacy said as she clicked the 'end' button on her phone.

Terrell called three more times before finally giving up and leaving a message. Jacy knew she was being mean to him but sometimes *that's how you gotta be to get a man off your back*, she thought. She had always talked to Terrell however she pleased, throughout their entire relationship. And he just took it. As hard and as well respected he was in the streets, Jacy had Terrell on edge behind closed doors.

She even thought that Terrell actually *liked* being verbally abused. He would smile as if he was enjoying his time being cursed out after doing something dumb.

Terrell was raised by a mother who was regularly lashing out on him and telling him he wouldn't amount to anything. He was always doing stupid things as a child to provoke his mother. It was no wonder why he probably thought the situation with himself and Jacy was normal. Jacy didn't understand why he acted so stupid sometimes, but she felt bad for him and even comforted him at times when he'd come over her apartment upset about something his mother said to break his spirit. Jacy would encourage him to do more with his life and told him how he had so much potential, which was part of the reason why Terrell loved Jacy so much. He just couldn't get past his vices though, he was ghetto born and raised; he couldn't help it.

Jacy pulled into her apartment building and walked up to her apartment. She thought about watching some late night TV, but she didn't want to take the chance of falling asleep on the couch. It was after 12 midnight, so she decided to just get ready for bed. She wrapped up her hair in a scarf, washed up, said a quick prayer for sweet dreams and jumped underneath her pink cotton sheets.

THE NEXT morning at work Jacy sat at her desk, completely fed up with her job. Her boss had just called her into the office to scold her for coming in ten minutes late.

"I can't believe this place, that woman is absolutely ridiculous," she thought out loud of her boss, throwing her pen on the desk. Despite being only 23, Jacy had been at her company for over seven years, starting out as a copy girl working part time while in high school in New Jersey, then becoming an intern, while in college at Seaton Hall, for the Assistant Director of Corporate Communications, and finally getting hired full time as a Communications Analyst at the firm's Philadelphia office. After all that time they were still giving her a hard time over little things, such as coming in a few minutes late.

"I hate this place," she mumbled to herself as she got up to get a cup of coffee from the break room. On her way to the large break room she passed Patricia, Robin, and Felix, the resident gay guy at the office, gossiping as usual at Patricia's cubicle. Jacy just shook her head and continued on to her destination. On her way back she heard her name mentioned in their conversation, so she moved to the side and listened to what they were saying.

"…she probably thinks she is just IT, just because she got an 'analyst' position. Big fucking deal that don't mean nothing. I could even do that job." That was Patricia. She and pretty much all of the black women at Jacy's job were secretaries.

"You know? Ms. Thing, walking around here trying to be all cute and shit. I bet she slept with the director to get that job," Felix said in his gay voice. Jacy could never understand why some gay men talked like that, it was as if they were trying to sound *overly* female.

"Well you know I talked to her a few times, and she seems like a pretty cool person," Robin said in Jacy's defense. Jacy thought back to the time she had stayed late with Robin to help her fix the printer so that Robin could print out a color version of her report for night school. Everyone else, even her so-called gossiping buddies, had left her high and dry since it was after 5pm.

"Well I don't think so, she seem like a straight up bitch to me," Felix answered rolling his eyes. "Patty did you ever find out who that dude was that came up to the office looking for her that day?"

Patty was the office busy body. She knew everything and everybody—even the higher ups at the firm. She was notorious for smiling up in people's faces and then dishing the dirt about them when they left. Most of the black people and a few whites at Jacy's job were complete gossips who feened for information about other people's lives since they didn't have ones of their own. And Patricia was their pusher.

"Oh yea! I forgot to tell you. Girl, he works at the post office down the street. I saw him in there the other day and I was like 'I knew I recognized that guy from somewhere.' Poor guy, looking all desperate coming up here with flowers looking for Jacy and she wasn't even trying to be bothered. I think she probably did some foul shit to him and it's too bad because he seemed like a pretty nice guy."

She couldn't be further from the truth, Jacy thought. The guy they were talking about, Desmond, from the Post Office, was a complete lunatic. Desmond had always flirted with Jacy when she came into the post office, and one day he finally asked her out to a happy hour after work. Jacy had made the half-way drunk mistake of letting him drop her home after the happy hour since she took the train to work usually, and after that he started popping up to her house unannounced. When she told him off and said she didn't want to see him anymore, she started to see his car parked to the side of her building occasionally when she left in the morning for work, and sometimes later on at night when she went out.

One day he approached her in the parking lot of her building and asked why she didn't call or answer his messages anymore. She screamed at him to leave her alone and stop stalking her before power-walking to her car. That was the day he came up to the office looking for her and Jacy was conveniently absent. After that surprise visit she told the security guards in her building to not let him up to see her ever again, and she hadn't heard from him since. She had since moved to a new apartment building to start anew. She also went to a different post office, in spite of the fact that it was a longer walk from her job.

"Damn you see? There ain't nothin' nice about that girl Robin. She probably didn't want to see him when she found out he work at the post office," he snickered with Patty.

Jacy shook her head and kept walking on to her desk.

AS THE El train hit the daylight again after being under the tunnel, Jacy's cellphone signal came back and only a few seconds later her cell phone rang. The number came up unavailable. Debating on whether she should pick it up or not, she reluctantly clicked the 'talk' button.

"Hello?"

"Why'd you bang on me like that last night? I swear you be treating me like I ain't shit!"

Damn, Jacy thought sighing, *I knew I should have just let this shit ring.*

"Jacy we need to talk," he continued, "I know I've done some dumb shit in the past, but I ain't never cheat on you or laid a hand on you. That's gotta count for somethin' right? I promise you, I'll do whatever it takes for us to be together and to get along," Terrell said trying to sound sincere.

"Okay then, how about this. What did you have to give me last night?" Jacy asked, setting him up.

"Wha...?"

"You know, you said you have something to give me. I'm on the El right now, three stops from your house. I'll come pick it up."

"Huh, oh, ummm. That's at my mama's house, I'll have to get that for you tomorrow. But I still want you to come by—"

"Negro please!" Jacy said laughing. "You never had nothing for me, so stop lying. Ooo. You are always doing that. But I bet you've *changed* right?" she asked sarcastically.

"Naw baby listen. I'm telling you—"

"Whatever." Jacy laughed again and then flipped down her phone. It was always little things like that that bothered the hell out of her about Terrell. He would say something one day, and then play dumb like he never said it the next, as if it didn't matter at all that he was lying from the beginning. Jacy didn't feel that she could really trust Terrell. Jacy understood the fact that if someone is your ex, there's a good reason why they are your ex.

Jacy got off the train and passed through the West Philly hood to get to her parked car. Where she got off wasn't far from where they called "the bottom," The bottom was exactly that—the worst *kinda* hood. You didn't want to be caught there after the sun set unless you knew somebody there who was well known on the block. Philly was big on 'hoods'—everybody knew everybody in each hood, and if they didn't know you then you'd better rethink your plans to visit.

"Ay yo shorti!" some guy with a thick beard yelled out from his permanent spot on the opposite corner as she passed. Jacy just kept walking involved in her own thoughts. "Fuck you then bitch." the guy said just as loud. Jacy just nodded her head, glad she hadn't bothered with him in the first place.

Jacy drove home in complete silence thinking about her life and career. What she really wanted to do was to own her own real estate business. But she had little connections in the field, didn't know any good carpenters that could fix up houses for cheap, and had a hard time finding the time to concentrate or take the actual steps towards her goal. She didn't know how much longer she could postpone her dream, and only hoped that it wouldn't leave her behind.

When she arrived home Jacy fed Muffy, then plopped in front of the television and started channel surfing. While getting into the episode of *Seinfeld* where George fights the bubble boy, her cell phone rang. It was Rich from last night.

"Sup girl. What you doin'," he asked over background noise from his car stereo.

"Nothin', just watching TV," Jacy said giggling as the townspeople ambushed George for sending the bubble boy to the hospital.

"I wanna take you for a ride."

"Where?"

"Just around, and to run some errands. We can get a bite to eat a little later."

"Uh…" Jacy hesitated, thinking about whether she felt like riding through the hood today and meeting his friends, which was obviously what he meant. But she kinda liked Rich and was curious to see him in action around his people. Plus she was hungry. "…Yea I guess. I can go for some Houlihan's pasta later ok?"

"Aiight. Imma come pick you up?"

"Naw let me change real quick and meet you at 56th and Chestnut. I'll park my car up there and jump in with you, okay?"

"How come you don't want me to know where you live?" Rich inquired.

"Cuz I don't know you very well." Jacy said bluntly.

"Well, I ain't crazy or nothin'," he said getting a little defensive. "What you think I'm gonna stalk you or somethin'? I ain't got no time for all that."

I bet, Jacy thought.

"So I'll see you in about 30-40 minutes, ok?" Jacy said out loud.

"Aiight."

WHEN SHE pulled up almost an hour later, Rich was sitting in his car, a rust colored '92 Pontiac Bonneville, talking on his cellphone. When he saw Jacy's car he ended the conversation, leaned back in his seat and just stared at her fixedly as she got out the car and strutted over to the passenger side of his car.

"Damn," he said, pulling his lips into his mouth, "I might have to give up my rules on this jawn, she got that model walk and everything." Lost in his thoughts Rich forgot to click the locks on the door for her to get in.

When he finally did, Jacy stepped in smelling like fresh flowers, filling his car with her sweet scent. Even though she was dressed casual in a pair of tight fitting jeans and a v-necked pink blouse, she still looked amazing. He continued staring at her not saying a word while Jacy started to fidget in her seat wondering what the hell he was thinking about. She finally broke the silence.

"So where are we about to go?" she asked. Rich didn't answer her right away, just looked her over.

"I gotta go see my man for a minute, then run some quick errands. After that we'll hit Houlihan's like you said aiight?" he said finally breaking his stare and turning the ignition. The music immediately started blasting Freeway through the speakers.

"Alright," Jacy answered. She admired the interior of the car that looked pretty plain and boring from the outside. It was a squatter. It was unimpressive on the outside, but nice and comfortable inside. The car was also very powerful and its pick up speed surprised her. He obviously used his money to hook the car up on the inside, while keeping the exterior looking basic yet clean instead of flashy, to avoid drawing unneeded attention to himself. Good, Jacy thought, he's smart.

They drove up a few blocks and finally made a right turn on a small back street lined with row houses. Kids that couldn't have been more than seven or eight years old played in the street recklessly, screaming and carrying on while grown folks sat on the porch talking or stood by the sidewalk waiting for something, anything to happen.

Rich swerved his car in front of a line of red brick rowhouses and jumped out, his tims pounding the pavement leading to his boy's house. Jacy still sat gripping the side door. Rich had been driving like a maniac.

"Timbo!!" he yelled mid-jog.

His boy came to the door dressed in a wife beater and some shorts and they disappeared into the house.

Rich and Timbo came out about ten minutes later laughing. Timbo came around to Jacy's side of the car and opened the door. He looked Jacy from head to toe. *Damn he's bold,* Jacy thought, *with his ugly ass self.* She sat still staring up at him waiting for him to say something.

"So you Jacy huh? Damn Roo wasn't playin' when he said yo ass fine! Shit!"

Jacy couldn't help laughing.

"Yo, put your eyes back into your head nigga." Rich joked, pushing Timbo aside. He reached his hand out to Jacy. "Come on out baby, I want you to meet some people."

Jacy grabbed his hand and stepped out in her baby pink blouse looking completely out of place on that worn down block which of course caused all the people lining the streets and sitting on the porches to turn and look, being nosey. She watched as Timbo shut the car door and then followed Rich around to the house. Timbo was walking behind her of course. She could feel him staring hard at her ass. The door was wide open so they just walked right in.

There was always something about Jacy that made people stop and take note. She had a 'presence.' Some people could stand in a room for over two hours and nobody would even know that they were there, because they had no presence. But not Jacy. When she stepped into a room she had the uncanny ability to win the attention of everyone in it.

They walked into the chilling area near the back of the house where there were about ten brothas and sistas sitting chilling, drinking and watching the Sixers playoff game on TV. They quieted down and all eyes were on Jacy.

"Ya'll meet my girl Jacy," Rich announced. Your girl? Dang, I just went out with you once, Jacy thought. "Jacy these some of my peoples: Don, Petey Pete, Box, Coot, Jimmy, T-dog, Trim…" he said running off their names. Jacy followed his finger with her eyes in the dim light as everybody said 'what's up.'

"What's up ya'll," Jacy said with a smile and a light wave in the air.

"What's the score," Rich wanted to know. One of the girls sitting on the couch got up as if by habit and Rich pulled Jacy over to the spot sitting her on his lap. Jacy sat down not thinking much of it. Everyone else went back to watching the game.

"75-70 my nigga. The Sixers playin' real sloppy right now."

"My nigga DC!!" a walnut colored brotha jumped up and screamed as Derrick Coleman slammed the ball in the hoop while everybody else "ohhhhed" in approval.

"It's about time—he been missing all his damn jump shots," a short coal black brotha said from his chair in the corner after settling down.

"Naw he just was having a bad run earlier, he be aiight."

"Yo that nigga Snow got four fouls already what the hell he doin'???" an annoyed rail thin light skinned brotha they called Trim yelled from the couch as the referee blew his whistle on Eric Snow.

"He betta get wit it and start hittin' those threes if they gonna win this shit, *early*!" another dark skinned brotha growled, never taking his eyes from the screen.

Just then Terrell busted in the front door with a light skinned girl who had a bad weave complete with pink tips running close behind, trying to catch the door before it closed. The girl had on a matching hot pink belt and shoes with skin tight jeans molded to her figure.

"Damn Terrell!" she said in her high pitched 'philly girl' voice nearly falling back outside from the door slamming back on her hands.

"What's the score!" Terrell yelled running into the living room with his eyes glued to the screen. He bent down with his hand on the top of the TV, still not even noticing that Jacy was in the room.

Oh Shit! Jacy thought, immediately feeling awkward at what would inevitably happen. Terrell was still staring at the screen when Iverson got fouled.

"76-72 Detroit up," the thin light skinned guy said leaning into the screen.

"What quarter—" Terrell said finally leaning back up quickly and turning towards the crowd. He froze when he saw Jacy sitting on Rich's lap.

Terrell was definitely not a bad looking brotha. At 6'3 he towered over most men in Philly, most of whom usually stood at about 5'10. He was a shade darker than caramel with big soup cooler lips that were always wet and muscles popping out from everywhere under his black wife beater.

"What the? Jacy what the hell you doin' on this nigga lap!" he finally said.

"Terrell don't even start," Jacy said turning her head and getting embarrassed as everyone turned to look. You could have heard a dime drop if the game hadn't been blasting on the TV.

"How you know my girl Rich?" Terrell said clenching his fists and giving Rich the look of death.

"Yo' girl? I thought *that* was your girl standing right over there nigga?" Rich said pointing over to the light skinned girl who was standing to the side with all her weight on one foot and her arms crossed. She didn't look happy, but still didn't say anything.

"Could ya'll take this shit outside or something I'm trying to watch the game!" Trim yelled out. His face was scrunched up in disgust. He seemed to always be annoyed.

"Shut the hell up man." Terrell yelled at Trim, never looking in his direction. Trim just sucked his teeth and leaned back, trying his best to focus on the game. "Jacy what the fuck?" Terrell said ignoring Rich's prior question and looking hurt.

"Terrell why can't you just let shit go?" Jacy said standing up, thoroughly embarrassed at having her business aired in a room full of people she didn't even know.

"What happen to Keisha ass?" Terrell questioned Rich hoping he had struck a chord.

"Me and Keisha done—been done dude," Rich said standing up too, becoming increasingly upset.

"Oh yea? And what about that jawn you was fuckin' with—"

"Rich can we go get something to eat now, I haven't eaten since lunchtime," Jacy interrupted grabbing Rich's throwback, trying to stop something before it had a chance to start. Terrell had some nerve—she had only dated him for a couple months but it was never officially serious between them. Why was he always acting like this? Jacy thought. Rich hesitated for a moment, looking dead into Terrell's eyes. He sucked something out of his back teeth and continued eyeing Terrell.

"Rich, come on. This is nothing, really." Jacy stepped in front of Rich to break the stare-down. Her tone was reassuring. Rich looked at her soft brown eyes, which were opened wide and pleading. He looked back up at Terrell.

"Okay baby, we gone. Ya'll stay up," he finally said grabbing Jacy's hand and giving several people pounds. If Terrell had been drinking water, steam would have been coming out of his ears. "Bo Imma get up wit you later doggie," Rich said walking out with Jacy in front of him. Terrell was speechless.

"Aiight then man, don't forget what we talked about," Timbo answered him, then focused back on the game.

Rich and Jacy had made their way outside when they heard three loud gunshots down the block not far behind Rich's car and a woman's blood curdling scream.

"Get in," Rich said nearly snatching Jacy's arm off throwing her in the driver's seat of the car. He glanced back at what had happened for a minute before he finally jumped in himself, pushing her to the passenger's side. Two men were running full speed down the block and turned a corner disappearing out of view. A woman, presumably the one who was screaming, ran down her steps to a man's lifeless body on the sidewalk. Rich's boy Timbo and a few others appeared at the door to make sure that Rich was alright as he pulled off down the block. He pulled an extra cell phone, not his usual Motorola, from under his seat and told Jacy to call for an ambulance. Some of the people on the street had taken cover but most were still standing around outside being nosey looking at where the shots came from.

"Don't tell them that you saw who did the shooting, just tell them the location and hang up aiight?" Rich said, navigating through the narrow streets. Jacy, shaking a little, did as she was told.

"Oh my God!" Jacy said with her heart beating through her chest as she finally clicked off the phone and dropped it. She was visibly shaken by all of what had happened in such a short time.

When they finally got back out on Chestnut Street they made a left and headed up towards the direction of Market Street. They kept riding north in silence, still slightly in shock. Jacy had been witness to a lot of shootings since she moved to Philly, and even in her old hometown, but had never been that close to the actual shooting. That was just *too* close.

"Do you think he'll be alright?" she said turning her head to look at Rich.

"Naw, that nigga got hit at least twice close range. He's done. It was probably those niggas from down 60th they had it out for that nigga for a minute..." he said trailing off. He had his left hand on his chin in deep thought.

They kept driving until they reached another red brick rowhouse on a corner.

"Stay here," he said hopping out again, and making his way around to the back of the house through a small alleyway.

Jacy sighed and pulled out a piece of Dentyne Ice to chew on. She looked out the window after him until he was out of sight.

She was more than used to this routine, but she was starting to grow tired of it quickly. Why couldn't she just meet a nice regular brother somewhere? Someone who wasn't down with running the streets all the damn time? Someone she didn't have to dodge bullets with? She already knew the answer though. Look at where she lived. Thug city—Philadelphia, USA. The vast majority of people in Philly were living below the poverty line and in misery. Crime flourished. Therefore her choices of types of men in the city were slim. Most of the professional brothas in Philly lived far out near the main line and in Germantown, Mount Airy and Chestnut Hill or on college campuses, but she had no business to attend to out there or a reason to be in those areas. In addition, from Jacy's experience those types of guys were usually the ones that pretended as if they were too good to approach a woman. Jacy needed a man, not a bitch.

In the part of Philly where she lived you couldn't even walk down your block without encountering a rough looking brotha standing on a corner, or a chicken head riding by in her drug dealer boyfriend's rimmed out Lexus. *Maybe I should seriously start thinking about moving out of this city*, Jacy thought.

Her cellphone rang and she smiled when she saw the caller ID. It was Rachelle, her very best friend, outside of her cousin Tammy of course. Rachelle had gone to school with her in Jersey and coincidentally got a job in Philly only two months before Jacy was transferred there herself. Rachelle and Jacy hung tight like sisters and could sit around for hours talking about whatever was going on in their lives.

"Hey girl!" Jacy said happily into the phone.

"What's up chick?? Whatchyou doin'."

"Nothing really, just sittin' outside this house."

"Oh yea, which?"

"This dude I've been seeing named Rich. I just came back from his boys' house and now I'm sitting out at somebody else's house waiting. He'd better hurry up. I tell you Chelle I don't think it's worth all this drama, for real," Jacy said getting angry as she realized 15 minutes had passed and she was still waiting.

"Damn girl. Is he at least cute?"

"In his own way I guess. He's got a little bit of a swagger about him—he seems to have the most pull out of his crew. And he most definitely has dough."

"Alright then girl just don't make him cry like you did that nigga Terrell," she said and then broke out laughing.

"Oh girl. You will never believe it. I'm at Rich's boys' house and why Terrell's black ass come through the door!"

"NO!"

"Yes! He was pissed! You should have seen the look on his face. I wanted to sink into the floor I was so embarrassed—in front of all those people. Nothing really popped off but they looked like they wanted to throw blows!"

"Oh lawd girl. You better be careful about that situation. Did you tell him you used to date Terrell?"

"No, but he knows now. Do you know I just went out for a first date with Rich yesterday and he's already talking about 'I'm his girl?' I swear these brothas get so damned possessive."

"Well you know that's how that goes. Don't want nobody else dipping in their jelly."

"I guess," Jacy said laughing. "And then I come outside with Rich and have to dodge bullets! Somebody just got shot on his block. Not even 15 minutes ago."

"What??"

"Yup."

"Damn girl, are you OK?"

"Yea, *I'm* fine. I feel bad for his mother, sister or his girl. Whoever that was. She was outside when he got shot," Jacy looked out the car window at an old man crossing the street. "We called an ambulance, so maybe he'll make it. I don't know. I hope so."

"Me too."

"So what's been up with you? I haven't seen you in a few days."

"Yea I know that's why I was calling to see what you were up to tonight."

"Why what's going on?"

"Well, Chemistry is supposed to be jumping tonight. They having a special 'Thursday Night Freestyle' bash. They're playing reggae, soca, hip hop, old school and plenty of down south hits. I think that rapper, um, what's his name. Konfidential might be performing live too. At least it said so on the flyer. Someone passed me his CD a while back, I like a couple of his songs."

"Oh for real? Now you know I'm down. We're going to eat in a little while, but after that I'll just tell Rich I have other plans."

"Alright then girl, just give me a call when you're getting ready."

"Okay, talk to you later."

Jacy hung up and literally two seconds later Terrell's number was popping up on her cell.

"Lawd," she said outloud to herself. "Let me get this over with."

"What!" she said into the phone.

"Hell no. Don't get no fucking attitude with me! That's the nigga you seein' now huh??"

"Terrell not that it's any of your business, but yea that's who I'm seeing. You happy now? Why does it matter so much to you anyway? We broke up almost three months ago!"

"I don't give a fuck. You ain't supposed to be fucking with niggas I *know*. Dammit Jacy why of all people you gotta be dating my cousin's best boy??"

Damn, Jacy thought. "How the hell was I supposed to know Rich is your cousin's best friend. I'm not psychic. It's not like he's *your* friend, ya'll are just associates from what you just told me, so you need to stop trippin."

"Tripping? No you gonna stop tripping acting like—"

"Terrell?" she said with her finger resting on the 'end' button while the phone was still to her ear.

"What?"

"Terrell, I'm really not in the mood for this babe. I just saw that guy get shot and killed and I'm not feeling this frivolous conversation right now," she said making an excuse to get off the phone.

He paused and thought. "Alright but I do want to talk to you about this shit later."

"Terrell there's really nothing more to talk about on this. I'm dating Rich, we're cool, it's nothing serious, you can't say or do anything to change that, and... that's all there is to it alright? Goodbye." she said firmly, then clicked off the phone before he could get in another word.

It had been a full 30 minutes since Rich went in the house.

"What the hell does he think I like to spend my day waiting in people's cars?" Jacy said outloud to herself, contemplating how far the walk would be to her car.

Just then the door flung open and Rich came out with a serious look on his face, as if he was crunching numbers in his head or something.

"What took you so long?" Jacy asked as he slid into his seat.

"What? I had some shit to take care of," Rich answered turning the ignition, hardly paying attention to her question.

"Don't have me sittin' in your car for that long again," Jacy said calmly then looked out the window again as he pulled off. Rich looked over at her in amazement as he drove.

"Girl you better chill the fuck out. I told you I had business to take care of. Shit!"

"Nigga?" she said turning to look at him like he had lost his mind. "I will hop out this car and *walk* to 56th street, do you really think I *give* a fuck!?"

"Fine then. Do that. I don't have no time for this kinda bullshit," he said calling her bluff. He pulled the car over, leaned back in his seat and rested his wrist on the wheel staring straight ahead. Jacy promptly grabbed her purse and unlatched the door getting out. Rich whipped his neck in her direction.

"Ma, ma, ma. Calm down," He said in a deep stern voice, quickly reaching over and pulling her back into the car by her arm. He gave her a crooked smile. "I'm sorry alright! I didn't expect that shit to take that long. I'll make it up to—"

"Look! Rich. I don't have time for this type of shit either. I told your ass I was hungry two hours ago and you still gonna have me riding around waiting in your car two hours later? Then gonna get an attitude with *me*? I coulda been home eating a TV dinner for all this shit. Don't disrespect my time like that again." Jacy said moving her head violently. Who the hell did he think he was? she wondered.

"Alright mami, damn, I gotchu. Just sit back and chill we headed to Houlihans right now aiight?" he said looking at her with his full attention and both his eyebrows raised. He was unnerved by the fact that she was actually about to walk over 15 blocks through 'the bottom' to get to her car in the darkness at almost 9'oclock at night. *This chick gully*, he thought. For some reason he found her very appealing at that moment.

"Naw, I don't even think I feel like going to Houlihans no more. Just take me home," she said settling back into her seat. Jacy was used to getting her way with men.

Rich paused for a couple of minutes still staring at her before saying: "Nope, we goin' to Houlihans." He turned around in his seat and pulled out towards City Line Ave.

AS THEY left the restaurant full from pasta, chicken, shrimp and wine and were headed to the car, Rich pulled Jacy close to him and wrapped his arms around her back straddling her as he leaned back against his car. He kissed her firmly on the mouth, trying to pry open her lips with his tongue. Jacy, feeling slightly tipsy from the wine and liking the forcefulness of his kiss, eventually eased her soft hands around the back of his head and kissed him back, slowly opening her mouth and letting him slip inside. She fought his tongue with her own, until he gave in, allowing his to retreat back into his mouth and giving her full control. If there was one thing Jacy knew, it was how to kiss. Teasing him, she traced his inner lips—first the top, then making her way around to the bottom never breaking the embrace. He moaned deeply as she explored the inside, finally playing with the tip of his tongue and allowing him to again push back into her mouth. She sucked on it, as if she was sucking on a lollipop, until she felt his now hard manhood rubbing against her thigh. She finally pulled back from the kiss, giving him one last peck on the lips before attempting to break free from his hold. She laughed a little and then looked off towards the street behind them. To her, it was a pretty good kiss.

Rich just held onto her tighter, eyes still closed. He felt as if he had just experienced the tip of heaven. Despite his extreme attraction to Jacy, Rich was trying hard to play it off as if she was just another girl he was seeing. But she wasn't. He had only been with two types of women: hoodrats who opened their legs and asked for money, and weak easily manipulated women who were curious about dating a 'thug.' Rich's personal motto when it came to women was 'Bitches ain't shit' and he and his boys would regularly laugh and joke about the last 'freak' they had been with in shameless detail. But Jacy, she was different, he could tell off the bat from the moment he met her at Club Flow. She was wearing an outfit that was sexy and showed off her shape, but covered her body leaving plenty to the imagination. She had a bright white smile that he could see clearly in the darkness of the club. He approached her on the dance floor face-to-face, looking her straight in the eyes and grabbing her by her hips. She just flashed that gorgeous smile and started dancing to the song that was on. She swayed with him for one more song after that and then turned around to tell him politely, "It was nice dancing with you." He pulled her back before she could walk away and asked her if she wanted a drink? Could he get her number? She smiled and said maybe later, walking away. Rich just could not get the image of her smile and eyes out of his mind the whole night. He kept a close eye on her the rest of the night getting stingingly jealous whenever she danced with someone else, even when he was dancing with someone himself. Towards the end, he finally came up to her, cellphone in hand and demanded her phone number. He was not going to let this one go. Jacy, tipsy off of Martini after Martini, just ran off her number and smiled at him one more time before leaving the club with her friend.

As he talked to her on the phone and was around her more, he began to see that his earlier hunch about her was correct. She was different. Definitely not ghetto, but not bourgie either. She wasn't naïve which he thought was very refreshing from a woman. She knew the game and the fact that he wasn't a construction worker as he originally told her when they talked on the phone, whereas most college educated women her age would have fallen for that hook line and sinker. She knew how to play her position, but still didn't accept any type of mess from him in the short time he had known her. He liked that. The hoodrats he usually dated acted hard in public but were still stupid enough to carry weight for him up from Virginia, his main connect, and allow him to smut them out on the first date, if there ever was one. He thought he had hit the jackpot with Jacy, she was a dime, smart, sexy, streetwise—the perfect wife. He would never even think of fixing his mouth to ask her to hold something for him. She was classy; a lady and deserved respect. Maybe she could even help him get out of the game and move on to some type of legit business.

"Rich?" Jacy said tugging him gently on his arms. "Rich?" she said again louder. He had been caught up in his own thoughts for a moment but still had not let go of his grip on Jacy. The wine they drank at dinner had definitely had its effect on him. He had never had wine before that night, but he had let Jacy convince him to have a couple glasses of Cabernet Sauvignon. He liked the feeling it gave him.

"Yo, let's go over my crib," he finally said loosening his hold and resting his hands on her shapely hips.

"I can't, I have something to do later," Jacy said running the palm of her hands down his chest lightly. She was thinking about the plans she had with Rachelle. She thought about what she was going to wear to the club. It was going on 10:30pm so she really had to hurry up and get changed.

"Doing what?" Rich said unable to hide the slight anger and disappointment on his face. He immediately assumed she was going to see some other guy, maybe even Terrell. *I ain't gonna be taking her out for dates then she go give another nigga the goods,* he thought, burrowing his eyebrows at her.

"I'm going out with my girl."

"Oh. Well tell her you catch up with her another time. I wanna hang wit you."

"I can't, I promised."

"What you don't wanna be wit me tonight or something? I thought we was spending time."

"We are. I'll hang out with you late another time. Besides, you're just trying to bed me," she said smiling wide, pointing her finger at him as she teased.

"Awwww girl it ain't even about that, you know," he said softening to her smile.

"Yea, OK," she said playfully rolling her eyes and smiling at him sideways.

"Listen, I want you to set aside Saturday all day. I'm gonna take you downtown to do some shopping, we'll eat and see a movie and all that, aiight?" Rich told her, not really asking.

"Umm. Alright, yea that's cool."

"You cool? You need any money to go out?"

"I'm alright. But I could be better," she answered. She didn't usually take money from guys she'd only known for a short time, because she knew what it meant. She knew what he was trying to do—lock her down before someone else could. But hell, she thought, I'm not seeing anyone else right now. Besides, she was finding herself becoming more attracted to him as time went on and thought he would be a good brotha to pass the time with, for the time being.

Rich pulled out a wad of twenties and hundreds from his pocket peeling off 4 or 5 bills and sliding it into her back pocket.

"Gimme a kiss," he said putting his arms around her back again, pulling her to him.

"Thank you sweetie," she replied giving him a peck on the lips. She looked at him for a moment, studying his features. He was actually a pretty good looking guy with his low cut hair, white teeth and slightly slitted chocolate brown eyes. He just had an edge to his look that made him look very rugged. A long scar reached from below his chin to his lower neck. He had a low cut fuzzy beard that tickled her when she hugged him and a sly sexy smile, big juicy lips that leaned toward the right side of his mouth when he was up to something.

"I need to get back to my house and change," Jacy said finally breaking free from his embrace and walking to the passenger side of the car. Rich started moving to the driver's seat.

"Aiight, why don't you call your girl and tell her you're on your way home?" he said still needing confirmation that she was in fact going out with a female.

"Yea let me do that," Jacy said pulling out her phone and getting into the car. She knew he only asked to see what her response would be. One thing about Jacy, it was a rare occasion if she ever outright lied to anyone over everyday things. She always kept it real and would only lie if it were a life or death situation. Rich quietly sighed in relief when he overheard a female voice say hello on Jacy's cellphone.

"Chelle, I'm on my way home. I'll be over there at about 11:30 alright?...No I'm about ten minutes away from home, I need to get dressed and take a shower...Alright. See you later." She clicked the end button on her phone and looked over at Rich who was faintly smiling that sly smile with his hand on his chin.

chapter 2
Real Life Drama

ALL THREE FLOORS OF THE CLUB were packed by the time Rachelle and Jacy arrived after midnight. It was only open until 2am so they had a little under 2 hours to mingle and do their thing. Rachelle was doing her thing as usual on the dance floor. She was a professional dancer who had once done an afterschool dance program at Julliard in New York City, her original home before moving to New Jersey for college. At 5'6 150 lbs, Rachelle was a beauty. She had long jet black hair, the complexion of Sanaa Lathan and a thick body to die for. She was outrageously smart, graduating with honors from Seaton Hall, Rachelle was a wonderful person, very giving and sweet—everybody loved her. Her only fault was that she was a little immature when it came to men. She was a sucker for a pretty face. It took her a while to realize when a guy she was dating was only playing with her feelings, and she was constantly getting hurt. Jacy tried to counsel her friend, and never hesitated to give her a piece of her mind when she was doing something stupid or being a fool for a man. But Jacy soon realized that sometimes the best way for a woman to learn is through experience. *How many experiences do you have to go through before you finally learn the lesson though?* Jacy would wonder to herself.

Twirling around and dropping to the floor with her arms waving in the air, Rachelle was really giving the crowd a show. She was wearing a light blue tube dress and stilleto sandals. She was dressed a little skimpy, but still managed to carry it classy. The guys were loving her, tripping over their feet to get near her to dance. She got up and finally chose one of them, whipping around to grind on his package while he held his drink high in the air.

Jacy stood to the side smiling, watching her best friend make the guy she was dancing with grimace as if he were about to come right on the dance floor. Jay Z had been blasting through the club speakers up until then, but then the DJ decided to change the pace to some old school music. Jacy moved over to the bar area and attempted to get the bartender's attention, but before she could try a second time a tall light brown skinned brother came up behind her and put his long arm up immediately getting the barkeep's attention.

"What would you like?" he said looking down at her with his brown eyes sparkling under the club lights. He was tall with short wavy hair, maybe even 6'5, and was wearing a blue button down shirt with the top button open and long flowing black slacks. He was gorgeous.

"Oh. I'll, um…I'm having a Courvoisier on the rocks. Thanks," she said thrown off balance by his presence. She had never felt nervous around a man before. He had caught her completely off guard.

He ordered her drink and his Hennessey and coke and when they came he asked the bartender the total for both drinks.

"Oh no, no I have mine," she said quickly opening her purse and pulling out a twenty from the money Rich gave her earlier to pay the bartender. He had slipped a hundred dollar bill in her pocket with the twenties so she had plenty of cash to buy her own drinks that night. Plus she felt a little guilty getting drinks from a stranger after just having seen Rich earlier.

"Suit yourself," he said smiling. "What's your name?"

"It's Jacilyn, but all of my friends call me Jacy," she said leaving a five dollar tip for the bartender. "You?"

"Kevin Trouvant. Nice to meet you. Did you come here alone Jacilyn?"

"No I'm here with my girl, she's on the dance floor over there," she said pointing to Rachelle. She liked the way he said her full name. His deep voice was commanding and confident as he spoke.

"I'm not keeping you from her am I?"

"No, not at all. So where are all your friends?" she asked walking back towards the dance floor with him.

"They're in that booth over there," he said pointing. Three brothas, two of which were wearing casual suits stared back over at them, then turned their heads to pretend like they were looking at something else when they got caught. "Don't mind them, they all were too shy to come over here and talk to you," he said smiling again.

"Oh so I guess you're the bold one?" Jacy said returning the gesture. She was slowly becoming mesmerized by the smell of his cologne. It smelled like Issey Miyake. Maybe even D&G.

"Yea I guess. But it wasn't too hard a decision for me being that you are so beautiful. I couldn't resist." he came back.

Jacy stopped guessing in her head what kind of cologne he was wearing, and just beamed in response at how casually he slipped that into the conversation, taking another sip of her drink.

They talked for another half hour, drank, and dancing intermittently, until one of Jacy's favorite dirty south songs, *Never Scared* by Bonecrusher, came on. Fully feeling the effects of the cognac she had been drinking all night, she pulled Kevin on the floor and started bouncing to the bass from the speakers.

Just then Rich and about 15 of his boys mobbed through the door. The girls lining the area near the door turned and stared, some shaking their asses a little harder, hoping that they would catch the eye of someone in Rich's crew. A few did, as a couple of Rich's friends left to dance with the girls that were wearing the least clothes.

The rest made their way up to the VIP area and a waitress nearly broke her neck trying to rush over to their table. They were obviously regulars at the club, and ballers. She took their drink orders—two bottles of Cristal, six bottles of Hennessy and several mixed drinks and then rushed back over to the bar smiling as if she had just won the lottery.

"Yo go get some bitches up here," Timbo yelled to one of the younger brothas in their crew they called Gold. They called him that because all he ever wore was gold jewelry, gold watches, gold chains, gold teeth. He went back down to the floor and handpicked a few of the best looking women he could find in that area, mostly hoochie-fied, some professional looking women. They quickly agreed and followed him back up.

As Rich was inspecting the women Gold had brought upstairs for some reason his eyes travelled over to the middle of the club and took in the sight of Jacy bouncing to the music on the dance floor. It seemed like every brotha around her was gawking at the sight of her jingling as she moved to the deep hard bass from the music.

"What the FUCK?" Rich said outloud causing two or three of his boys to turn from the women and look at him. His face got hot with rage as he watched a light skinned brotha turn her toward him by the waist and move his hands towards her behind. He had seen enough.

Rich rushed out towards the dance floor almost flying, roughly pushing everybody out of his way until he finally reached Jacy. In his blind rage he didn't have time to notice that Jacy had pulled away from Kevin, resisting his embrace. Grabbing her by the hand he snatched her back through the crowd and over to a corner of the club.

"What in the hell you doin' out there lettin' niggas feel all over your ass and shit!!" he screamed and stepped forward at her, throwing his hands down to emphasize his point and causing Jacy to back up a little. She stumbled, still tipsy from the Courvoisier, and then finally regained her composure.

"Rich, what the hell are you talking about? Coming in here screaming and shit! You betta calm the fuck down." Jacy demanded. She didn't know what he was capable of but still wasn't going to let him punk her out in public. If she did he would do it all the time.

"I'm talking about YOU letting that light skinned nigga feel you up! How you gonna just disrespect me like that in here!"

"First of all I didn't let nobody 'feel me up' and I'm NOT your girl so how in the hell am I disrespecting YOU??"

"Jacy this shit ain't gonna work," he said lowering his voice a bit. He was so angry that his words were wavering. "You are *gonna* be my girl and I don't want you in no club grindin', on no niggas!!"

As much as she hated to, Jacy had to admit to herself that she was turned on a little by Rich's impulsive display of jealousy. She also could tell by his words and emotion that he was *really* feeling her, hard. Which meant she already had him in the palm of her hands. It was a new record for her, only three days.

"Well like I said I wasn't letting nobody feel on me, I pulled away from him, so just calm down ok," she said crossing her arms and turning back towards the dance floor. Kevin was standing at the edge, staring at the two of them waiting to see if she was alright. She quickly turned in another direction hoping that Rich would not follow her eyes and try to make a charge at Kevin for still looking her way. Even though Kevin, a muscular 210 lbs, looked like he could hold his own.

Rich paused eyeing her for a long while before grabbing her by the waist and pulling her towards him. He made sure he had full eye contact with her before speaking to her again.

"Look baby, I'm sorry for flippin' but I don't wanna see you going out like that. You got *way* too much class to be in a club."

"Rich. I met YOU in a club!" she leaned forward with her hands out to emphasize her point. She had a look on her face that said "are you serious?" She started talking faster to throw him off. "Why all of a sudden is shit different? If you think I'm gonna stop going to clubs or something you're really tripping. If I want to go out and have fun with my girls that's just what I'm gonna do. Believe that." When she finished, she gave him a look with her eyebrows up and then walked back out towards the dance floor to find Rachelle. Rich grabbed for her but she was out of his reach, so he just shook his head, pulled his hat down over his eyes and watched her walk away. Finally deciding he didn't want to cause any drama in the club that would scare Jacy away, and noticing that the security guards were now watching him like a hawk, he headed back over to the VIP area.

Rachelle was at the bar writing down her number for a baby-faced peanut butter colored brother when Jacy found her.

"Hey girl, you about ready to go?" she said before Jacy could open her mouth.

"Yea let's get outta here! Please!" Jacy replied sighing as she turned to look in the direction of VIP, where Rich was sitting slouched in a chair with his boys, his eyes barely visible under his hat as he stared back in her direction. Timbo was trying to get his attention about something.

Rachelle said her goodbyes to the brother she was talking to. "Oh yea, before I forget cuz you know my memory's shot. Some fine light skinned brotha named Kevin just came over and told me to give you this." She handed Jacy a white business card with Kevin's home, cell and pager number written on the back. The front of the card revealed that he was a consultant at Deloitte. She turned fully around facing Rachelle attempting to hide the card from Rich who was still looking her way. She smiled and tucked the card in the front pocket of her purse and they both headed towards the door.

chapter 3
Change

T HE DAY AFTER their night at the club, Jacy sat at her desk on 1530 Walnut Street. She was absolutely through with her job at Summit Financial, and it showed. She was so tired of working a 9-5 where she was getting paid in beans compared to how much the company was profiting off of her work. To top that off they treated her as if her work didn't even really matter to them. They didn't appreciate her efforts, which was even harder to bear than any other issue she had with her job. She needed a change, and she needed one quick.

When she got home she called her favorite cousin Tammy in Maryland who worked for a new mortgage finance company in Annapolis. She was hoping Tammy could give her some solid tips or contacts to the real estate world to get her started in the business. Tammy picked up on the second ring.

"Hello?"

"Hey Cuz! It's me! How you doin'?"

"Jacy!! What's up chick? When you gonna come back down here and see your big cousin again?" Tammy always got right down to what she was thinking. She was one of those people that said exactly what was on her mind. She was a fast talker, extremely blunt and quick witted, never really caring much about other people's feelings when she spoke. But she and Jacy had always been tight, ever since they were little girls. Jacy thought of Tammy as a sister and Tammy always gave her 'little' cousin the utmost respect.

"Soon girl, probably in the next couple of weeks even. Look I wanted to ask you about something— "

"What's that? Ain't nobody stalking you again is it? Cuz, I don't care what you say this time I'm gonna get Ray and his boys to come up there and beat the hell outta whoever—"

"No! Tammy," Jacy laughed. "Nothing like that. Actually I wanted to ask if you could help me out in getting in contact with someone who can help me get started on this real estate thing."

"Oh! So you really about to take that step huh? Congratulations, I always told you you'd be great at selling houses! You have honest eyes, and it doesn't hurt that you're cute. You know I'll help you in any way I can. In fact..." she said as Jacy heard her pumps hitting the hardwood floor, then the sound of rustling papers. "I have a friend down at a mortgage company in Philly, Germantown I think, who knows a great team of carpenters that fix up houses for cheap out there. And you know I can help hook you up with some financing once you get a business plan together."

"For real? Tammy that would be great. You just don't know."

"Yea let me just see where I put his number. Hold on a minute," Tammy said putting down the phone.

Jacy couldn't figure out why she never asked her cousin about real estate contacts before. Tammy was a social butterfly and a corporate raider all wrapped in one, and knew just about everyone there was to know in her business. She had been working for real estate and mortgage companies for over ten years, starting out as a receptionist and working her way up to her current position as a VP of the new mortgage finance company she worked for, EverGreen Financial. Jacy admired Tammy for achieving such a high position at the young age of 27. She began to daydream about what her next step would be. She had to touch up her business plan. Little did Tammy know that Jacy had already written a full blown business plan complete with financials. Owning her own business and making her own money. Thinking about that concept made Jacy want to shriek out in joy.

"You there?" Tammy said flipping pages in a book.

"Yup."

"OK, take down this information. Jason Colridge...C O L R I D G E Germantown Mortgage...215-745-3214. Got that?"

"Yup!"

"Alright girl, just call him and tell him Tammy referred you. Tell him what you're trying to do."

"Tammy. Thank you sooo much I don't know what I'd do without you girl!" Jacy's second line started beeping. When she saw that it was Terrell she quickly pressed 'end.' He always seemed to pop up whenever she had something special or new going on in her life.

"Hey no problem. Now tell me when are you coming back down here?? Ray's friends Rod and Daniel been asking about you and you know Lisa misses that Chicken Alfredo you made the last time you came down here."

"With her greedy ass. She only wanna see me for my food!?" Jacy said laughing and twirling a piece of hair on her finger.

"Naw bitch. You know that girl loves you." Lisa was Tammy's best friend of six years. Two years prior, Jacy and Tammy had helped Lisa through a crisis with her boyfriend of eight months, Thomas, who had been beating her by then on a regular basis.

After Jacy visited them in Maryland and Lisa finally broke down in tears admitting what was going on; no longer being able to lie about why she had red and black marks all over her face, arms, and chest, Jacy made it a point to call Lisa every week for almost two months to encourage and help her get the courage to leave her piece of shit boyfriend. Finally, one day Lisa just completely snapped. Thomas had punched her full force in the mouth for questioning his whereabouts. After she recovered from the blow, Lisa, holding her lip from the bleeding, grabbed one of those heavy coal black African statues from her window sill and busted Thomas with it on the back of the head as he walked away from her. Lisa, a pretty healthy sista in size, then proceeded to kick and punch him wildly screaming at the top of her lungs until one of her neighbors called the cops. Thomas suffered a concussion and two broken ribs from Lisa's wrath. Since it was seen as self-defense Lisa only had to spend a night in lock up after which a judge quickly dismissed the case. It was obvious from all the bruises they found on her very light complexioned body. Lisa had not seen Thomas since that incident and met a great new guy that she had been with for over a year and a half. He was treating her like a queen, and was even a little scared of her after hearing about what happened to her last boyfriend.

"Well I'm gonna see what Rachelle is doing, maybe we'll drive down there for July 4th. Maybe we can do Kings Dominion again."

"Yea do that! Just let me know so I can plan to take off of work. Alright lemme go. I got to pick Ray up from the airport. I'll check you later," Tammy said hanging up.

Jacy jumped up from her seat and headed for the computer. It was time to start researching some properties.

IT WAS 11am Saturday morning and Jacy rolled over in bed half awake and still half dreaming. She had been dreaming about a backyard barbeque at her parent's home in Somerset, New Jersey where all of her old friends and aquaintances were chilling when the *Yu Gi Oh* cartoon characters showed up to the party and started fighting the guests with their cards. She could hear their voices clearly, and finally awoke fully to see that the cartoon was on TV. She smiled and rolled over again staring at the bright sunlight coming from the window.

She finally pulled herself up and moved towards the bathroom. On the way she saw her cellphone light flashing. She then remembered that she had put her phone on silent the night before after speaking to Tammy so that she could concentrate on her plans to start her real estate company. She would have to go into the department of Licenses and Inspections Monday morning to apply for a permit to perform real estate services.

The caller was Rich. She took note of the fact that she had voice messages seen by the little envelope at the top of her phone and clicked the 'talk' button.

"Hello."

"Jacy where you been I've been calling you since 10 o' fuckin clock last night!" his deep voice boomed into the phone. Jacy could hear a lot of background noise on his end.

"I'm sorry, I had my phone on silent. What's up?"

"Are you dressed? We're going downtown today remember?"

"Oh yea!" she said looking at the clock and getting happy at the thought of new clothes. "Naw, you gotta give me like another hour to get ready, I just woke up."

"Aiight. I'm coming to pick you up today. I don't wanna hear nothin' about it neither."

Jacy paused for a minute mulling over whether she was ready for him to know where she lived. It probably wasn't the best idea in the world, but she had decided to deal with Rich, at least on a "friends with privileges" basis. And outside of his jealous streaks she could tell that he was actually a good guy, with a big heart underneath all of that outer roughness. At dinner the previous night he had opened up to Jacy about his family. How he had never known his father, and how his mother ran off with one of her abusive boyfriends, leaving him and his brother and two sisters to fend for themselves. Eventually he and his siblings moved in with his aunt and her six children. Life was rough for him living in a three bedroom rowhouse with nine other kids forced to share beds. He was constantly getting into fights in school and had officially dropped out of high school his junior year to start hustling full time and help out his aunt, despite his decent grades. He was a really smart brotha, probably more intelligent and intuitive than most college educated brothas, but due to his circumstances he never had a chance to show those talents anywhere else but on the streets.

"Alright," Jacy said then gave him directions for how to get to her apartment complex. "I'll be ready about 12:30 ok?"

"Aiight baby. I'll see you in a little bit," he said before he hung up.

When Jacy hung up she saw 14 missed calls on her phone.

"Damn!" she said to herself as she found that nine out of the 14 were from Rich. *He is serious*, she thought. The others were from her Mom, Rachelle, an unavailable number and two from Terrell, of course.

At 12:15 Rich called to say he was outside. Jacy told him she'd be right out and finished putting on her eye shadow and MAC lipgloss. Ten minutes later she was engulfed by the warm sunshine and a light breeze tickled her forearms as she walked down her apartment building steps to reach his car. Rich was shuffling through some CDs when she got in.

"Hey baby. What you feel like listening to?" he asked looking up at her from under his baseball hat. He gave her a crooked smile, again slightly taken aback by the strikingly beautiful face sitting across from him in his car. Jacy had high cheek bones and a face that contoured like that of a model. She had almond shaped eyes that formed into slits whenever she smiled. Which she was doing right at that moment. That bright smile. He was trying to figure out how he was able to actually get a woman with all of her qualities all wrapped in one. He wouldn't let her get away.

"What you got?" Jacy responded grabbing the CD's out of his hand. Rich put the car in gear and headed off toward Center City. "Wow, you listen to Floetry?"

"Yea, those chicks are pretty nice. I liked that song *Say Yes* on the radio so I went out and got the original copy. I gotta support the sistas like that. I'd buy an album like theirs in the store way before I went and spent 20 bones on some of these rap niggas. Just so they can brag about how much loot they got, as if we don't already know," Rich went on laughing. "Fuck that, I'll just get all their shit on bootleg then. When they decide they wanna rap about some real shit I'll reconsider."

Jacy turned and looked at him carefully, for only the second time since she had met him. "That's great Rich, supporting the non-mainstream artists. They gotta rely on the black community to go out and buy their albums."

"Yea, but most of these niggas out here don't care about that shit. All they wanna hear is that scruffy nigga remind them of how poor their asses are. 'Oh yea, just in case you forgot niggas, I gotta home in San Tropez. And I won't even lay my shiny ass foot in a six.' Old horse mouth muthafucka. Nigga can't even hardly close his mouth selling millions of records. Meanwhile, half my boys can rhyme circles around him *and* his artists."

Jacy chuckled and put Floetry in the CD player. "And you'd think rappers that grew up poor would know better. They know how it feels to be poor. Now that they got money and connections, you'd think they would do something positive with it, rather then just rubbing it in poor people's faces. I know they do some charity work, but... man if I had 100 million dollars I'd probably be giving ten to fifteen on people in need alone. *And* that money is tax deductible."

"Those niggas don't care about that shit Jacy. As long as people keep putting money in their pockets they're gonna keep doing exactly what they wanna do. The bling sells records cause there's a lot of simple ass muthafuckas out there that don't know or care about nothin' else."

"All you need is a catchy beat, some braggin' ass lyrics and you got a hit." Jacy sighed and bobbed her head to the music as she looked out the window. "If I had more money I would probably try to do something for the homeless people downtown. Like an institute where they could learn basic job skills. When I first came here, I was shocked at all the homeless people in the city, it's crazy."

"Yea, I might have dough now and spend it, but I don't just keep all that shit to myself and I don't brag about nothin' I have. All the kids on my old block, not just my family, got the things that they need. They need a bookbag for school, some new clothes or kicks, a new football helmet for practice, all they gotta do is ask and Mr. Rich or one of his boys get it for them. They wouldn't get that stuff any other way cause don't nobody else give a fuck, sometimes not even they own mamas."

The more Rich talked, the more turned on Jacy was becoming by his words and the way he spoke. She was becoming more turned on by a lot of things about Rich. She admired his confidence, and he was definitely the quiet, thinking type. She loved that in a man. She liked the way his lips felt, and his strong masculine hands. And how he seemed to know how to keep her interested from one point to the next in the short time they had been together. Jacy continued the conversation.

"There are only a few rappers whose albums I might actually buy. I like the ones that don't be talking about all that bling blinging shit all the time. Like Common. I like Freeway and Outkast. Nas to an extent. The Roots. And I've seen some Philly underground artists I like. Nina Ross is hot. Oh yea, and there was this one guy my friend told me about, what was his name...Mike let me listen to a song off his CD a couple weeks ago..."

Rich just listened as he made a swift one-handed left turn, wondering more about the friend she mentioned than the artist she was trying to recall.

"Oh, Lexx Luthor. That's his name. He has a song called *What do we do now.*" Jacy sang the chorus a little. "That song is kinda hot."

"Who's Mike?" Rich asked ignoring the rest of what she had said.

Jacy turned and looked at him. "He's a friend of mine, he works down the street from me. I've known him for years."

"Ya'll were dating?"

"No. Why?" Jacy wanted to know.

Rich made a grunting sound in the back of his throat and rubbed his chin. He never answered.

"So we're going downtown?" Jacy said breaking the silence.

"Yup."

"What's my budget. Cause I don't think you know, I get a little crazy when I get around clothes."

"You get what you want baby."

"Okay Rich. Don't say I didn't warn you though." Jacy smiled and looked out of the window.

They continued their conversation throughout the ride to the Rittenhouse Square district, one of the more ritzy areas of Philadelphia's Center City. Shops lined the streets between 20th to as far down to 11th Street on Chestnut and Walnut Streets, and on Broad Street. There were small boutiques, department stores, a movie theater, jewelry shops, food places, designer stores, anchor stores like the Gap, H&M and a small mall in the area on 16th and Chestnut called Liberty Place. Rich parked the car in a free space on 20th and Spruce, not bothering to put any money in the meter.

Jacy, a natural born impulse shopper, attacked the stores snatching up just about anything cute, pastel-colored and body-hugging from the racks while Rich sat engrossed in cellphone conversations. As promised, he bought her whatever she wanted, including a new signature tote bag from the Coach store on Walnut and a two-piece bathing suit from the Burberry Store at 16th. The rest of her wares were from small fairly inexpensive boutiques that she liked to shop at downtown. Store after store Jacy came out with more bags of clothes and shoes. Rich finally had to head back to the car to put some bags back in the car before heading further down Walnut where he bought himself two brand new throwback jerseys from the flagship Mitchell & Ness store on 12th Street and a New Jersey Nets cap. They finally stopped at a seafood restaurant on Broad Street, for a late lunch. Famished and tired, they tore into their food.

"Damn girl, you can shop," Rich said shaking his head as he ate a forkful of pasta and shrimp. "We only been down here a little over an hour and a half. I'm about ready to hit the sheets after this."

Jacy smiled deviously and cut her eyes at Rich. "Oh no you don't, not until you get me that pearl necklace I want."

"What pearl...necklace?" Rich stopped and eyed Jacy curiously. He swallowed as he watched her place her fork down in her food. She leaned forward and traced a circle around her lower neck. The shimmery lotion she wore caused her dark brown skin to radiate with tiny gold flecks.

"I want it to fall right here. Don't you think that would look nice on me?" Jacy continued. She was smiling at Rich, who was sitting completely still and looking back at her with a serious look on his face. Rich swallowed hard. His fingers lost their grip on the fork he was holding up and it dropped to the table. Jacy laughed.

"I'm playing with you," she said starting on her food again as Rich looked down at her plate then back at her face in disbelief. He finally twisted his lips to the side in a smile and fought back the urge to swallow again. He could tell he was going to like this one. She had actually managed to catch him off guard. Even his aunt, who he considered to be like his mother, hadn't been able to do that since he was a child.

"I'm starting to get tired too, we should call it a day. Rich I *love* all the stuff you got me. Thank you so much sweetie!" She blew him a kiss across the table. She smiled at him for a while, and then took a sip from her glass of soda.

"No problem baby." Rich picked his fork back up and dug into his pasta.

* * * * *

When they left the restaurant, Rich grabbed Jacy's hand and held their other bags as they crossed Broad Street on Chestnut.

Some guys slowed down to gawk and stare at Jacy. They were beeping their horn and yelling "Chocolate!!" before speeding off as the light changed. Jacy had been attracting attention like that all afternoon because she was wearing a pair of plaid short shorts that showed off the full shape of her behind, and a baby tee that revealed her flat stomach and half moon belly ring that had a pink gemstone on the end. At 85 degrees it was hot enough to justify her outfit, but *Niggas will be Niggas*, she thought. She couldn't help how her clothes fit her, and that her body was fit and well proportioned. She always said that she wouldn't hide her body to please other people and loved outfits that complemented her figure. But Rich did not agree.

"Jacy why did you have to wear that lil' skimpy ass outfit. I know it's hot but you know your ass is too big to be prancing around in those booty shorts," he said with an annoyed look on his face.

Jacy immediately got on the defensive. She turned to him with a screwed up expression on her face. "So you tell me what I'm supposed to wear in 80 degree weather? Some sweats and a t-shirt? Not happening. Sorry Rich but if you don't like how I dress that's tough shit," she said in a fairly normal voice rolling her eyes and taking her hand away as she looked in the opposite direction.

"You know what? You gonna stop gettin' smart wit me Jacy," he said in a serious tone. "I'm only tryin' to look out for you I don't need that fuckin' lip every time I tell you some shit."

"If you don't want no lip then don't say no smart shit to me like 'stop wearing booty shorts.' It's MY ass, and I'll wear what I damned well please!!" she said raising her voice.

"Well 'your ass' had bet' not to be on display next time *I* take it out!"

"Well maybe we just won't be going out no fucking more then!"

By then they were having a shouting match in the street. Picking up her pace and walking slightly ahead of Rich, Jacy thought about catching the 21 bus home. She couldn't even believe how belligerent this simple argument had become in such a short time. A smooth-looking brotha, standing about 6'2, who looked a little on the spanish side wearing dark sunglasses approached. He walked close towards Jacy and put his left hand on her waist attempting to pull her towards him.

"Heyyy Miss Chocola—"

It all happened so fast. Before he could even get the word out Rich had come from behind them and slammed his right fist between the stranger's eyes. His sunglasses immediately broke and fell to the sidewalk. The blow was so hard that the man stumbled and fell into the street and Jacy had to jump to get out of the way. Luckily cars had been waiting at the light at 16th so the street was clear. Rich came after the guy as he was trying to get up and commenced to whooping his ass right in the street. Jacy was in shock and stood with her hands by her side. Their bags were strewn all over the sidewalk. Cars began to come through the green light and slowed down to look as they manuevered around the scene into one lane.

"Rich!!" Jacy finally found her voice. "Rich!!!" She moved into the street cautiously because Rich's arms were flying fast and hard as he hit the guy over and over with all of his power. The other guy unsuccessfully tried to fight back. At first he had gotten a small hit in from just balling up his fists and swinging wildy, but Rich, only getting madder, got the best of him punching him square in the jaw causing him to hit his head back on the pavement. Jacy heard the faint sound of sirens a couple blocks down as she pleaded with Rich.

"Rich, baby please! Please stop! The police are coming!" she screamed, almost crying.

Rich, seeming to suddenly snap back into reality, finally stopped and backed up from the wounded man as he saw police cars coming down from the direction of Market Street. Traffic was backed up on Chestnut from people rubber necking, some just completely stopping to watch the fight. Rich sighed and reached in his deep pockets.

"Here," he said in a low voice to Jacy as he handed her his cellphone then his keys and a couple of dime bags of weed from his pocket, all slightly covered with blood. A few seconds later a couple of black officers jumped out of a patrol car and ran down the street towards Rich. "Go home and call Timbo. NOW," Rich demanded. Jacy backed up, discreetly putting the items in her purse, picked up the bags Rich had dropped, and slightly blended into the small crowd that had formed on the sidewalk. She looked over at the brother who was slowly attempting to get up, shaking his head quickly causing more blood to splatter. The officers caught up with Rich who already had his arms up in the air and immediately put him into handcuffs as they asked him what was going on. Jacy slipped through the crowd and began walking at a normal pace towards the car. Fortunately, no one tried to stop her or ask her if she'd seen what happened so she continued on down the street to the car never looking back. A few more ignorant brothas bothered her on the way but she just ignored them and focused on her destination. As soon as she got to the car she took a deep breath leaning her head back on Rich's leather seats.

"I can't believe this shit!" she screamed and hit the steering wheel. She finally picked up her purse and found the cell phone Rich gave her trying to wipe away some of the blood with a tissue from her bag. It took her a minute to get the hang of the phone but finally came upon his phonebook. She scrolled through the numbers seeing name after name, every other entry was a female: Aisha…Asia…Brenda….Calia…*Hoochies*, she thought feeling a slight tinge of jealousy, but then quickly corrected herself saying outloud "He ain't *my* man."

There were hundreds of numbers in there so she finally pressed the '8' button for T's. Timbo's name finally popped up and she pressed 'talk.' The phone rang six, then seven then eight times before it finally went to voicemail. Jacy hung up and called again.

"Pick up the fucking phone!!!" she yelled into the receiver as if someone could hear her. As if someone had, Timbo picked up the phone after the first ring.

"Roo!" he barked into the phone.

"Timbo it's Jacy. Rich is in trouble, he whooped some guy's ass in the street and now the police have him he told me to call you, I'm sitting in his car right now…" Jacy rambled on without taking a breath.

"Oh shit. For real?? Damn! I told that nigga he need to learn to control his motherfucking temper! Where you at?"

"Downtown. He's at 16th and Chestnut." She sighed into the phone catching her breath. "I don't know where they're taking him."

"Aiight look. Go home Jacy. I'll take care of it," Timbo directed, hanging up in her ear.

chapter 4
What can you do?

I T WAS ABOUT NINE O'CLOCK in the evening, the same Saturday of Rich's fight in the street. Jacy was sitting on her couch Indian style flipping through the channels, but not really thinking about what was on the screen. She was thinking about how quickly and completely Rich had flipped out earlier. It kind of scared her. She considered how it all happened because of what she was wearing and the attention it drew.

"Whoa, this could be a real problem," she said to herself.

She was even more concerned about what would happen to Rich as a result of the incident. She thought in a stream of consciousness: I guess he was just trying to defend me. Maybe they'll just treat it like a regular fight. He just overreacted. Damn, he has a temper. He beat that dude's ASS. And he had about 4-5 inches and several pounds on Rich. Damn he's strong. He was probably agitated from our argument. But I wonder if he would ever try to beat on MY ass? Whoa I'd probaby get knocked out with one hit. But I'd still try to KILL his ass when I woke up. I wonder if he's gonna have to go to jail. For how long? I guess I'll go visit him, cause he did get in trouble over me. But if they try to put him in there for years... I am NOT his girl. Damn, what is *taking* them so long. Would they even call me? Yea, cause I have Rich's car and phone. What if they really keep him locked up for years over that shit? I hope he's OK...

Jacy sat still and continued turning the channels aimlessly. Fifteen minutes later Rich's cellphone rang. She didn't know if she should even look because his phone had been blowing up with calls since she got it from him, some from females, most from random numbers. She finally looked at the screen seeing that it was Timbo and hurriedly clicked the talk button, fingers shaking.

"Hello?"

"Hey baby. It's me—"

"Rich," she breathed a sigh of relief. "I've been worried sick about you. What happened?"

"Yea, my fault, I shoulda called you earlier. I'm at Timbo's. He bailed me out a couple hours ago."

"How did he find you?"

"Oh he know some people. One of his cousins works at the 19th precinct and one of his friends at the 26th. He brought our lawyer down there when they found the place I was being held at."

"So what's gonna happen? What did they say?"

"Well, they ain't say exactly. But my lawyer said they would normally try to slap me with an aggravated assault charge since I beat dude so bad. And that's some serious time, like a few years. But he said because it was kinda like self-defense—since I was defending you, and since I didn't use a blunt object—he might be able to get a lesser charge. I'm probably gonna have to do a few months, even less if I have good behavior, and maybe some community service. But I'm probably gonna be on probation for another two, three years." He paused for a moment and the silence seemed to go on for hours. They were both involved in their thoughts. Finally, Rich spoke up. "Jacy?"

"Yes," she said into the phone, her eyes focused on the coffee table in front of her.

"I'm sorry you had to see me like that. But dude had no right to put his hands on you. I know you probably like 'whoaaaa what the fuck is up with this nigga,' but yo. I'm not usually like that. I just lost it for a minute, ya' mean? I know we ain't known each other for that long, but I'm really feelin' you and I know already I want you to be my girl. Just MY girl, cause I have a feeling you still out there dealing with other niggas and I don't like that shit."

Jacy was silent.

"You hearing me?" he questioned.

"Yea, I'm just thinking."

"I think I have a lot I can offer you. No, matter fact I *know*. But we're gonna have to have an understanding."

Jacy continued listening to what Rich had to say.

"And, not that this should even be a question, but I want you to know that I would never, ever raise a hand to you. That's not me, I don't hit on women," he said as if he were reading Jacy's thoughts.

He continued. "So if I do gotta go to jail, I don't want you to just forget about me aiight? It'll be OK, I'm gonna make sure you taken care of for the couple months I'm up, and hopefully I'll get to see your pretty face in there sometimes? It won't be long baby."

Jacy let go another deep sigh through the phone and there was silence for a while as she thought about what he was saying.

"We'll see what happens Rich, I'm just happy to hear you're alright. I'm not making any promises about anything, but we'll see."

"Aiight. I guess I'll take that for now. Imma come scoop my car up from you right quick. You gonna be home in 20 minutes?"

"Yea just call me when you're on your way," Jacy said wondering if he really understood what she meant about not making any promises.

"I'm on my way now, Bo's dropping me off. I'll call when I'm outside. Matter fact, what apartment you in?"

"It's 2B, just ring the buzzer I gotta come open the door anyway."

"Aiight then. One," he said and hung up.

ANOTHER HALF hour later Jacy's buzzer rang shaking her out of a light nap. She slid into her flip flops, unlocked her apartment door and started down the steps to the main security door.

When she opened it up Rich came in with his right hand bandaged, and grabbed her by the waist lifting her high up off the ground.

"Rich!" she shrieked out smiling as she held onto his shoulders. He set her down, looked at her with cloudy slitted eyes, and kissed her lightly on the lips. He smelled as if he may have been smoking a blunt earlier.

"I'm sorry baby. Imma be smarter next time I promise."

"Alright. And I guess I don't have to dress *as* skimpy as I did today, but you gonna end up buying me a whole 'nother wardrobe in that case," she joked.

"I ain't got no problem with that baby just let me know when you wanna go," he said, semi-serious.

They went up to her apartment and she sat down on the couch summoning him to her. He sat down and let out a big sigh resting his hand on her bare thigh and looked around the room.

"Baby you need some money for some home design shit? This place is empty as hell!" he teased. "You need some pictures or something on the wall!"

"Shut up," Jacy laughed and playfully pushed him upside the head. She had to admit, her house did look like kinda empty and boring. Jacy was still in 'college dorm mode' when it came to her living space so all that she had was the basics—couch, TV, entertainment center, stereo. She needed home decor badly.

"Well you know for real, my sister is into all that interior design shit. I can get her to hook you up with some really tight decorations. African art and all that shit."

"Yea, I guess I do need a little help huh? That's cool Rich," she said giving him a wide cheery smile.

Rich was beginning to crave her smile. He was becoming addicted to her presence. He found himself thinking about her more and more throughout the day and wishing he could be around her. She had a magnetic aura that made him feel comfortable and relieved, completely relaxed when she was close. They gazed at each other for a moment, feeling a sexual tension begin to form.

"C'mere, let me give you a massage," Jacy pulled him between her legs as she moved, resting her back on the side arm of the couch with her right foot beneath her. He let his body get loose. "You had some day today huh."

Jacy began to slowly rub his shoulders, focusing deep pressure through her thumbs onto the area on either side of his spinal cord. With each movement Rich released tension, leaning his head farther and farther back to show his approval. After a few minutes she pushed him forward and moved down his back slowly working out the tightness as Rich let his head fall forward. After finishing his lower back she ran her hands back up to his neck pulling him towards her perky breasts.

As she massaged him she thought about the energy and force he used to throw blow after blow on the brother from earlier and felt a gush involuntarily. He didn't seem to ever tire, even though they had been fighting for over ten minutes. She also thought about the fact that up until that moment he had never even mentioned sex to her, though he had wanted her to come over to his house a couple of times. She had known a few men that actually tried to coerce her into sex on the first date. There was never a second date with any of those men.

"Looks like you need a pedicure too," Rich teased holding up her left foot who's third toe had a small chip on the paint. The rest were immaculate.

"Would you hush!" she said smiling, abruptly ending the massage and roughly pushing him forward on the couch.

"Oh you wannabe strong huh?" Rich said turning around on his knees and grabbing her by the waist lifting her over his head. Jacy shrieked and laughed, punching him lightly on the back when in response he started raising her up high and then back down. He did this a few more times before getting up and dropping her back down on the couch. He looked down on her and put both fists in the air in a victory stance turning around to gloat. She got up and jumped on his back pulling him back on the couch. They wrestled for a while until Rich finally just let her win. She sat atop him holding his arms back on the couch.

"Now what!" she taunted him, strands of her hair falling in her face.

They both chuckled and smiled wide at each other. The only sound besides their heavy breathing was the Avril Lavigne video on TV.

Jacy leaned in and kissed him once on the lips. She opened her eyes only a couple of inches from his face and stared him down. She could already feel his erection forming. Rich reached up and kissed her penetrating her lips with his wet tongue. He moaned, wrapping his arms around her waist tightly pulling her towards his body. He ran both hands down to her round behind and grasped it firmly.

Jacy came up for air and grabbed his chin with her right hand holding it tightly for a moment, glaring at him before jerking it to the side and licking him from his collar bone to the tip of his ear making his heart beat faster. She then tickled the inside of his ear with her tongue while Rich began to caress her breasts underneath her shirt, which were just big enough for a handful. She groaned and threw her head back as he squeezed her flesh in his hands. He looked up at her facial expression, and then moved to her nipples rolling them between his fingers causing her another stream of wetness. She stood to unhook and remove her strapless bra and then pulled her shirt over her head exposing her bare breasts standing at attention. Rich jumped up and scooped Jacy by the legs in one motion, carrying her to the bedroom. He couldn't get there quickly enough. He was ready, feeling as if he were about to burst. His attraction to this woman was so strong. She continued to kiss his neck, his face and his ears running her hand over his head.

He threw her on the bed with fire in his eyes and a rise so strong it was nearly busting the zipper on his loose Girbaud jeans. He pulled off his bright white t-shirt and wife beater revealing the rippled muscles running down his arms and bare chest in the dim light. Jacy laid on the bed looking up at him in anticipation. He took off his jeans and boxers exposing the nine inches that had been fighting to get out, then went over to shut the blinds completely so that no one in the apartment building across the street could see in through the window.

Oh boy, Jacy thought to herself as she noted his thickness and immediately felt bad for her throbbing walls. For a split second she thought about telling him she had changed her mind, but Rich climbed on the bed and removed her shorts in what seemed like no time. He parted her legs diving in to bite her on her spot through her pink thongs. She shook with pleasure trying to close her legs but he would not permit. Moving up he licked her belly button while playing with her nipples with his bandaged hand. He finally reached her breasts grabbing them both with either hand and lightly licked and sucked the tip of each. Jacy, about ready to scream, wrapped her hand around his manhood and caressed it slowly while reaching into her night stand for a condom. It was snug but she managed to slide it on nearly to the bottom.

Rich moved her panties to the side and slid his finger inside. "Oooo," he shuddered and whispered. That was it, no more waiting. He somehow managed to slip her panties off in record time, and opened her legs so wide that she was almost in a split. Holding her down he was able to guide himself in without ever losing his grip. Pushing in slowly at first he gasped at how taut she was. Jacy trembled and groaned pushing him in the chest as he forced himself in further. He blinked in disbelief at the wall behind them as he registered what he was feeling at the moment.

After much effort on Rich's part, Jacy's walls finally gave in to the pressure and she felt completely filled. He picked up his pace still holding her down. He would hit the bottom from time to time making Jacy yelp out in submission. She didn't know how much more she could take.

"Ohhh…shhhhhhittt," Rich whispered with his eyes squeezed shut trying to psyche himself out of an imminent climax. Jacy realized what he was doing and began urging him on to come because she didn't know if she could take it anymore. She whispered dirty words and phrases that no man could resist hearing. After several more strokes he looked down at Jacy's glistening brown body and couldn't help himself anymore. He quickly looked back up but it was too late; he had to immediately pick up the speed.

"Fuck, I'm comminggg...Ungghhh..." he grunted with one last solid thrust. He shook as he felt himself shooting out.

Jacy felt him throbbing as he came and was relieved as his body shook with pleasure. He finally collapsed on top of her breathing heavily.

"SHIT!" he exclaimed loudly one more time shaking the bed and then grasping Jacy tight to his sweaty body as he recovered.

A few minutes later when they had both caught their breath Rich spoke.

"Baby?...damn. I don't even know what to say," Rich chuckled and then sighed, resting his head on Jacy's shoulder.

"Did you come?" he asked after a few more moments, as she stroked the back of his head.

"Naw, I can't come like that. But I enjoyed watching you," she said softly and kissed him on the top of his head.

"Huh? What you mean you can't come like that? You ain't never come like that?" Rich inquired.

"No, I need direct stimulation to my clitoris," she said feeling like a sex ed teacher. "I know it sounds strange right? But it's true for a lot of women. Sucks for me huh?"

"Well tell me what I gotta do next time for you to enjoy yourself too," Rich said knowing that good sex was crucial in making it harder for a woman to push on. If he wasn't able to please Jacy in the bed, it was inevitable at some time in the near or far future that he would lose her. That's just how it went. *I can't go out like that*, he thought.

"I will."

"Your shit is tight. You ain't no virgin are you?"

Jacy laughed, Rich's head rising and falling as her body trembled. "No, not quite."

"Man, you got that good stuff."

Jacy inhaled long and sighed. She was feeling sleep coming on. "Come on," she demanded pushing him up and out from her.

Rich got up and went to the bathroom as Jacy wrapped her hair in a scarf and turned off the TV in the living room.

"You got to be somewhere?" Jacy asked with her eyes cut towards him as they met in the hall and she attempted to pass.

"No, why?" he asked stopping her.

"Just asking. I thought you might have to do something. It's only around midnight."

Rich looked at her for a moment. *Damn what's she trying to kick me out?* he thought. "You want me to leave or something?" he asked her frowning. Jacy was really starting to mess with his head.

"No I didn't say that. Look, never mind. Come on to bed," she said motioning with her left hand as she walked back into her bedroom. He followed her in thinking that he probably *should* leave and hit the streets, but he really didn't want to. He had been looking forward to falling asleep holding her. He felt like a bitch all of a sudden.

Jacy climbed under the covers and rolled onto her side. Rich came up behind her and laid his arm around her waist, nestling his nose in her neck.

"Goodnite," she sang.

"Nite baby."

chapter 5
Scandalous

MONDAY AFTERNOON Jacy took a late lunch break and went into the Department of Licenses and Inspections. The place was crowded with people trying to get their permits to run businesses—mainly food related. She stood on line for almost an hour waiting to see someone, and when she finally got to the front she was waiting an unusually long time for someone to call her. There was one woman left running the counter. She was chatting it up on the phone, cackling and gossipping, a classic Philly girl, seeming to have no conscience at all about the people waiting on line for her. When she finally finished her lengthy conversation, Jacy fed up with all the waiting, walked right up to her window.

"I'd like to submit this application for a real estate license?"

"Sorry, we're closed," the woman said uninterested, not even looking up from her paper. The people behind Jacy groaned and some cursed before slowly dispersing.

"What?!" Jacy said a little loud, getting the attention of the security guard standing nearby. "I've been waiting on line for almost an hour. Can't you just take this last application?"

"Miss, we closed at 3' oclock," she said with attitude pointing up at the black and white clock on the wall that read 3:12pm.

"Why couldn't you tell me that 10 minutes ago?"

"Come back tomorrow and then we will process your application. Goodbye!" she said smiling and sounding pleased with herself. Jacy felt like reaching over the counter and strangling her with both hands. Her stringy neck would probably snap right off her head. But she knew that was why there were so many security guards in the building. Philadelphia city workers were extremely ignorant. They figured they could do and say whatever they wanted to people just because they worked for the city.

Jacy shifted her weight to the front and leaned forward onto the ledge. "How are you gonna be talking on the phone, with all these people on line, for ten minutes, and not tell anybody you're closed? I have been waiting here my entire lunch hour." Jacy said glaring at the woman. The woman didn't respond, just took a glance over at the security guard. "Fucking bitch." Jacy said under her breath as she walked away when it finally sunk in that her rantings were hopeless. The security guard eyed her, but sympathized with her at the same time. He knew he'd be pissed if he had wasted his entire lunch hour waiting on line. Lunch was the highlight of the 9-5 work day.

Walking back to her office Jacy felt a little discouraged. She had called Jason Colridge earlier that morning but only got his voicemail. She left her number and Tammy's name but knew how people could be about answering their messages. She would have to harass him with calls, she guessed, until he finally picked up the phone. Bless the person that invented *67, she thought.

"There always seems to be something standing in my way. Why does everything have to be a constant struggle," she said to herself as she stepped into the elevator and pressed the button for her floor and ran her other hand over her hair.

When she got off the elevator she passed Felix who was heading down.

"Heyyyyyyy girl!" he said in his fake gay voice.

"Yea," Jacy replied dryly and kept walking. *Two faced muthafucka*, she thought.

When she got back to her cubicle she noticed that her red message light was flashing. Checking her messages, this is what she heard:

Hi, Jacy this is Jason Colridge. I received your message and I'd be happy to help you out with your real estate venture. I'm leaving the office right now, but give me a call in the morning I should be in the office around 10am. And tell Tammy I said hi and to give me a call. Bye."

"Oh thank God," Jacy exclaimed. She was relieved that she didn't have to harass Jason as she had planned. He sounded very pleasant on the phone, very professional.

"Hey Jacy?" said someone from behind.

Jacy turned around to face Cara, one of the office assistants. She was the bubbly busy body of the office. The white girl that was always extra happy.

"Oh hey Cara. What's up?"

"Nothing much! I just need your signature on this release before I send it down to Marketing." she said smiling so hard it looked like her cheeks would pop.

"No problem," Jacy looked over the materials, signed the form and handed it back. She caught Cara sneaking a peak at her real estate application on the desk. Cara quickly tried to play it off, looking away.

"Thanks," she said walking away so fast that she tripped on the rug and damn near fell. Jacy snickered and turned back to her screen. *That's exactly what you get*, she thought.

"Ohhhkkkkkk," Jacy said consuming herself with work once again. 40 minutes later her cellphone rang and when she found it, Rich's number flashed on the screen. She thought for a minute, and then pressed 'ignore.' It wasn't that he was bothering her, she just would rather call him later. Rich had stayed over until 2pm Sunday after spending the night and Jacy was kinda happy to have the house to herself again. She enjoyed his company, but had been looking forward to spending the day planning for her real estate business. She thought Rich was definitely a good shot. She was still walking funny at work after two whole days. But he still had to prove that he could bring her to climax in order to keep her interested in that department. Plus he was just a little too large and rough for Jacy's size and taste. Thinking about their episode the other night made her shiver in pleasure, but the actual act had just hurt more than anything. *He might just be better as a friend*, she thought, but knew deep down that would never happen. Rich left a message. Jacy finished up her work day and headed out the door at 5:15pm.

When she arrived home, Jacy did her normal after work chores and sat down at her computer. Slipping in the disk that held her business plan she got to work on updating it. Halfway through her task her cellphone rang. It was Terrell. She threw the phone back down and continued working.

After a few hours of typing and two computer restarts, she decided to find out what Rich had called her about earlier. She didn't want him to start panicking and thinking she was trying to dip out on him or something. One thing Jacy was learning was that Rich had a temper even worse than hers, and she didn't want to evoke it over small stuff. His voice was breaking up on the message.

"....want to see.... call.... do something after work you...how come... calling you since Sunday night!...holla atch.... One."

"Damn, either he or I needs to get a better phone," Jacy said to herself. Her cell phone service was always breaking up and dropping calls all of a sudden. Both she and Rich had the same cellphone service, so she was able to leave a message for him without calling.

"Hey Rich, it's Jacy. Just calling you back. I'm not gonna be able to get up with you tonight—I have some work to do. But maybe I'll catch up with you later this week. Talk to you later."

Jacy dropped the phone on her couch and went into the bedroom to strip for a nice warm bath. Typing again after a long day of work was making her head hurt and she needed a break. She put on her pink robe, ran her bath water and put in a Jill Scott CD. As her bathroom filled with the smell of soothing pear and watermelon scented bathsoap she sat on the side of her tub, closed her eyes, and ran her fingers through the water slowly.

BAM BAM BAM BAM!

The sound of someone knocking loudly at her door shook her out of her reverie and almost caused her to fall in the tub. She reached over to turn off the water and fixed her robe. She wasn't expecting anyone, who could it be?

"Who the hell is it!" she yelled annoyed that someone was interrupting her meditation as she stormed toward the door. How did they get past the security door?

"It's Terrell! Open up."

"Terrell? What the hell do you want? I'm about to take a bath!" Jacy replied through the closed door hoping he would just go away. Yea right, she thought.

"Just let me in for a minute baby, it's important," Terrell said in a serious tone. Jacy peeked out of her peephole and saw Terrell's tall figure, big head and lips at top, small feet at the bottom. She giggled to herself at the distortion and slowly opened the door. She had never known Terrell to be a threat, so she didn't have a problem with letting him in her house, even after they had broken up.

"What you want?" she demanded.

"Mmmmm. I forgot how good you look in that robe..." he mused before pulling a dozen soft pink roses from behind his back. "These for you. I know pink is your favorite."

"Awww Terrell. You didn't have to do that," Jacy couldn't help but smile. Terrell was looking good in a neatly ironed white cotton button down short sleeved shirt with a white wife beater underneath and brown slacks. She let him in and went in the kitchen to put the flowers in a vase before coming back out to the living room. "How'd you get past the security door? And what you all dressed up for?"

"Somebody was coming in. I just left my Aunt Sarina's birthday party. You know she kinda bourgie—she don't like nobody coming to her house parties looking any ole way."

"Yea how's she doing? How old is she now?" Jacy asked guiding him to the couch.

"She say she 37 but we all know she like 44, 45—she look good for her age too. So what's up with you though? You still seeing that nigga?" he asked sitting down.

"Oh lawd. Terrell, if you just came here to start on that you might as well leave."

"Nawl... I just hope you know that nigga got more freaks than Luke!" he emphasized the last part of his sentence as he reached behind him to adjust the couch pillow.

"Oh really?" Jacy said chuckling. "Well good thing I'm not his girl, otherwise I might give a fuck. But I'll keep what you said in mind, cause I ain't trying to be sexing—" Jacy stopped herself in her tracks and put her fingers up to her mouth, hoping he missed that last part.

"Oh...so you *are* fuckin that nigga then? I knew it!" he said looking at her in disbelief.

"Terrell even if I was what the hell would it matter to you?" she said shaking her head and looking back at the TV.

"What do you mean?? Come on now, of course it matters to me Jacy!" he yelled jumping up from the couch to face her. "Girl, I want you to be my wife one day! Of course Imma care what niggas you fuckin'!"

"Well just don't hold your breath Terrell," Jacy said rolling her eyes and going off on a rant. "Cause I'm sorry to be the one to break it to you, but we are *never* getting married. You got way too many issues. Shit I might not ever get married period. Look what I have to choose from? These random dick-led black ass niggas out here. Acting like they ain't got no damn sense, including you, baby boy." She said calling him by the nickname she had given him when she learned that he still lived with and off his mother.

Terrell paused looking at her curiously, and Jacy thought that he might have actually absorbed what she had just said. That she might have actually hurt his feelings enough to get him to lay off of her a bit. Of course she was wrong.

"Jacy, what that nigga got that I ain't got? Huh? Is he giving you money? I can get you some dough. His dick bigger than mines?" he still stood and stared down at Jacy, his elbows high in the air as he pointed to himself. She just shook her head at him. Then, as if someone had flipped a switch in his narrow mind, something new and strange developed in his eyes. As if he had just gotten a great idea. Jacy pulled the top of her robe together more securely and looked up at him with the 'something stinks' face.

All of a sudden, Terrell pushed back Jacy's huge black coffee table with little or no effort. He got on his knees and quickly grabbed either one of her thighs with his bulging arms before she could get away. Jacy squirmed and resisted but Terrell's arms were holding her so tight that she could only move her upper body. He looked up at her and smiled. "I bet you this, I can still do this better than any otha nigga can," he said licking his lips. He finally dove in. Jacy gasped at the feeling.

"Noooooo!!! Terrell please don't do this. I can't do this. I cannot do this," Jacy whined even though her body was telling her different. She pushed at his head and shoulders but it was like trying to move a 500 pound boulder. Terrell took his tongue out and licked her from the bottom to the top until he reached her spot. When he started his hyper-quick movements Jacy began to remember why she had stayed with him so long.

"DAMN!" she cried out already on the verge. The soulful sound of Jill Scott's *Is it the Way* in the background was turning her on even more. Terrell stayed focused on his task never loosening his grip. He parted her with his fingers then moved his tongue back down before going back to her spot which was standing at attention by then. He consistently hit the same exact spot for several minutes until finally it was time. "Terrell pleasssssse! Oh, this is so wrong...I really can't be doing this. I can't be *doin'* this...ooooooohh... OHHHHH!!!"

Jacy screamed out as the waves of pleasure hit her one by one. Terrell only held her tighter and continued flicking, which caused her whole body to shake prolonging the release. After a few more minutes, he finally gave her relief.

Terrell, satisfied, lifted his head and smiled like the cat that ate the canary. He licked his lips as he glared at Jacy, waiting for her reaction.

"Get up!! You ass!" Jacy yelled at him, finally able to push him off. She curled up on the couch to recuperate looking away from him. She sat shivering. Her whole body felt refreshed. It had been a while since she'd felt like that.

"Now you know ain't no otha nigga ever gonna make you feel like that. *In your life.*" Terrell said cockily getting up and heading towards the door. "See I ain't even gonna try nothing else wit you tonight, cause all I want is for you to feel good and be happy. That's all I ever wanted. That nigga Rich can't say the same. He don't even know you like I do."

"Just go, you make me sick." Jacy said, her feelings of annoyance returning.

"Yea whatever boobie. Imma sleep well into the night tonight thinking about you in that robe." He licked his lips in a circle at Jacy, chuckled and then opened the door and shut it behind him before Jacy could respond. She lifelessly threw a magazine that had fell on the floor at the door. She was so weak that it barely made it to the foyer.

"Shit!" she said feeling as if he had gotten the best of her, even though she hadn't actually had sex with him. She hadn't willingly consented to the act...had she? Damn it felt good. *Why?? Why is he always popping up in my life at the wrong moments?* she thought, as she drifted off to sleep.

* * * * *

A few hours later Jacy's phone rang half-waking her up out of a good dream. She sleepily reached around herself on the couch for the phone and clicked 'talk' without looking at the caller ID. She answered the phone groggily, still thinking it was a dream.

"Hello?"

"Sup. Why you ain't call me? I'm feeling some type of way about that," Rich asked in a low voice as if he were thinking about something. Jacy could make out Juelz Santana from Dip Set's new hit playing in the background from his car stereo.

"I called you, didn't you get my message?"

"Your number ain't come up on my phone."

"Oh. That's because I just sent a reply to your message. What's up?"

"I'm about to come through."

"Ummm. I don't know maybe tomorrow. I have to finish up a little work and then I'm going to bed. I'm not gonna be much company baby," Jacy said standing up and stretching.

"Oh yea? You heard from Terrell lately?" Rich inquired in a way that said he knew something. Jacy paused for a few moments, and she cursed silently for giving herself away. She sat back down.

"Yea, I see him around. Why?"

"No reason. I just saw him down 60th street at the corner store cheesing at me like a damn fool. He said he was coming back from 'round your way, wanted to know how you was doing?" Rich said letting his words hang as he waited for a response.

"Oh yea?" Jacy said trying to sound disinterested. She hadn't even taken a bath after Terrell left and felt scandalous, to say the least. She felt as if she had gotten herself into some deep shit even though it wasn't really her fault. Rich was cool, but he had a temper and she did not want to agitate it with something like this. It could get ugly. *I couldn't have done anything about it anyway though,* she thought, feeling less guilty but still a little concerned.

"What was up with you and that nigga?" Rich inquired.

"We just used to date."

"How long ago was this?"

"Like. A few months ago. Why?"

Rich was quiet for a few moments during which all Jacy could hear was the music in the background. "You still seeing him? Don't lie to me Jacy."

Jacy sighed deeply before going on. "Rich, I see him every once in a while, but I'm not fucking him if that's what you're asking—"

"What?" he asked raising his voice an octave. "That nigga was just over there wasn't he?"

Silence.

"He was, wasn't he? You fucked him? Please don't tell me you're fuckin' him Jacy. I don't think I could handle that right now." Rich said, losing it. His voice was shaking.

"No Rich calm down, I just told you I wasn't! Look he was just over here because he was in the area, his Aunt—"

"Oh so then why he smiling ear to ear when I seen him just now? Askin' me about you when he just seent your ass!? And why was you just acting all surprised when I mentioned his name?" Rich said emphasizing his point by banging on his steering wheel as he spoke.

"I'm tellin' you it wasn't nothing Rich, really. I promise you, I did *not* have sex with him okay? That was just Terrell being Terrell you should know not to pay him no mind! And Rich, I'm chillin' with you right now, but I don't think you're really understanding when I say I'm not tryin' to get serious with anyone right now—" Jacy tried to get a much needed point across but was interrupted.

"Oh so now you gonna just try to dump a nigga. Terrell's ass come over there and all of a sudden you ain't tryna get serious? And you ain't fuck 'im? Gonna tell me you got some 'work' to do. I bet." Rich scoffed.

"Rich would you calm the fuck down I'm not trying to *dump* you—"

"Incredible. You actually think, Imma let some nigga be at my girl's house while I'm sitting up here like a fucking nut? Fuck nawl. Yo, you buggin' Jacy," Rich's voice faded away at the end and then she heard the line hang up abruptly in her ear.

Jacy shook her head as she sat still holding the phone to her ear in disbelief. Men never took her seriously when she said she wasn't looking for a serious relationship. She felt like a broken record.

Jacy preferred freedom. If she had to choose between being single, sane and having freedom to play the game, or being in a relationship based on drama and unhappiness, single was the life for her. Why couldn't she just enjoy the company of her thug. Have some fun. No strings attached. It was always only a matter of days before they started trying to put the lock down on her. She had held to a strict policy of not sleeping with more than one man at a time, which was very difficult at times. But even with a guy she chose to be intimate with, she preferred to leave out the formal 'girlfriend' title if at all possible. Jacy shook her head and finally put down the phone. She headed towards the bathroom where her bath water sat stale.

While emptying the tub she started to think about relationships. She thought about what it meant to be in one. She thought about how all of the relationships she'd ever seen come to be, in her family, her friends, and her own, had failed horribly. Some of her family and friends may have still been in those relationships, but their lives were depressing. Maybe if Jacy had witnessed just one relationship or marriage that turned out right, she wouldn't be so jaded about the subject.

She thought about the type of women men like Rich and Terrell were used to. Dependent. Clingy. Easily influenced. Fake hard core. Complacent. Naïve. She wondered if any of the women they dealt with ever stood up to them. *It's such a shame how women spoil these grown assed men,* she thought, *they're picking up right where their mamas left off.*

After emptying the tub she stripped off her robe and took a long shower. Her mind wandered to her father, a tough construction manager who always took care of his family financially. While he was always there for his four children, proving to be the ultimate breadwinner, he had brought Jacy's mother through complete hell throughout their 27 year marriage. They had married young despite protests from their parents. Her father was a player in his earlier years, latching onto every pretty young thing that crossed his path, and didn't let marriage stop him. Her mother had been a bright virtuous young woman with aspirations of becoming a lawyer that were dashed as she got stuck with the reponsibility of taking care of four children that were all around the same age. Jacy's older sister was 26 and now living in California, her younger sister was 21 and her younger brother was 20. Throughout their childhood, their parents were constantly fighting, the relationship was verbally and physically abusive at times, causing Jacy and her siblings to constantly be on edge. While their home life wasn't perfect, they still always received love and support from their parents which fostered their growth into educated, mature adults. While she was grateful to her parents for their dedication to their children, she vowed to never be put in a situation like theirs, a relationship so cold and problematic. She had been very selective with boys from a very young age, and made it a point to learn as much as possible about them. She wasn't wildly popular in grade school and only had a couple of real boyfriends during her high school years that didn't last for long. They were just dumb high school boys to her, after all. While people wrote her off as 'stuck up,' Jacy never hesitated to be there for her friends and even strangers when they needed her. She had had a couple of heartbreaks in school, like any other young girl, but quickly learned how to suck it up and move on to bigger and better things. Smart as a whip, she breezed through college breaking the hearts of unsuspecting college boys and revelling in her independence.

She stepped out of the shower, delicately dried off her curves, moisturized, brushed her teeth, then went into the room to pull on the big white t-shirt that read "Princess" in big pink letters she had gotten last Christmas from her cousin. Just as she was about to pull back the covers her cellphone rang. It was Rich again.

"What?" she demanded.

"I'm coming over, that's what. Fiesty ass." Jacy heard some male voices in the background yelling and conversing. Then it got quiet as Jacy assumed Rich went inside a house. "You know you turn me on when you get like that. Listen, I got a little hot when I saw that nigga and he said your name, ya' mean. But for real? I thought about it, I know you wouldn't do no trifling shit like that to me. I'm coming to see you."

"Naw…I really don't feel like any drama tonight Rich—"

"No drama. I told you I'm sorry right?" Rich said in that way of his that told you he wasn't playing. Jacy was quiet. "Did you eat?"

"No, you know, I didn't even have a minute to eat." Jacy said putting her face down into her hand and rubbing her forehead.

"I'm about to bring you some crab legs and baked potatoes from the seafood place, I'll be there in 20 minutes," he said hanging up before she could say anything else.

Jacy sighed and slung herself under the covers. She flipped the channels finally stopping at an episode of "The Golden Girls," and patiently awaited his arrival. She remembered that she would have to move the coffee table back into its original position.

* * * * *

Rich walked through the door wearing a fresh new Phillies baseball throwback jersey, dark jean shorts that reached his mid-calf and a new pair of butter colored tims with short white ankle socks underneath. The tat on his lower arm was magnified by the muscles and veins visible there. He brought with him a crisp manly scent—a cologne oil that he had bought from the Muslims on 52nd Street. He had a fresh cut and his Cartier roadster watch shimmered and gleamed with every step. Damn, he's looking kinda good right now, Jacy thought. When she turned back around from closing the door he was right there.

He forced her backwards slowly onto the door without ever using his hands, one of which held a white plastic bag full of crabs, and softly kissed her on the lips. The only thing connecting him to her were his lips as he carefully turned his head to begin giving her a deep passionate kiss that lasted for what seemed like hours. Jacy's defenses melted and she kissed him back while beginning to delicately trace his chest with her index finger. She tasted a hint of Hennessy on his tongue and began sucking on it lightly. He took his other hand and guided hers down to the bulge in his jeans. She outlined it with her fingers for a few seconds, and then pushed him out of the kiss. He eyed her as she went around him.

"What kind of crab legs did you get?" she asked.

Rich finally broke his trance and followed her into the living room. "I got three pounds of King, and two pounds of Dungeness. I hope you hungry."

"Mmmm." Jacy bit down on her lower lip. "Yea, let me get some hot sauce."

They sat in front of the TV and watched *The Fifth Wheel.* For once, the couples were black. There was a light skinned guy with freckles that seemed to be the player, a tall dark skinned bald brotha who was the quiet and sensitive type, a sista with auburn dreads and honey colored skin to match who was the 'independent' woman and another brown skinned sista with a long straight silky weave who wasn't too cute in the face and seemed at first to be innocent, but as the show went on she was groping all over the two brothas, showing them the tattoo on her butt, and tongue kissing them on her individual dates. The player was loving every minute of it, but the sensitive guy was more reserved about her actions. He seemed to be easily intimidated and almost too shy to even talk to the women. The other sista ranted on about how she was just on the date to see what's out there, and how she didn't need a man to satisfy her needs—she talked too much about her dildo, named Wally. He, she claimed, was all that she needed. *Yea right,* Jacy thought. When the fifth wheel came out, a pretty brown skinned woman with a curly short do, a big bright smile and a nice body the expressions on the women faded. She had a carefree attitude, and seemed to have the two men wrapped around her finger. They immediately gravitated towards her, but she was disappointed in them. According to the fifth wheel the sensitive guy's breath was stinking and he was too passive. She also said in her interview that the playa was so obvious that she could predict his every next move and word, and that his freckles bothered her.

"Sometimes it's so obvious why people go on these dating shows," Jacy said cracking a crab leg open.

"Oh yea? What you mean," Rich replied dipping a sliver of meat in the butter sauce and throwing it in his mouth.

"I mean how the one guy is a wannabe playa and the type of woman he *really* wants to be with can smell him a mile away. The girl with the dreads is on that independent kick that no man is trying to hear. The other girl is hoing herself off, so she probably *gets* men but can't keep them for long—"

"Hey, hos need love too," Rich smiled.

"Oh do they? And I'm guessing you know this from first hand experience?" Jacy teased but really did want to know.

"There's hos everywhere Jacy. They in the supermarket, in college, on the corner, in the bakery—they popping out the cement cracks in the hood. Of course I know!" he said counting the places on his fingers as he talked and getting animated.

"Really. So I guess you just give them the love they need?" Jacy shook some hot sauce on her crab meat. She ate it and then dipped her fork in her hot baked potato, which was drenched with butter.

"Naw I'm not the nigga. Let them get that shit from some weak nigga down the street. What I look like with a ho for a girl? I need me a smart chick, like your sexy ass," he made eyes at her and licked his lips. Jacy couldn't help but laugh at him. Rich chuckled and then sucked some crab meat into his mouth.

"Well. *I* heard you got girls beating down your door playa. You don't know nothing about that huh?"

"Where you hear that?" Rich said turning to look at her curiously. He already had an idea of where though.

"Don't worry about it," Jacy replied, beginning to regret having dragged the subject on. But she wanted to hear what he had to say about it, or if he would just skirt the issue, which would be a dead giveaway. If she was going to be exclusively intimate with a man, she wanted to be sure that he was doing the same. She couldn't see herself messing with a male ho.

Rich continued eating and was quiet for more than a minute. Jacy just assumed that he had dropped the subject. But finally he said: "Yea there's a couple broads that's trying to get a piece of me and my crew, but its all because of loot. My baby momma included, she *always* at me—"

"I didn't know you had a child?" Jacy interrupted.

"Yea she's five this December. That's my heart." He paused in between shuffling some shells around in his plate. "Why, is that a problem?" he asked looking at her out of the corner of his eye.

"No, not at all. What's her name?"

"Shelly, short for Michelle. She fiesty—and smart. Take right after her daddy!"

Jacy laughed. "You are just too modest!" she teased. He smiled back at her.

"You know my court date is this Friday at 9am. You don't have to come, but my lawyer thinks it would help my case if you said something to the judge about how dude grabbed on you. You ain't gonna get a subpeona or nothin', because I told him I didn't want to force you to get involved. But do you think you could come though?"

"Of course I will Rich! Why didn't you tell me sooner?" she said in a surprised tone wiping her fingers on a tissue.

"I don't know. I just didn't want you to get all wrapped up in my shit. But I'm glad you gonna come, I'll feel better with you there, period."

"Awwwwww. Rich," Jacy said smiling and grabbing onto his arm. He turned his head and she pecked him on the lips. Then she got serious again. "Do you really think you'll have to go to jail over this?"

"Probably ma. I got priors. But like I said, it won't be for too long," he responded looking back up into her eyes.

Jacy stared back for a minute before speaking again. "I'm gonna take off of work on Thursday and Friday morning. We can spend the day together up til the case alright?"

Rich grinned wide and then looked back down at his food to grab another King crab leg. "Alright, I'd like that. You ain't gonna get in trouble at work or nothing?"

"Fuck them. I'm thinking about leaving that job anyway."

"Do it. You know I got you." he said casually, cracking open the leg. "How much is your rent and utilities anyways?"

Jacy thought for a moment while she stared at the television screen. Both men had chosen the fifth wheel and the other two girls were salty, but the fifth wheel decided not to choose either. Jacy chuckled in amusement.

The offer from Rich was tempting but no, she thought, she couldn't quit her job based on promises from a man. What if something happened, which it most probably would, and he was gone from her life? Then she'd be truly assed out. On the other hand it would be cool if he could pay her bills while she saved her own earnings…

"Jacy? You heard what I said right?" Rich said, not about to let the subject pass them by.

"Yea. Yea I don't think I'm gonna quit my job just yet, but it would help alot if you could take care of some bills for me right now." As soon as she finished her sentence she felt a little regret. She knew what it meant. That first $650 rent payment would represent the first day she was officially 'Rich's girl.' She felt the air around her decrease, and involuntarily her heartbeat quickened and her lungs seemed to tighten. What was she getting herself into, really? She leaned forward a bit and looked down at the table to compose herself.

"Aiight. When you get your bills let me know. If I'm not around in the next couple months, you gonna call Timbo and he's gonna take care of it okay?"

"Well you know maybe…I—" Jacy stammered.

"You know what?" Rich shoved his left hand deep in his pocket to retreive a thick stack of bills. He counted 12 hundred dollar bills from the wad and put it on the table. "That should at least cover your rent and utilities for this month. I'm gonna give you more on Thursday."

Jacy eyed the money spread out on her coffee table. She sensed that Rich was trying to close the deal, just like he did in the streets. She could see why he was so successful at it. What could be so bad about trying Rich out for a while, she asked herself. She didn't have to stay with him *forever*. Maybe it would be a good idea for her to settle down for a little while as she worked on her new business. And the money she saved probably could help her buy her first house in Philly without having to get a loan or present a business plan to the bank...

"Thank you sweetie," she said and leaned over to kiss him again.

Rich smiled a satisfied smile and sucked the meat out of his last crab leg. He was happy that he finally had a way to keep Jacy around indefinitely. He had been a little uneasy. Uneasy after he saw Terrell in the store earlier and heard confirmation that he had been in Jacy's apartment. Uneasy when he didn't bring her to climax in bed. Uneasy when she went almost two days without wanting to see him. He was amazed at how deep his feelings were developing for Jacy after only a little under two weeks. He had never felt that way about a female—it was very new and different for him. She did something to him—even made him feel vulnerable at times, and he liked it. When other brothas so much as looked in Jacy's direction he wanted to bang their heads against a brick wall. Money was no object for him when it came to Jacy because he knew she was not dealing with him just because of his dough. She hadn't ever really asked him for money—he always did the offering. That was unheard of. When he told his boys about it they looked at him in disbelief. "Does she have a sister?" one of them asked. He felt proud of Jacy, it was as if he'd found a rare beautiful flower growing out of a row of rough prickly bushes.

"Jacy we gotta be clear on some things though. I don't want you fuckin' with no other niggas no more aiight? That ain't cool. It's me and you—we supposed to be a *unit*, ya' mean? don't let *nobody* come between that. I'll be very, very upset if I find something out I don't wanna hear," he said gravely and looked fleetingly at his cell phone that was ringing. He pressed the ignore button, glanced back up at the TV in thought and then focused on Jacy again.

"Yea OK Rich. But we gotta be clear on some other stuff too." Jacy retorted, leaning back on the couch and looking squarely into his dark brown eyes. "Don't expect me to sit in my house all the time just cause you don't want me to be around other men. I'm young, I'm going to have fun and go out, but if I'm dealing with you… I'm dealing with just you okay? What I'm saying is, I do have a couple of male friends and I'm not going to stop hanging out with them occasionally—but you have my word that I won't be fucking with anybody but you, alright?"

Rich shook his head 'no.' "Why do you need to have male friends though? If you have me?"

"Rich…" Jacy turned her head from him and shook her head, thinking again that this wasn't going to work. She didn't even know what else there was to say to him.

Rich was held in his thoughts for a few minutes. He was now resting back on the couch also, staring at the leftover food on the coffee table.

"Aiight," he finally uttered.

Jacy looked over at him. His expression definitely wasn't happy, but at least he was willing to compromise. She turned her body towards him and ran her open palm down his chest. He looked down at her hand and watched her delicate fingers trace the heavy material of his powder blue 1976 Phillies jersey, then looked back up at the TV. He didn't move and continued looking forward resolutely as she kissed his cheek and whispered comforting words in his ear, biting that same ear intermittently. He tried to continue being stubborn, pretending as if she wasn't affecting him. But that didn't work for long. He finally closed his eyes, enjoying her attention.

After a few more minutes of coddling, Jacy asked if he was cool. He answered with a simple "yea." She leaned over more and kissed him on the lips. First a peck, then more and more passionately. He was loving every moment, but still trying not to make it obvious. He still wasn't so sure he liked the idea of Jacy having male friends.

Jacy finally reached forward and cleaned up the mess in front of them before heading to the kitchen to put the leftover food in the fridge. She put the dishes in the sink and filled up Muffy's bowl of water for the night. It was beyond 1am at that point and she was past tired. She passed Rich and went back into the bedroom to get ready for bed, again. After redoing her nightly ritual—brushed teeth, washed face, scarf on her head—she came back out to see what Rich was doing.

He laid there on the couch slumped slightly to the side fast asleep. She stood for a few seconds looking at him. *He's probably been up since early this morning running around,* she thought. Finally she turned off the TV, went back to her linen closet, pulled out a sheet and took one of her pillows from her bed. She took off his boots and laid his feet out straight on the couch. He grumbled a little. She placed the pillow under his head and threw the crisp clean white sheet over his body, which was moving up and down as he breathed heavily in and out. She kissed him on the forehead and whispered "goodnight" before turning off the light.

chapter 6
Good to Bad to Ugly

"... **S**O JUST START doing research on fixer upper houses available in the area, get an idea of what your price range will be and even go take a look at them if you can. Just so you can get an idea of what you want to work with. Make sure you get that license this week so that you can be prepared in case something comes up immediately. And we'll meet on Saturday right?"

"Right. One o'clock at Ms. Tootsies on South Street," Jacy replied smiling excitedly. She had finally gotten in touch with Jason Colridge and he had been giving her some wonderful tips on how she should start up her real estate company. "Thank you so much Jason, you don't know how much I appreciate this."

"No problem I'm glad to help. What were you thinking about naming your company?"

"You know, I haven't really thought about that yet. Something catchy like 'Good Livin' Realty,'" she laughed with him.

"Well you might be on to something there. You want to get popular through word of mouth. People who are looking for a house to live in, or who are considering selling their own house will remember a name like that. Look I gotta run Jacy, I have a meeting at 2pm that I need to prepare for. But I'll see you on Saturday."

"Alright, thanks again Jason, I'll talk to you later!"

They hung up and Jacy bounced in her seat a little. She stared at her computer screen for a second and then turned to get up but was surprised when she met eyes with her boss, Caitlin Heines. Caitlin was a hard nosed white woman who was over-obsessed with her career. While she was fairly pretty and young for someone in her position at only 42, her inner ugliness negated everything else positive about her. She had strawberry blonde hair, blue eyes, a long thin witch's nose and deep lines in her face from stress. She confirmed the theory that some white women just didn't age very gracefully. She had never been married, but owned a huge house on the main line and drove a maroon 2003 CLK55 Mercedes Benz coupe. *Lucky bitch!* Jacy thought to herself.

"Jacy did you sign a release form for Marketing to use the statement we drafted for the Jackson account?

"Drafted? You told me that was final."

"No, I did not. The statement included a number of grammatical errors. Erin Brockville just called me and was upset that he had to make several changes on his own."

"Caitlin, you saw that statement yourself, marked it up with a few minor changes and told me everything else looked okay after—"

"I think that we're going to have to 'touch bases' in the near future about our communication Jacy. I expected you to look over it one final time after making the changes and have me look over it once more before sending it down."

Jacy looked at her boss with a blank stare. She was cursing Erin Brockville in her head. That man was always trying to get her in trouble. They had been cool with each other at first, but after Jacy told him she was unavailable to help him with a minor project, which he thought was more important than the one she had been working on, he began continuously going to Caitlin with any and all errors he could find with Jacy's work. He had even caused Jacy's schedule to be changed because one morning he called at 8:45am needing a short statement to be drafted by 11am and Jacy was not due in until 9am. Ever since then she was required to come in the office at 8:30 instead of 9am. It made no sense at all because Jacy was still able to get him the draft by 11am with no problem. Jacy despised him for that because she really needed that extra half hour in the morning to prepare for her day. These were some of the reasons Jacy needed to get out of that place. They were always bitching about minor things, ignored the positive major things she did for the department, and didn't respect or value her as a *person* instead of just a worker. Everything was so bureaucratic.

Caitlin continued. "I would like you to go down and get the version with Erin's changes so that you can take note of the errors and place them in your own final version on the drive."

"Alright Caitlin," Jacy replied shortly, and Caitlin walked away.

Jacy sat back down in her chair and leaned back. She let out a heavy sigh and closed her eyes fighting back the anger. She wanted to hit something but the last time she banged her fist on her desk four or five people came around to her cubicle to see if everything was OK. And she had caused a boil to form on the side of her hand that pained her for weeks. She felt as if she would go insane if she didn't leave her job soon.

She picked up her card key and took the elevator down 12 flights to the 10th floor where the marketing department of the firm resided. She pushed open the large glass doors and made her way over to Erin's office, located in the far corner of the floor. When she got there Erin was on the phone talking about nothing as usual. When he saw her he put up his finger to say "hold on." Jacy, standing in his doorway, crossed her arms and put all her weight on one leg as she stared out of his window at the view reaching out to West Philadelphia. Two minutes later he was still talking on the phone so she mouthed "I'll be back later," rolled her eyes and turned to walk away but he stopped her.

"Wait a sec Jacy…Brian could you hold on a minute?" he said moving the receiver away from his mouth. Jacy stopped and came into his office. He handed her a folder with a small smirk forming on his face underneath his thick rimmed glasses. "Here is the statement with my changes."

Jacy grabbed the folder and turned around to leave without a word.

"Jacy? There's also another piece on the common drive that I had my secretary write up that I need proofread. Could you take care of that? It's under the Fulasi folder named Fulasi_Draft2."

Jacy, inwardly enraged, simply nodded her head and left. She was not a proofreader. The people at her job were always trying to make her do things that were not in her job description, which pissed her off. Jacy was a skilled copywriter, and her official job title was a Communications Analyst, meaning she was only responsible for creating material and scrutinizing whether or not her company should say certain things in their communications to clients and the media. Yet more and more she was being asked to take on a role that the secretaries at her company were supposed to take care of, editing. Simple edits such as putting a semi colon instead of a comma, things that a secretary could easily handle, especially since that was in their job description. She tried to talk to her boss Caitlin about it once, to no avail. All Caitlin said was: "Being that you work so closely with the documents it would be helpful if you could take care of the editing. We're thinking of making that the norm."

Jacy couldn't believe that four years of college and tens of thousands of dollars invested in her education had only led to this; editing documents in a dead end job. She regretted majoring in business communications and minoring in finance. She found herself wishing she would have chosen a flimsy major such as management or even something totally unrelated such as art history. It seemed as if people who chose easy majors became the managers and bosses at most companies, simply due to the good grades they received in school from taking such simple classes. Jacy had busted her behind throughout college ending up with a GPA of 3.14, taking impossible classes and working part time for nearly all four years. She did have one vice however, and that was partying. Jacy went to just about every party that was held on campus and off, especially after pledging Zeta as a junior. Her sorority sisters called her *Blue Vixen* because of her reputation of acquiring and then dropping men. Social activities were the one aspect of college Jacy didn't regret. But she was still starting to wonder if the whole experience was even worth it.

Jacy went back to her desk and opened the file. There were two errors noted on the paper before her. One was a missing comma, the other had changed an 'an' to a 'the.' She shook her head in disbelief as she made the changes on her online file in less than two seconds. She wanted to go back into her boss' office and throw the paper in her face to see the simple errors they were fussing about, but knew that it wouldn't make a difference. So she just opened her email and wrote an email to Erin copying her boss:

The following changes have been made to my online document:
comma after "gross revenues of $120 million"
and
'an' was changed to 'the' in the third paragraph

Right before Jacy was about to lock up her desk and leave for the day, Rachelle called on her work line.

"What's up girl?" Jacy asked.

"Nothing, I'm just calling to see how you're doing. I haven't talked to you in a minute."

"Yea, where you been?"

"Oh, just doing this and that. Girl I wish I would have never met that nigga Steven from the club."

"Who?"

"You know that guy I gave my number to before we left. He's a jerk."

"Oh really," Jacy said preparing herself for another one of her stories. "What did he do?"

"On our second date he stood me up! Can you believe that shit? I was waiting up in the house dressed for two hours before I finally called him and he was just getting up from the motherfucking bed! He said he never 'confirmed' that we was supposed to be going out. Yea fucking right. A man's supposed to make a good impression on the first couple—"

"You didn't go out with him again did you?" Jacy interrupted.

"Naw, he said he'd make it up to me, so we made a date for last night. We went out to Copas down on South Street. But Jacy, he was staring at every chick that came in the bar! He even excused himself like he was going to the bathroom and when I looked up he was talking to some white girl!"

"Oh Lord," Jacy said putting her head in her hand. She was upset more that her friend had gone out with the man again, and so soon. At least let the nigga sweat for awhile! she thought. Jacy could tell just by looking at the guy that night that he was a dog. Why couldn't Rachelle see that?

"I finally told him I didn't appreciate that shit and he had the nerve to flip it on me like I did something wrong! He said I was making a big deal out of nothing and always complaining, already. I was like how am I always complaining and I've only known you for a week?......"

Jacy listened as her clueless friend went on and on about her horrible night out. She had even had sex with the fool after all that. Then was dumb enough to be shocked when he didn't want her to stay over. He made her trudge home half drunk at three in the morning. She had been calling him all that day but kept getting his voicemail.

"Chelleyyyy. When are you gonna read the signs. I can't believe you slept with him after that shit at Copa's. He didn't deserve that! He damn sure didn't appreciate it! He's probably making a date right now with that white girl, and look, you sitting here stressing about his funky ass!" Jacy almost yelled, and looked around the office taking a mental note to lower her tone. There were gossip vultures throughout her company, continually circling a target for their next prey. No need to feed them voluntarily, she thought.

"But I really like him Jacy. He's a professional type, works at an advertising agency, owns his own house and everything. And he's so cute. I thought we might have something good going..."

"And he thought he might be able to get some quick ass. He got what he wanted from you, and now he's going to avoid your calls. Dammit Chelle stop calling his ass if he's such a jerk like you said yourself. Leave him alone! Stop being so desperate," Jacy spun off letting off her frustrations from work that day on her friend.

Rachelle paused for a moment in thought. "Well sorry we can't all be as strong as you Jacy. But I like him and I think he'll call me back. He's probably just busy at work," she began defending him. Classic bullshit women always pulled. Wasn't she the one just saying how he was a jerk and she should have never met him? Jacy wondered.

Jacy rolled her eyes back into her head. "Don't hold your breath because you'll die waiting on that call. Better yet, mark my words, he *will* call you. It'll be when he needs some more ass."

"Whatever Jacy. I'll holla at you later," Rachelle said with an attitude and hung up the phone.

"Auggghhh." Jacy made a sound of disgust and frustration. She dropped the phone on the receiver and then laid her forehead in her hand.

* * * * *

When Jacy got home she did some basic chores around the house to occupy her time and mind. She was still thinking about her exchange with Rachelle earlier. Her cellphone rang in the next room as she was washing dishes. She dried her hands and walked into her living room. Picking up the cellphone she saw that it was Rich.

"What's up, what you doin'?" he asked, apparently in a good mood.

"I was just washing dishes. What's up."

"Oh. That's my girl doin' the domestic thing. You need to come over here with that," Rich said grinning through the phone.

"Yea whatever, I wash my own dishes and that's about it!" she laughed.

"Imma come get you, I want you to come hang at my crib tonight."

"Oh really?" Jacy said realizing that she hadn't yet seen his home. "Where do you live anyway?"

"With my cousin and brother off Market Street. You gonna be ready when I get there?"

"Yea give me like an hour."

"Aiight."

Jacy went back in the kitchen and finished off the dishes before pulling her work clothes off and jumping into the shower. She made the water more cold since it was really hot outside and the dish water had heated her body. It was the third day of June and it had gone from comfortably hot to unbearably hot in Philadelphia. Toward the end of her shower Jacy shrieked as she turned the knob to all cold and eased herself underneath the intense stream of water. She laughed, and jumped back to safety, then reached around the stream to turn off the water completely.

When she got out, she dried off, lotioned with a new scent from Victoria's secret and pulled on the white velour short shorts set with the zip up top Rich bought her with a matching pair of solid white K-swiss and a small white clutch purse from Unica. She pulled her hair up in a ponytail, attached huge silver hoop earrings to her ears and applied a light coat of clear Mac Lip Glass to her lips, as well as a few strokes of mascara. After dusting her lids with a dark tan color not far from her complexion she was satisfied with her look. Posing in front of the mirror, she finally decided to put a silver charm anklet around her right leg before she threw her cell phone in her bag and sat down to wait for Rich.

40 minutes later, nearly an hour and 45 minutes after their initial conversation, Rich called her cellphone.

"Yo. I'm outside."

"What took you so long?" Jacy said not moving from her spot on the couch.

"What? It's only a quarter to eight. Come on."

"Yea, whatever. I'll be down in a minute," Jacy clicked the end button the phone. She sat and watched the last ten minutes of *Will & Grace* before getting back up to check her makeup in the mirror. Her cell phone rang as she was leaving the house but she ignored it.

Rich dialed her number twice more before he finally saw Jacy appear at the entrance of her apartment. He was extremely annoyed but pushed that to the back of his mind momentarily as he watched her approach the car in her all white outfit. *Sexy little thing*, he thought. She pulled open the door nonchalantly and slid in flipping down the car visor in the same motion to get some mascara out of her eye. Her unapologetic attitude from making him wait caused his feelings of annoyance to return.

"What the hell took you so long? I been waiting out here for like 15 minutes!"

Jacy just glanced over at him with a look that said it all. Rich sighed, then smirked to himself and put the car into drive.

Rich pulled up Chestnut and made a left onto 56th Street, then a right on Market and finally a right onto a small block called Ruby Street. He passed several more short blocks before pulling up behind a dirty red Ford pickup truck on the right. They got out of the car and Rich grabbed Jacy's hand as they approached a group of four guys hanging on a stoop covered with a fake green turf mat. The bars covering the porch in the front of the rowhouse they were sitting at were covered with chipped dark green paint and a female in her early 20's stood behind the white trimmed torn porch screen door, watching Jacy and Rich's every move. Still holding tight to Jacy's hand, Rich came up and reached down to give one of the men sitting down a pound.

"Sup Roo," the brother responded as the others studied Jacy like an expertly cut piece of filet mignon. Rich cocked his head to the side and glared at them with a look that said "what the fuck are you looking at?" They quickly acknowledged him, then chose to look in any direction but Jacy's.

"What ya'll getting into tonight?" Rich asked directing the question at the first brother.

"Probably go down to the bar later. You know the game on tonight, we about to go in now."

"Yo where Jimmy?" Rich asked starting to walk off towards the rowhouse next door.

"I 'oun know I haven't seen his ass for an entire week dog."

"Well when you see that nigga tell his black ass he better see me," Rich said with a tinge of annoyance in his voice as he walked up the stairs to his house and opened the door with a single key.

"Aiight man."

"Take off your shoes," Rich said as they walked into the foyer. After Rich took his off, he reached over to the wall near the door to slightly open the shades and let some light into the house. He disappeared into the back while Jacy made herself comfortable on the couch.

"You hungry?" Rich yelled from the kitchen.

"Yea a little," Jacy replied as she scanned the room. It was nicely decorated for a bachelor's pad. She was sitting on a deep dark blue leather couch with a matching leather loveseat to the left side in the middle of the room which was turned facing the 53 inch flat plasma screen affixed to the wall. Underneath the wall-mounted television was a long short black entertainment center holding several VCRS, a DVD player, an entire cabinet full of CDs and DVDs, a five CD changer and surround sound stereo system. Two tall silver poles stood on either side of the entertainment center with silver and gray silk flowers flowing from the top. A long glass coffee table with silver trim sat in front of the large couch which was in front of the staircase leading up to the next level of the house. Sleek africanesque pictures of shimmering silver black and blue were hung everywhere and the large stark white rug placed in front of the couch set the whole scene off perfectly. The house smelled faintly of nag champa incense. The room and house was not large, but not small and they had made the best of a limited space. Rich came in with a tall glass of lemonade.

"Here baby. The remote's on that stand over there. Use the one for the cable box."

"Thank you Rich," she said smiling and picking up the remote. "I'm impressed, it's really nice in here."

"Thanks." Rich was pleased to have her approval. "I'm about to make us some steaks, so sit tight."

Rich went in the back and Jacy heard him clanking some pans together. She flipped through the channels and stopped on MTV which was playing a rerun of the Real World. The picture was so vivid that it was as if the characters were right there in the room with her.

An hour later Rich came in with two large plates of food that had the house smelling like heaven. He sat the plates down along with the A-1 sauce from under his arm and went to get small wooden eating tables from the closet. When he sat the plate before her Jacy closed her eyes and took in the magnificent smell. There was spanish rice, french cut green beans and two large thinly sliced beef steaks smothered with fried onions.

"Rich! Sweetie this looks sooo good. How did you make it so quick?" she said picking up her fork and knife before placing it back down on her plate to prepare to say Grace.

"I just threw it on the George Foreman Grill, that's my shit," Rich picked up the bottle of A-1 and started to shake it on his plate, but saw that Jacy had put up her hands to pray. "Oh," he said putting the bottle back down and closing his eyes.

"Lord we truly thank for the food before us. Let it give us nourishment in Jesus Christ's name Amen."

"Amen."

Rich switched the TV to the Sixers game and they began eating in silence. Jacy went into the kitchen to get paper towels to cover her white outfit before getting down on her plate.

Hours went by and Jacy had fallen asleep in the late fourth quarter of the game, which the Sixers had lost miserably by 15 points. When it was finally over, Rich cleaned up the mess and then picked Jacy up to carry her to the second floor bedroom. She woke up as soon as she felt his arms lift her from the couch and grabbed onto his neck.

Rich's room was lavishly decorated with expensive dark oak furniture. A huge bureau sat in the corner by the window and his king sized oak canopy bed covered with white 300-count sheets jutted from the back wall into the middle of the room. The carpet was a plush light tan color and an oak entertainment center with TV, DVD, stereo system and other costly electronic equipment made up the final large attraction of the room. A large gold framed picture of a midnight black man and woman interwined hung near the door over an attractive artificial green-leaved plant. Admiring her surroundings, Jacy pulled off her shirt and then headed to the bathroom down the hall to freshen up for bed with her purse in hand.

"You need a t-shirt?" Rich asked coming in the bathroom behind her to check the toilet for surprises.

"Yes please," she answered as Rich came up behind her at the sink, grabbed onto her waist with his right arm and stared into the mirror. Jacy had splashed some water on her face to get rid of the excess mascara and other makeup, and was drying her face off with a small towel as she leaned up. They both looked in the mirror for a minute. Jacy was obviously much shorter than him without high heels on. He took the ponytail holder out of her hair, which fell to her shoulders, leaned in and pressed the left side of his face into her hair taking a long whiff of its scent. His eyes never left the mirror. She smiled as she looked back at him, and like him she was considering whether they looked as if they belonged with each other. Jacy cocked her head to the side slightly. A little to her surprise, they kind of did. After a while, she lowered her eyes and went back to what she was doing. Rich stepped back and watched her pull a small wide toothed comb out of her purse to wrap her hair.

"Do you have a scarf or doo-rag or something?"

"Yea I got one in the room," Rich said smacking her behind and watching it jingle under her white shorts before leaving the bathroom.

Jacy closed the door behind him and relieved herself. When she came back out into the bedroom he had everything laid out for her. She thanked him as he left the room again.

After stripping, wrapping up her hair and getting under the covers Jacy fell asleep almost immediately when her head hit the pillow. She had literally sunk into the soft mattress and fresh clean sheets. She thought it was a part of her dream when Rich slid in behind her enclosing her with both arms and moved close. His manhood was fully aroused, and he rubbed it against her backside as he brought his hands up to fondle her breasts underneath the t-shirt he had given her. Jacy was beginning to get aroused at that point, but was more tired so she tried to play 'sleep' for a while. But she knew that Rich was not going to give up that easy, especially since he was already erect before getting into bed.

She turned around and kissed him fully on the mouth, while stroking the back of his head. He swung his body over on top of hers and they began moving together in a perfect rhythm. A bright Philly moon shone through the window as Rich moved down her soft body with his lips.

THE NEXT morning Jacy was awakened by the sound of a car door and men talking loudly outside. She became aware of her surroundings and frantically searched for the alarm clock. 9:15am.

"Shit!" Jacy screamed flying up from the bed and waking Rich. She was over 45 minutes late and wasn't even dressed or prepared for work. As she gathered her clothes like a mad woman she heard someone open and close the door downstairs.

"Baby, what's wrong?" Rich glanced at the clock and didn't need an answer. "What time were you supposed to be there?"

"8:30. This is just what I need," Jacy shook her head as she pulled on her shorts and zipped up her top. She remembered that her cellphone was on the table downstairs.

Flying out of the room and down the stairs she bumped right into Rich's cousin Cochese. He smelled of sex.

"Whoahohoooo slow down there lady!" Cochese smiled wide looking Jacy up and down with a look of approval in his eyes. Cochese was a fine specimen of man with a very close cut, goatee, caramel complexion and tall lean muscular body. He wore a cream colored linen outfit—he was just getting in after a long night of partying. Born in Philadelphia, Cochese had lived most of his life in Chicago with his father, before moving back to Philly two years prior to live with his cousins and be closer to his mother and grandmother, who needed him.

"I'm sorry, I'm late for work," Jacy apologized before going around him and heading down the stairs. Mid-descent she said, "My name is Jacy, I'm here with Rich."

"Oh ok, nice to meet you Jacy," Cochese still had not taken his eyes off of her. He decided to be curious and go back down to introduce himself.

"I'm Cochese, Rich's cousin. Did Rich tell you about me?"

Jacy snatched her cellphone off of the table and started pushing in numbers. "Yea a little. He told me you live here with him and his brother, excuse me for a minute?...Yea, hi Lauren it's Jacy. I'm running late. I'm probably not going to be in the office until about 10:30 or 11 could you tell anyone who asks to reach me on my cellphone until then? ...Thanks, see you soon." Jacy clicked off her cellphone and turned back to Cochese who quickly moved his eyes back to her face.

"You need a ride or something? I wouldn't mind taking you since I'm already up," he offered.

"No that's alright, I need to go home and get dressed first. Thank you though." Jacy headed back up the stairs towards Rich's room. Rich had rolled over and went back to sleep. She went over and shook him firmly.

"Rich, I need you to get up and drop me back home to get dressed for work!"

Rich peered over his shoulder with his right hand over his forehead. His eyes were red with sleep. "Jacy I thought I told you to quit that job. Take the car, you can take it to work I don't care. I ain't doing much today before five."

Jacy stood over his bed and looked at him. "Fine. Where are your keys," she demanded in an annoyed tone of voice.

"Downstairs on the entertaiment center," he responded sleepily as he rolled back over to go back to sleep.

Jacy gathered the rest of her things and left the room without another word. *He's already starting to show out,* she thought. She considered accepting Cochese's earlier invitation to ruffle Rich's feathers a bit but decided against it. She didn't want to start any drama between family.

GLIDING INTO the parking lot beneath her buliding, Jacy took her ticket and searched floor after floor for a parking spot. Finally finding one, she pulled in and locked Rich's car. Powerwalking to the elevator, she tripped over a groove and fell knee first onto the cement floor of the garage. Her brand new stockings now had a run that led from her knee down to her ankle and her knee was scraped and starting to bleed.

"Shit!!!" she screamed so loud that one of the parking attendants came over to see what was wrong.

"You okay miss?" the attendant looked at her strangely.

"No, I just ran my stockings and I'm late for work," she pouted trying to decide whether she should go out on the street to the Riteaid on the corner to get a new pair of stockings before going into work, or just go into work to check in and get a new pair later. Either way she was going to be embarrassed.

"Is there anything I can do?" the parking attendant, a middle aged man, asked.

"Unless you have a pair of cocoa brown stockings in there I don't think so!" Jacy responded chuckling a bit to relieve the stress that was building. "But thanks anyway."

She decided to take her chances on the street and get a new pair. She held her head high against stares from people on the street and giggles from other black women that passed by. *Damn. I wish I had just worn sandals!* she thought. Once inside Riteaid she rushed to the back aisle where the stockings were and picked out the darkest brown pair she could find. She went to the first aid aisle and picked up a couple of packets of alcohol swabs and a box of bandaids. Hoping the stockings would match her skin tone she came back to the front where there was just one line backed out to the toothpaste aisle.

"Great," she sighed looking at her cellphone. It was 10:57am.

Ten minutes later she finally was next on line. A RiteAid worker, a black girl of about 16, came up to the front and opened up a new line just as the person in front of Jacy was wrapping up.

"Oh now they open up a new line," Jacy said outloud to herself looking around in disbelief and throwing up her hand. By then her knee was bleeding profusely and dripping down her leg. She searched her purse for more napkins but couldn't find any.

"Next on line," the girl said with a disinterested attitude.

The tall white man behind Jacy broke his neck to be first in the new line. Jacy looked at him, but he stared straight ahead as the girl lifelessly rang up his items. *This is going to be a great day*, Jacy thought sarcastically.

The man ahead of her finished and she went up to purchase her stockings. She asked the lady behind the counter for some napkins, but of course she claimed to not have any. She left the store with blood dripping down her leg and rushed into her office building, past the security checkpoint and into the elevator. Once there she breathed a sigh of relief. When the door opened on her floor she flew out towards the bathroom and prayed that she wouldn't come across anybody she knew on her way there. No such luck.

Patty, the office gossip, came sauntering out of the bathroom as Jacy was on her way in.

"Jacy! What happened?" Patty questioned masking curiosity with concern.

"Nothing Patty, I just have a little scrape."

"Do you need the first aid kit?"

"No I'll be fine Patty." Jacy pushed her way into the bathroom.

Jacy threw her purse and the bag onto the green marble bathroom counter and stripped out of the old stockings quickly. She then grabbed the bag and went into a stall to clean up.

When Jacy finally came out of the bathroom all cleaned up and fresh again it was 11:30am. The stockings were about a shade off but they would have to do. She went to her desk and found a post it note on her computer screen that said:

"Please see me in my office, Caitlin."

Great, Jacy thought as she turned on her computer. She then prepared herself for the worst as she headed towards Caitlin's office. She knocked lightly on the open door.

"Caitlin? Hi, you wanted to see me."

"Yes Jacy, please close the door and come in."

Jacy did as asked and sat down at the table in the center of Caitlin's office.

"Jacy I can't afford to have you coming in at 11:30am in the afternoon. What if one of the consultants needed your help this morning?"

"Caitlin, I apologize. I called in as soon as I could and left my cell phone number for anyone that needed me. I tried to get here as soon as I could but I had a few mishaps this morning."

"You can't really proofread documents or do other computer work over the phone Jacy. I'm sorry too, but I'm going to have to put you on warning," Caitlins tight thin lips looked like a flexing rubber band as they moved up and down releasing cold rehearsed words. "Any further unplanned absences or other problems with your work and we are going to have to take disciplinary action. Now I see that you took off for the next couple of days but we may need you to be on call to work at home if needed during the day. The big news conference about the Unified Contracting account is happening on Tuesday and we have to be fully prepared. Are the numbers we have for you, 215-564-4123 and 267-377-9103 correct?"

"Yes they are correct," Jacy said clenching her teeth to remain calm.

"Good. Marsha Collins from corporate in New York is the point person for Unified. She has a good relationship with them so she was insistent on preparing most of the statement we will be using at the news conference. I would like you to start work on proofreading and applying the revisions I've already made to these few pieces I received from her this morning. I sent the Word document to you this morning via email. She will be sending down potential questions to be fielded later today via email as well."

Jacy was tempted to ask her what the secretaries were doing today and why they couldn't handle proofreading and editing the document, but she knew she was already skating on thin ice. Boiling inside, Jacy stood and received the folder Catilin was holding out for her. She told Caitlin she'd have the changes done by 3pm and walked out of the office.

Jacy finished the assignment with time to spare and waited for the final pieces from Marsha. During her downtime she searched real estate sites for available properties in Philadelphia. She found a few and emailed their MLS listing numbers to her home address. At 4pm Marsha still had not sent anything to either her or Caitlin.

Jacy picked up the phone and dialed the operator in New York.

"Summit Financial how may I help you?" the operator sang into the phone.

"Hello, I'm calling from the Philadelphia office. Could you please connect me with Marsha Collins."

"Sure, hold on a moment." Jacy heard two beeps.

"Marsha Collins."

"Hi Marsha, this is Jacy Thomas from the Philadelphia office. I am waiting on your final copy for the Unified conference. Do you have that ready for me?"

"No, I'm still having my secretary type up a few more questions and answers. I'll have that for you within the hour. Sorry about that."

"No problem, I will be waiting for it. Thanks."

5:13pm rolled around and still nothing from New York. She redialed the New York office and was transferred to an automated service where she dialed in Marsha's information. A minute later she heard Marsha's voicemail pick up. She sighed at the sound of Marsha's generic voice and left a message explaining that she had a commitment to meet that night and could not stay at the office for very long so she needed to get that information in the next ten to fifteen minutes or she would have to be contacted at home the next day to work the revisions. She left her home email address and both her work and home number and then hung up the phone. Pissed at herself for not expressing her urgency more to Marsha when she talked to her earlier, she began to pack up and get ready to leave. Just then Caitlin appeared at the entrance to her cubicle.

"You aren't about to leave are you?" Caitlin inquired with a puzzled look on her face.

"Caitlin I can't stay late tonight, I have my friend's car and he needed it back at 5pm."

Caitlin shifted her weight to one side and folded her arms. She looked down at her shoes for a moment in thought and then looked back up at Jacy.

"Jacy I need you to stay here and wait for Marsha's document to arrive. Since you won't be here tomorrow and Friday I need you to be here as late as needed in order to get that last piece finalized."

"I left a message with Marsha telling her to send the documents to my home email address and I will do the revisions there. As you said yourself I'll be on call for those two days anyway."

"I know that, but I still think it's best if you stay here to receive the very first version so that there will only be minor changes tomorrow."

"Caitlin." Jacy paused and dropped her head down a little while rubbing her forehead back and forth. She looked back up and said firmly with slight frustration in her voice. "I'm sorry but I really do have to leave. I can't keep my friend's car from him indefinitely while I wait for Marsha to answer her phone or send me these files. I left her my home email and number to send the files, I will work from home tomorrow to get those completed and back to you by the end of the day. If you have revisions of your own you can just send them to me through email or fax. The press conference is not until Tuesday and I guarantee you that all of the statements will be prepared and ready for that date."

Caitlin first looked at Jacy with her eyebrows raised, about to challenge her again, but then her expression relaxed. She looked back down at her $250 shoe, and then back up at Jacy's computer. "Alright then, Jacy," is all she said before walking off.

* * * * *

Jacy pulled up at Rich's house at 5:47pm. He was standing on the porch talking to one of the guys they passed from next door the day before. She slammed the car door shut with all her power and trudged up the stairs. Rich looked at her with his mouth open as if she had lost her mind.

"What you slamming my car door like that for?"

"Look just take your keys," she said with a look of disgust on her face and threw the keys at his chest. Jacy was definitely not in the mood, anything added to her day at this point would send her off the deep end. He caught the keys in his hand up against his chest wearing the same look of amazement on his face. "Bye," Jacy said sarcastically, turning her back to him.

Sensing trouble, the guy Rich was talking to told Rich he would get up with him later, to deaf ears, before walking off to the house next door. Jacy had since made it down the steps and was headed in the direction of Chestnut Street.

"Girl, where the hell do you think you going!" Rich leaped down all six cement porch steps and charged towards her lunging for her right arm and turning her to face him. She flung her arm out of his grip.

"I'm going the fuck home. I'm taking the bus," she said in a frustrated tone then turned and continued on her way hoping he would just leave her alone at that point, let her stew in her anger. What a day. There had been a ball of fire growing constantly in the pit of her stomach since earlier that morning and she knew it was bound to let loose if Rich did or said the wrong thing. *If he would have gotten his lazy ass up and took me to work, I wouldn't be in this mess with Caitlin, I wouldn't have skinned my knee and I wouldn't have to work from home tomorrow*, she blamed in her head. To top things off she had barely missed an accident on the way to Rich's house that would have caused sure death—a man ran a red light and would have hit Jacy dead on at the driver's side if she would not have stopped in time. Her heart had almost jumped through her chest and she had to pull over to thank God for her life.

"No you're not. I'm taking your ass home so get in the fucking car!" he grabbed her hand roughly and pulled her towards the car.

"Rich! Get the FUCK off of me!!" Jacy snatched her hand back like a wild woman. The lit fuse had hit bottom. "I'm about TIRED of you always trying to tell me what to do! Who are you my daddy? Your lazy ass didn't want to take me to work this morning so don't worry about taking me no fucking where right now!" Jacy screamed at him in a way that actually shook Rich down to his Nikes. She then turned and powerwalked down to Chestnut Street. Rich stood speechless as he watched his future wife march away from him. One of his next door neighbors, his boy's sister Neecey, watched the whole scene through a dark screened window upstairs. Rich's cousin Cochese came outside to see what the commotion was about.

"Yo man what's going on out here? Was that Jacy?"

"Yea I don't know what the hell is wrong with this girl! She came over her wilin' out, talking how I ain't take her to work this morning."

"Oh. Well you know how womens is. She probably had a fucked up day and taking it out on you. Where she going?"

"She said she's taking the bus but fuck that, I'm going to get her ass and straighten this shit out now." Rich picked the key to his car off of the ring and held it in between his thumb and index finger placing it into the lock. He hopped in the car and pulled off screeching down the one-way street towards Chestnut.

Figuring she was taking the bus that ran down 52nd, he headed in that direction and found her standing at the bus stop on 52nd and Chestnut. Some young knucklehead was trying to talk to her but Jacy, who was looking bored and annoyed at the same time, was completely ignoring him. Rich swerved up to the bus stop and hopped out with a quickness.

"Get outta here young bul," Rich waved him off. The boy thought about protesting but then listened to his gut instinct and turned around and left looking mad. Jacy looked straight ahead holding the strap of her purse with her right hand as if she didn't see anything that was going on around her.

"Jacy. Baby. Could you please tell me what's going on?" Rich came up to her and put his hands around her waist leaning back and straining to look into her eyes under the rim of his hat. She avoided his stare and didn't say anything. He smiled a little at her antics. "Jacy, come on now. Whatever I did I apologize, I won't do it again. I promise, I'll take you to work everyday if you want! Come on in the car so we can talk."

Jacy finally moved her eyes back to his after a few seconds of pensive thought. She saw his smile and her look became warmer and her features softened, but she was still almost frowning.

"Rich, I'm sorry for screaming on you like that. I just had a bad day and I'm ready to just go home and go to sleep."

"Alright then come on baby. I'll take you home." He let go of her and opened the passenger side of his car for her to get in. She stepped in and threw her purse on the back seat. As she leaned her head back and closed her eyes she heard him open the driver's side door and get in. "So tell me what happened today."

Jacy went through her story from the tear in her stockings to the almost fatal accident. Rich chuckled when he heard Jacy had fallen on her knee, but then quickly shut his mouth into a tight smile when she shot him a look to kill. He genuinely felt bad for not waking up to take her to work even though he didn't think it was a big deal. But he was happy that they would have Thursday and Friday together with no interruptions from Jacy's work schedule—that is until he heard that Jacy would have to work from home the very next day.

"Jacy," Rich started as he pulled up into her apartment complex. "I want you to leave that job. I told you I'm gonna take care of you, you ain't never gonna have to lift another finger if you don't want to. Forget that bitch Katey, that job ain't doin' nothin' but bringing you down baby. I don't like seeing you like this, you looked like you was about to punch a nigga before!"

Jacy laughed and felt some of her tension releasing. She reached back to grab her pocketbook. "Don't think I won't—keep acting up and we'll see."

"Don't make me have to body slam you on this grass girl," Rich teased as they both hopped out of the car. Rich walked with a slow cocky stroll slighty ahead of her on the lawn as they moved toward the entrance to her apartment building. Jacy took two quick steps and jumped onto his back with a mock strangle hold on his neck. He grabbed onto her legs and spun around, dipping and shaking her from side to side as she giggled helplessly. He finally made one final hop to adjust her on his back and headed for the door.

chapter 7
Moment of Truth

IT WAS 7:12am, Friday morning and the alarm was going off for the third time. Jacy reached over and turned it off, then slowly opened her eyes and enjoyed the sight of the newly risen sun shining through her window to her left for a few moments. Looking further down her eyes rested on the back of Rich's low cut head. He was sprawled out on his stomach with his right hand dangling over the bed, snoring loudly. Rich had been so loud the previous night that someone from across the courtyard at Jacy's building hollered for them to be quiet. Mad because he ain't gettin' none, Rich figured. That night he had done his best to stimulate Jacy in the way she needed but was unable to hit her spot in a regular fashion, so after 15 frustrated minutes Jacy had pulled his head up and let him get his. He gets an A for effort, she thought. But as always, his shot was on point, so she had no problem staying aroused throughout the session.

It had turned out that Marsha Collins would not have anything ready to be edited for Jacy until Friday afternoon after 3pm, so Jacy did not have to work from home after all on Thursday. It was a good thing Jacy hadn't stuck around and waited for her the day before because Marsha hadn't even called or tried to contact her that night. During the early afternoon Thursday, Jacy and Rich bumrushed the King of Prussia mall and even went into the Louis Vuitton store to buy the new Monogram Multicolore Alma bag and a pair of matching mules Jacy had raved about after seeing it on the Style channel. Jacy's face blushed a deep Indian red when she saw the amount of money Rich laid out for just those two items. She wasn't a 'name brand leech,' and felt a little embarrassed to accept the gifts, but figured, what could it hurt to splurge and get some high quality shit for once. She let him decide on a few outfits per her agreement to wear less revealing clothes, but she still got her way with a few exceptions. Rich beamed the whole time as he watched her bounce from store to store. Most of the time Rich had more cash than he could even spend, so he was happy to drop a couple thousand on this last shopping trip before his court date.

After the mall they took the hour ride out to Six Flags in New Jersey. They rode just about every ride together, except the Freefall which they both knew they'd probably get sick on. After Six Flags they drove out to Camden where Rich had to make a run, then finally headed back to South Street in Philadelphia to eat dinner at Uno's. It was a full day and they really enjoyed their time together. Tipsy and fully satisfied with their day, they sat at Jacy's apartment afterwards and talked until late in the night.

This was the big day—Rich's trial was less than four hours away and Jacy was nervous for him. She again began to feel a piercing guilt for the whole situation, which may have been avoided had she worn a more conservative outfit. But why should she have to change how she dressed? She rolled over to her side towards Rich and rubbed him on his back. He stirred a bit, rubbed his nose and grasped underneath the pillow with his right hand. There was a few seconds of silence and then he began to snore again.

Jacy slid out of the bed trying not to wake him and went in the bathroom to wash up. She emerged several minutes later and headed to the kitchen where she began to pull out eggs, bacon, butter, milk and cheese. She whipped together some pancakes, dropping a touch of vanilla into the mixture, while the bacon fried in her non-stick pan. She whipped together the eggs and poured them into a smaller pan to fry. She left the pancake mixture to the side to wait its turn. Venturing back into the bedroom, Jacy turned on the TV and shook Rich to move him from the third to the first realm of sleep.

By the time the last pancake was flipped out of the pan, Rich was in the bathroom relieving himself. When he came out he stretched his arms above his head and walked toward the steaming plates of food being set on Jacy's glass dining room table.

"Awwww shit! You know this is the very first time you've cooked for me, Princess," Rich smiled his crooked smile and walked over to Jacy to hold her and give her an appreciative kiss. Jacy smiled back up at him, still swirling with thoughts of what would happen that day. She really didn't want to see Rich go to jail.

"Well I wanted to do something special," Jacy said in response as she went back into the kitchen to turn off the stove. She then joined Rich back at the table, prayed over his and her own food, and commenced eating.

"Do you have everything you need to bring with you today?" she asked him.

"Well, I really don't need to bring anything, if they hold me after the trial they're gonna take everything from me anyway," Rich said cutting up his pancakes and then putting a large portion of them into his mouth.

"Is Timbo going to make it there?"

"Yea he'll be there, probably late, but he'll be there. That's my nigga."

"Well did you tell them that I'm willing to speak as a witness?"

"Yea I told my lawyer, have you ever sat as a witness before?"

"No, I just have to state my name and swear on the Bible and all of that right? What if they cross examine me, do you think it'll be too bad?"

"Probably not. They're probably gonna ask you something about the fight, just tell them the truth about what caused it. That's all you can do."

"Alright," Jacy felt a shot of anxiety run up her back and into her throat as she put some eggs to her lips. What if she said something to mess up his entire case?

"Don't worry Jacy," Rich said almost reading her mind. "You gonna help the case a whole lot more than you can hurt it. They already got witnesses from the scene to testify about the fight itself."

Jacy nodded her head silently.

They finished up their meal and showered. By the time they were all dressed and ready it was closely approaching 8am. Rich was sitting on the bed pulling on his shoes when Jacy came into the room brushing her hair. She studied him for a while as he sat before her in the white Ralph Lauren oxford shirt and dark blue cotton slacks he had brought in an overnight bag. She had never seen him dress up even a bit, and he looked pretty good. But even now he looked far from formal. He still had on his trademark baseball cap, a black White Sox hat. His demeanor gave the outfit a street appeal, sort of like a *Fresh Prince of Bel Air* feel. He had a fresh shave and his light mustache and goatee were well-shaped. She thought of the possible outcomes for today and wished the whole ordeal had never happened. For some reason his appearance was giving her a rise. A sly grin was plastered on her face while he was still bent down tying his shoes. A naughty thought crossed her mind and she decided to act on it before she had a chance to change her mind. She put down her brush and walked over to him and pushed him up to an upright position. He looked up at her with a confused expression as she started to unbuckle his pants. He tried to say something but she shushed him with a finger to his lips. He held his hands up in submission as she completed her task. She hiked up her purple and yellow knee length summer dress and straddled him. It didn't take long for the blood to leave his brain and engorge his lower body. Jacy reached over into the drawer and pulled out a Magnum which she slid on before lowering herself onto his lap. She rode him quietly for 15 minutes, her tight walls pulsated around him. He just clenched his eyes closed alternating between a low moan and quick breaths. She finally whispered words into his ear that made it impossible for him to hold his climax a minute longer. He grasped her tightly as he lifted his head towards the ceiling, shaking and choked up with pleasure at the warm sensations overtaking his body. His body went weak and he held Jacy's body close to his. His lips grazed, kissed and grasped at her right ear in desperate passion as he began to whisper words that rattled Jacy.

"...I love you... Jacy...I love you," Rich breathed out in pained hushed tones as he manicly rubbed his cheek and mouth against the side of her face.

Looking out towards the window with a chaotic expression, Jacy didn't know what to do except continue holding him. She didn't want to ruin this moment for him, she wanted him to have positive thoughts going into his trial. She figured he was just caught up in the afterglow. The love-making had been so good that Jacy almost felt herself on the verge of peaking at one point. Unheard of. She bent her head down and kissed him on the back of the neck, then the side, then came around to the front to plant a big wet juicy kiss on his lips. When she broke free from the kiss, he looked up at her with a mixture of curiousity and concern in his eyes but she quickly eased it with one of her winning smiles. She pecked him on the lips once more before lifting herself up from his embrace.

She went back into the bathroom to take another quick shower before any tension or questions surfaced. It was now 7:52 and they had to get a move on to make court by 9am. Rich followed her into the bathroom and re-washed. When they finished up they made their way out the door and to Rich's car.

They had agreed that Jacy would keep Rich's car after the trial if he was taken into custody. Once outside, Rich called Jacy over to his driver's side for a moment. He emptied out his pockets and handed Jacy the stack of money that remained from their shopping spree.

"This should cover at least your next 2-3 months rent. Remember call Timbo if you need *anything*, he is going to take care of you aiight? You have his number?" Rich asked, peering into her eyes under his cap.

"Yea I have it in my phone. Thank you Rich," she said, then nervously put her hands on her behind, looked away and sighed a sigh that said her emotions were trying to take over. She was a tough little chick, but didn't want to see anyone have to go through this.

"Baby, I'm gonna be fine. For real," Rich said sensing her inner battle and opened his arms to give her a hug.

"Come on, let's go," Rich said when they finally released and Jacy went back around to her side of the car. Once they were both inside, Rich put the car in gear and they headed towards downtown Philadelphia.

* * * * *

The drive was shorter than they thought, as they arrived at the courthouse on 13th street which was used only for misdemeanor trials that lead to sentences of five years or less. The time was 8:23am and they had plenty of time to make their way to the courtrooom. When they passed the security checkpoint, Rich immediately saw his lawyer standing by the courtroom doors.

"How are you doing Mr. Wilkins," his lawyer, Tom Addison, a tall thin faced pale white man said reaching for his hand.

"Doin' fine, just ready to get this thing over with." Rich reached for Jacy and introduced her. "This is my girl Jacy, the one I told you about."

"Right. Jacy I wanted to go over a few things with you really quick this morning before the case is called. It should be pretty straightforward. Can you guys follow me?"

They followed him into a back room behind the courtroom and they discussed what would be asked of Jacy and what she could expect from the prosecution. A new set of butterflies found their way to Jacy's stomach during the conversation. Tom tried to ease her anxiety by assuring her that her testimony would add a lot of value to Rich's case.

The plan was to plead guilty to simple assault in order to accept a lesser sentence of between 30 and 180 days. They went over a few more details and then headed back into the main courtroom to await the case. Tom excused himself and went out into the hall to make a phone call.

A few minutes later Timbo came strolling into the courtroom in his standard attire, a Roc-a-wear t-shirt and tims.

"Ay Roo," he said just a little too loud and the court clerk shushed him as he went over to Rich. Rich stood up grinning and gave his best friend a half-hug.

"Look at this nigga, showing up on time." He laughed and Jacy shook her head and smiled at their candor in the courtroom.

"Shut up the hell up man I be on time for shit," Timbo replied. This time the clerk asked that the two gentlemen be quiet and have a seat. They listened and sat down. They spoke briefly in code. They knew that there was a strong recorder that taped all personal conversations in the courtroom so they didn't say much. Rich reached back over and put his arm behind Jacy as they sat on the wooden benches awaiting his case to be called. Rich was the definition of cool; he had obviously been through this process many times.

20 minutes later everyone was seated in the courtroom and the court tipstave officer called the courtroom to order. The first case was called, a 35 year old white man being charged with public lewdness for flashing people in the art museum area. He would mainly target tourists who were visiting the Philadelphia Art Museum as they descended the stairs from the large building. The judge charged him a $700 fine and 60 days in jail for the aggravation he caused families with small children. Another case was of a 42 year old black man charged with 1 count of aggravated assault and 1 count of domestic violence. He had attacked his live-in girlfriend with a Louisville slugger bat in a drunken rage and sent her to the hospital with a concussion. It had all stemmed from an argument he started because he was furious with his girlfriend for cooking him chicken and not fish as he had wished. The judge charged him on both counts and sentenced him to the max, 5 years in jail with the possibility for parole in 36 months, on testimony from his girlfriend, who had been fed up with his abuse. Her family members also testified

about his previous abuse and were probably the main ones who were finally able to convince her to press charges against her crazed boyfriend.

A few cases later, Rich's lawyer brought him out of the courtroom to let him know that he was up next. He went over some last minute details and they then went back into the courtroom just as his case was being called. Jacy felt her heart leap back up to her throat upon hearing his name.

"The case of the City of Philadelphia v. Richard Wilkins. All parties please take your seats."

The trial proceeded smoothly and as Rich's lawyer expected. Samuel Torres, the man who Rich had attacked, testified with his head partly bandaged up, presumably to win sympathy from the judge, but it didn't seem as if it was working. The most damaging to Rich's case was pictures of Samuel's bloody face and completely shut eyes at the time of beating. Finally, Rich's lawyer called Jacy to the stand. She swore in and took her seat on the witness stand. She had perfect posture and sat with her legs crossed and hands on her knees.

"Please state your name and city of residence for the courtroom," Rich's lawyer requested.

"Jacilyn Thomas I reside in Philadelphia, PA."

"Ms. Thomas, were you with Mr. Wilkins on the day in question."

"Yes I was."

"Could you explain in detail what happened that day?"

"Well Rich and I were walking down the street, minding our own business, when the plaintiff, excuse me, Mr. Torres? He just walked right up to me and grabbed me by the waist. He had no right to put his hands on me."

"And did you know Mr. Torres prior to the incident, Ms. Thomas?"

"No, he was a complete stranger. What right does he have to come up to me and grab me, especially with my boyfriend right there?" Jacy looked over to Rich who had his chin resting on his fingers and was smiling back at her like a kindergartener.

"So in your opinion, Ms. Thomas would you say Mr. Wilkins was acting in defense of you, his girlfriend?"

"Yes, Rich was just defending me from someone who put his hands on me without permission. For all I know this guy could have been trying to feel me up or sexually assault me on the street."

"Thank you Ms. Thomas. That is all," Rich's lawyer smiled at her and went back to his seat.

"Would the prosecution like to cross-examine the witness?" the judge, a large black man in his 60's with stark white thinning hair and blotchy skin asked. Terry Surgis, the brown haired female district attorney, hesitated at first but then stood with her response.

"Yes your Honor," she said and approached the witness stand. "Ms. Thomas, do you think the force with which your boyfriend used on Mr. Torres was necessary?"

"Objection your Honor, there is no way for her to determine—" Tom Addison began.

"Overruled. Please answer the question Ms. Thomas," the judge said looking at Jacy admiringly.

"I believe it was fully warranted based on the way Mr. Torres behaved on the street that day." Jacy felt herself slipping into the professional speak she only used at work and when she was at her legal studies classes during college. "Besides, he was not completely innocent or helpless. As you can see yourself Mr. Torres is a pretty tall well-built man, my boyfriend is 5'10 and Mr. Torres is well over 6 feet tall. He was fighting back and Rich had to continue to defend himself and me as best as he could. So yes I believe anything required to restrain Mr. Torres in that situation was necessary."

The district attorney hesitated for a moment as if she was going to ask another question, but then stopped herself reasoning that continuing to talk to this woman might hurt her case more than it helped. Upon hearing that the defendant's girlfriend would be testifying Mrs. Sturgis had figured her for a common uneducated woman from the ghetto. But she was now slightly shaken by the well put together responses Jacy was giving—she had even brought out something that the prosecution had hoped to avoid being brought out, the fact that Mr. Torres was taller and had pretty much the same muscular frame as Mr. Wilkins.

"No further questions Your Honor," she said, and glanced back at Jacy one more time before heading to her seat. Rich's lawyer nodded once in Jacy's direction with a tight thin-lined smile on his face.

The two sides gave their closing arguments and finally the judge took the floor to determine sentencing.

"Will the defendant please stand," Rich stood defiantly and awaited his sentencing. He had already plead guilty so it was not a matter of *if* he would go to jail for the assault, it was *how long*.

"Well Mr. Wilkins I have considered your testimony, and since you have plead guilty I will now hand down sentencing. There are several factors I'm taking into account in this case. The two points working against you are one, that you are *not* a first time offender, and two, the extent of the injuries inflicted on Mr. Torres. Not to mention the disruption you caused the residents of the city. Now based on these three things alone I would normally sentence you to a minimum of 6 months in jail and a $1,000 fine. But because you were obviously acting in defense of your girlfriend, and Mr. Torres was completely out of line for putting his hands on her, I am going to lessen the sentence to a maximum of 30 days in a nearby correctional facility with a possibility for early release for this offense and a $500 fine. Your parole will also unfortunately be extended for two years. I can personally relate to the frustration of having another man show disrespect to you and your female companion, and I would advise that you and Ms. Thomas bring charges against Mr. Torres for his conduct in case he attempts to sue you for medical bills and other charges," he looked sternly at Torres and then glanced at Jacy before continuing. "This case is now closed. Bailiff please take the defendant into custody," the judge said banging his gavel onto the table.

Rich grinned and then turned around to clasp hands with Timbo. He gave him a half-hug saying a few last minute words. He then kissed Jacy several times on the mouth before the bailiff came over and put him in handcuffs.

chapter 8
Time to Make Some Serious Moves

IT WAS SATURDAY MORNING and Jacy was parking her car on South Street. She was meeting Jason Colridge that day to talk about her real estate venture. She had tried to find a spot nearer to Ms. Tootsies but the only available parking down on 13th and South was a paid parking lot. She had finally found a spot near 10th and South but had to walk three blocks and pay the meter. She stepped out adjusting her skirt and rounded her car hitting the alarm chirper. She filled the meter with four quarters—all the quarters she had on her at the time—and headed towards the restaurant.

As she walked down the busy South Street she noticed a young black couple of no more than 16 or 17 years old walking down the street arguing. They were being loud and acting as if there was no one else on the street. The sister was pushing a stroller and holding a one year old baby, tears streaming down her face. The young brother who was wearing a long white T-shirt and a baseball cap was walking slightly in front of them to the side of the stroller throwing his hands up and being animated. He seemed as if he just wanted to walk off, and he very well could have. Poor girl, Jacy thought. Hopefully she'll wake up and smell the coffee *sooner* than later.

Jacy thought about the occurrences of the past week as she passed 11th Street holding a manila folder under her arm. After Rich's trial she had gone back to her apartment and sat in silence—no TV, no radio—for a good couple of hours just thinking, before she would have to turn on her computer and get to work on the file Marsha Collins had sent her earlier that afternoon. She thought about how fast everything had happened. It had only been a few weeks since she had met Rich and they were now officially together. Through prison walls at that. She had dated a lot of thug types, but had never stayed with one while he went off to jail. She never took them that seriously. But with Rich things were slightly different. Since she was trying to leave her job and start up a new business the money Rich was giving her to pay her bills was helping her out tremendously. She would have over $5,000 saved by the end of the next two months, combined with the nearly $4,000 she already had saved up for this venture and an investment from her family of $2,000 leaving her with a grand total of over $11,000 to buy and fix up her first rowhouse in Southwest Philly. Fixer upper homes went for as low as $3,000 in that part of town, but she was hoping to get one that did not require an extraordinary amount of work. She figured the carpentry required to turn a $9,000 home into a $15-20,000 home would cost her about $3,000. If she was able to sell that house at a profit she would immediately buy another and another until she was able to build up her portfolio of investment properties.

Besides the financial security he provided, Rich was really growing on her. Despite his anger problem and fits of jealous rage, Rich could really be a sweetheart. He took care of his responsibilities, including his daughter who he had spent the night with the day Jacy went off on him in the street. He had wanted to stay with Jacy that night but knew he had to make time to see his daughter before he went away. So he had left Jacy's around 8pm, picked his daughter Shelly up from her grandmother's house, where her and her mother lived, and brought her back to his house to stay over the night. Jacy was proud of Rich for doing that because most men would have put their penis before their child in a heartbeat. At least he knew where his priorities were at.

Her cellphone rang as she continued walking down South Street and she opened her purse to grab it. Terrell's number popped up and she immediately pressed ignore to send him to voicemail. "Just give it up Terrell!" she said out loud to herself and then went back to her original train of thought.

The only big problem with Rich was that she found herself arguing with him alot. They were usually small spats that dissipated in a matter of minutes, but they arose nonetheless and on a regular basis. They both were hot-tempered people which meant a lot of head bumping. Jacy liked Rich, but in her opinion, life was too short to constantly be arguing with someone. During their day together on the Thursday before his court date, the two argued over some of the clothes they had each picked out on their shopping trip. They argued about why Jacy had taken so long in the bathroom at the amusement park. They argued about how long Rich took in the house he made a stop at in Camden. They even argued about where Rich should park when they went to eat on South Street. It had become mentally tiring and Jacy was beginning to get a little fed up with Rich always questioning her whereabouts like a jealous madman. Rich was getting tired of Jacy always challenging his authority and insisting on looking like a sexpot in public.

Jacy's mind drifted to her parents as she stepped up on the block and approached the restaurant. Growing up, arguments were commonplace in her household. Her parents would argue about some of the silliest things: "Why isn't my toothbrush in the holder?" "The garbage cans are supposed to go on the *left* side of the driveway." "You're supposed to use neosporin on a cut not hydrogen peroxide!" That was in addition to the large arguments over her father's cheating and lying to her mother, and her mother's impulsive shopping habits. She didn't want to end up in a relationship like that. She wanted a man like her father—a man that who knew his reponsibilities, and was strong and protective over his family—but at the same time she absolutely *didn't* want a man like her father. Selfish, disrespectful and unfaithful. She wanted a responsible, loyal and giving man that could keep her in check but was still respectful of her and her needs. She could do without having to argue all the time too. Possibly an unreachable goal.

She finally stepped up to the outdoor area of the restaurant where several high chairs and tables were set out for patrons that wanted to enjoy their lunch outside. Standing to the right of the door was a tall, handsome, young looking, light brown-skinned man with hazel eyes, in a pair of loose tan rayon pants and a solid white short sleeved button up dress shirt with a wife beater visible underneath. Naw, this couldn't be him, Jacy thought. Jason Colridge was in his late twenties, this brother didn't look a day over 21.

When Jason saw Jacy he formed his mouth in an "O," popped the inside of his cheek with his tongue and looked generously over her outfit. She was wearing a straight flower patterned knee length skirt which fit loosely around her brown thighs and a fitted sky blue sleeveless shirt to match the colors of the skirt.

She stopped near the entrance and looked around her so that she would appear to be looking for someone in case the man before her actually was Jason Colridge. A big smile grew on his face as he realized who she was and he immediately stepped up.

"Are you Jacy?"

Jacy was definitely surprised at how good looking the man was. It wasn't often that you saw good looking professional type men in Philadelphia. But from what she knew he lived in Mount Airy, one of the more ritzy upper class areas in the Philadelphia region where black people resided. There was something about him though that sent warning signals to her brain. Sniff sniff, she thought. She smelled a dog. Definitely a man that would lick his balls and then lick your face. His shifty aura had been oozing out of him ever since she spotted him leaning against the wall outside the restaurant waiting.

"Yes, you're Jason? Nice to meet you." She reached her hand out and he grabbed it, turning it around to kiss the back.

"It's a pleasure to meet you as well," he replied looking at her with mischief in his eyes. His whole tone of voice and demeanor had changed from when they spoke on the phone. He no longer spoke like a professional—instead he sounded like a man trying to smooth talk a woman. Jacy was not impressed.

"You didn't have to wait out here for me, you could have gotten a table," right after saying that she noticed that there were a few scattered people waiting to the far right close to the street.

"No, no I put our names in, we have to wait for a table out here. We're behind one more couple and then we're in there," Jason explained. Ms. Tootsies was so small that it could only hold about ten tables closely arranged. It was a normal occurrence for people to have to wait outside on the sidewalk in order to be seated.

"So, Jacy, tell me more about yourself?" Jason said pulling her to the side and then shoving his hands in his loose pockets as he turned to face her.

"Oh, well there's not much to tell past what we discussed. I'm a communications analyst, originally from New Jersey, went to school at Seaton Hall I've been in Philly for going on two years—"

"So what do you do out here for fun?" Jason inquired.

"Oh a little bit of everything, I try to keep myself busy." Jacy answered, moving herself slightly to the side, out of his direct line of fire. He looks good, but whoa—his breath is really kicking, she thought. How can you not taste that shit smell in your mouth?

"That's good, you only have one life to live. Are you single, married, divorced?"

Well he doesn't waste any time, Jacy thought. "Not married, but I'm seeing someone right now." A couple was called into the restaurant by the short light skinned hostess who had a scarf wrapped around her head.

"Oh, well he's a very lucky man. I hope he's treating you right," he said. Jacy had to stop herself from rolling her eyes. Classic lines.

"Yes, he is," she said smiling and remaining polite. She didn't want to cause any problems with a man that could potentially help her reach financial independence. She tried to change the subject. "So how's business?"

"Oh it's alright, home purchases have been surging due to the low interest rates. People are trying to get in while the getting's good. I'm always busy."

"I see. Well hopefully I'll be able to get my operation up in time to take advantage of the current market."

"It's possible. But with the properties you're starting off with you'll probably be dealing with customers that require sub-prime lending. Their rates will be high regardless of the low mortgage rates."

Jacy nodded as she considered his comment. She guessed he was right since it was unlikely that someone with excellent credit would be looking for a house in the ten to twenty thousand dollar range. Still, she wanted to get things started as soon as possible. Just thinking about leaving her dead end job made her giddy with delight.

"Jason, party for two," the short hostess called out from inside the door frame. They followed her into the restaurant and sat down at the small table she gestured towards. Once seated Jason went back into his inquisition.

"So. Jacy Thomas. Hmmm. Why does a beautiful woman like you have to work anyway? You look like the type of woman that should be getting taken care of."

Jacy was a little taken aback by the comment, but decided to just take it as a compliment. She wasn't happy with the direction their meeting was going. "Well, thank you, I guess. I don't want to depend on a man for my living. At least not without being married to him," Jacy answered wondering if he even really needed to know all that information.

Jason studied her features and shapely upper torso. "A man would be a fool not to lock a woman like you up in the house. You'd never have to work a day in your life if you were my woman," Jason was obviously not one to mince words.

Jacy smiled weakly and then looked down at the folder before her, opening it up to reveal some papers.

"I found some properties in the area I'm targeting on some real estate sites online," she said changing the subject awkwardly.

Jason was looking at her so intensely that she thought a laser beam might shoot out at any moment. She handed him the black and white printed page of information for the property she was considering and he looked over the semi-detailed list. "I drove by a few of them, and they look decent enough. This rowhouse was for $8,500, but it's going to need some work on the exterior. The lawn is pretty messed up and a few windows on the bottom floor are broken."

"Well that's all fine and good if there's no major interior work to be done. The lawn is no biggie but depending on how many windows are broken and the severity of the outer appearance of the house, paint job and all of that—"

"The entire front of the house is brick. So no paint job needed. But it does need some new shutters and some new spray paint on the porch railings. That shouldn't be *too* much trouble."

"Oh okay. But still consider how much that will be in addition to the inner modifications you'll have to have done."

"True," she sat back and thought for a minute. She would definitely have to make an appointment to see the interior of that house soon. A few minutes later she sat back up in her chair.

"So I guess the main help I would need from you is the names of some reasonable carpenters in the area, who aren't going to try and take advantage of me because I'm a woman," Jacy said.

"Shit, once they see you they might do the work for free!" Jason chuckled and sat back in his chair with his hands spread out on the table as the tall buxom brown skinned waitress wearing a black t-shirt tied in a knot at the back with the words 'Ms. Tootsies' written on the front brought two ice cold glasses of water.

"Are you ready to order?" she asked looking only at Jason.

"Ummm, no not yet, could you come back in a few minutes?" Jason asked.

"Sure," the waitress smiled, winked at him and turned away. Jason followed her backside with his eyes and then turned back to

Jacy who was pretending to be preoccupied with sipping on her water and looking at her menu.

"I think I'm going to get the fried chicken and macaroni," Jacy decided.

"Yea I was thinking about getting that too, but I've had the worst craving for catfish since last week." He looked over the menu one more time to be sure of his choice. *He damn sure hasn't had a craving for toothpaste lately,* Jacy thought and fought a smile by pretending to suck something out of her back teeth.

When the waitress came back several minutes later they ordered. A half hour later their food came and they pushed the paperwork aside to eat. They talked about a few more details concerning Jacy's proposed business over their lunch and when the check came Jason snatched it up immediately.

"Oh that's okay Jason, I can get that. You're here to help me remember?" Jacy said smiling and opening up her purse.

"Jacy, now I couldn't imagine letting you pay the bill. This was definitely all my pleasure," Jason assured.

Jacy continued to search through her purse never looking up. "Alright, well at least let me put up the tip." Even though that bitch didn't even regard me throughout the entire meal, she thought. At any cost, she wanted to put something up for the dinner so that Jason would absolutely, positively, not consider it a bona fide date.

"No, you don't have to—"

"I insist," she said pulling out a $5 bill and two singles and laying the three bills on the table.

Jason got up to pay the check at the counter and as they were finally making their way out the door, the waitress that had served their food hurriedly came up behind him and slipped a small piece of paper into his hand as she muttered a few words. He turned around to regard her as Jacy shook her head and kept walking out of the door. Some women were shameless. She could care less about who Jason Colridge decided to take a number from, because this was all business, but who was to say she wasn't actually on a date with the man or something? That woman didn't know. No respect at all. A few seconds later he came back out and put his hand in the small of Jacy's back to lead her to her car.

"Where'd you park?" he asked.

"At 10th street. It's alright, I'm a big girl. I can make it there," she chuckled.

"No it's no problem. I don't mind the walk," Jason reassured her looking down at her from the side as they walked and talked. Three blocks later they finally arrived at her deep red 1998 Mitsubishi Eclipse.

"What are you doing later?" Jason asked as they stood in front of the car on the sidewalk.

"Uh, actually I have a lot of work to do today on a speech for a big press conference my company is holding on Tuesday," she fibbed, knowing that there really wasn't much more she could do on the file without getting Caitlin's final changes back on Monday.

"Well what about tonight. Maybe we could go catch a movie or hit a club or something?"

"Ahhh I don't know, I'll have to get back to you on that."

"Oh come on. It'll be fun," he paused as Jacy smiled and looked up at him with an expression that said, "Sorry, but the answer's still no."

"Alright. Well I have your cell number. I'll give you a call a little bit later on then," he said again giving her that intense look that made her slightly uncomfortable. It was as if he thought his eyes would mesmerize her or something. It was just annoying to Jacy.

"OK, I'll talk to you soon. And thanks again Jason I'm going to call up the carpenter you told me about next week." His eyes never left her body as she rounded her car and beeped the alarm to get in when she noticed a fresh new parking ticket sitting on her windshield. She looked down the street and saw a black female parking authority officer hurriedly walking down the street from her car. She glanced at her watch. It had only been about three or four minutes since the meter expired. "Evil bitch," she said under her breath. She snatched it up and said a few more choice curse words under her breath.

"Give me that, I'll take care of it," Jason offered.

"No it's OK, it's only $20." She didn't trust someone else to take care of a parking ticket for her anyway. They were towing people's cars left and right those days in Philly. Never mind the fact that the city of Philadelphia charged nearly double your ticket if they didn't receive your payment within eight calendar days.

She waved and slipped into her driver's seat before Jason could say another word. He waved back in a short motion and then watched her drive off down the block and make a left onto the next block. Jason put his hands back into his pockets.

"Whew!" he exclaimed aloud lowering and shaking his head once she was out of sight. "I have GOT to hit that, if it's the last thing I do on this green earth!"

chapter 9
Trouble is Brewing

"SO THEY'RE NOT GONNA release me early, all because of that dumb muthafucker! I'm heated!" Rich's deep voice boomed into the prison phone.

"Rich, sweetie, it'll be OK. It won't be long now, it's only two more weeks. Just keep minding your own business and don't let anyone get to you like that again. Besides, nobody's gonna be messing with you after that. You said they had to take him to the infirmary right?" Jacy held the raggedy black phone tightly and looked back at him through the thick plexiglass window.

"Hell yea that nigga got his shit rocked. But he started that shit, and they punish ME? What am I supposed to stand there and let some nigga put his hand on me? Hell to the muthafuckin' nawl!"

Another prisoner they called Baines had tested Rich during lunch after the very first week he was locked up. Baines was slightly taller and much chunkier than Rich. He taunted Rich and jabbed him in the chest with his chubby forefinger. In the blink of an eye Rich had hauled off and punched Baines in the face so hard that his big ass had flown back onto the lunchtables, on top of everyone's meal trays. The guards, who had witnessed everything, immediately broke things up, taking Rich back to his cell and Baines to the prison nurse to treat his face. Two days later they had notified Rich that he would not qualify for early release any longer. It was now Thursday, and Friday would mark two weeks since he was initially incarcerated.

"Well I know you don't want to have to be in there Rich, but it's just a couple more weeks. Be glad they didn't put you in the hole or whatever. Promise me you won't blow up on anybody in there til then?" she held her head to the side and looked back at him with those puppy dog eyes that made Rich want to give her anything in the world she wanted.

Rich sighed, leaned back in his chair and was silent for a minute. "Yea I promise baby, but you know I'm not gonna let no nigga get by on me. I feel bad cause now I might not be out in time to do somethin' with you on July 4th. I was gonna take you to a few barbecues and then maybe down to the shore to watch the fireworks. But they might not let me out until that Saturday right after the fourth."

"Awww." Jacy sighed. "Well that would have been nice but it's not the end of the world sweetie. We can just do something that weekend okay?"

"I miss you." Rich settled down and rested his elbows on the table in front of him as he held the phone loosely in his hands and gazed back at Jacy through the dirty window.

Jacy smiled. "I miss you too." They were silent for a moment.

"I been having nasty thoughts," he said in a lower voice, almost a whisper.

"Oh yea?" Jacy chuckled.

"Yea. I been thinking about what I'm gonna do to your little chocolate ass when I get outta here." He pulled his lips into his mouth to wet them and scanned her upper body, pure lust in his eyes. Jacy felt a tingle run up her thighs and in her Victoria Secret's. "Stand up a second," he demanded.

Jacy looked up at the ceiling and sighed with a trace of a smile on her lips. She stood placing the phone down on the table in the same motion, and turned around like a QVC model to show off her tight pink cotton wrap shirt and short fitted jean skirt.

"Mmmmmm," Rich moaned searching her coke-bottle body, round backside and supple brown thighs. *Oh! This is torture*, he thought. He closed his eyes for a second, took a deep breath and one of his arms left the table. He opened them again as Jacy was sitting back down in her seat. Suddenly a frown formed on his face.

"When you leave out of here I want you to take your ass STRAIGHT to the car. I mean directly. No talking to these perverted guards and shit. Don't even *begin* to entertain their minds. Do you hear me Jacy?"

Here we go, Jacy thought. He wanted her to be sexy as long as she was invisible to all other people in the world.

"Jacy, I said. Are you hearing me?" he probed.

"Rich..." Jacy sighed not really knowing what to say in response to that. "I'm not gonna start an argument with you. I just came by to see how you're doing, but if you're gonna start tripping I'm leaving. I don't need this shit everytime I talk to your ass." She sat back in the chair and crossed her legs looking at the partition separating her from the next booth.

"Jacy why do you always wanna resist what I tell you? I'm just looking out for you! You out here dressed in that eensy weensy little mini skirt and we in a prison full of horny ass muthafuckas! Don't get it twisted, I will kill a nigga in here if he try something with you. I will straight KILL his ass. So when you come back here I suggest you remember to put some more clothes on before you leave the house. Do you understand?" Rich was talking through partly clenched teeth and trying to maintain a normal voice so as to not alarm the guards but leaning into the window as he tightly held the phone so that Jacy would understand the seriousness of what he was saying. Jacy glared back at him with her left arm crossed under the right one holding the phone, and shook her head.

"Well maybe I won't come back here, if you're always going to have such a problem with the way I'm dressed Rich," she said with an attitude and put the phone down, grabbed her purse and stood up to leave. She was sick of arguing.

"Jacy!" Rich's voice was louder now.

Jacy blew a kiss. "Rich I'll speak to you later, stay out of trouble," was what she said, but it was barely audible to Rich since she wasn't using the phone. She turned and walked out of the small room as Rich stood up and yelled after her.

"Okay buddy, time's up." The prison guard quickly made his way over to Rich and tried to grab his arm but Rich snatched it away violently and steamed towards the door leading to the row of cells.

JACY TRUDGED into the office that Friday in one of her worst moods. She had to put her car in the shop that morning and the mechanics were telling her that not only did she have some serious transmission problems, but that she also needed new belts and brakes. Tricky motherfuckers, she thought of the mechanics, but didn't want to take the risk of them being right and her brakes failing. She knew she should have just waited to talk to Timbo so that he could go down and talk to the mechanics but he hadn't answered her message from the previous night yet and the mechanics were right down the street from her job. So she had gone in early that morning to drop it off and they had given her the estimate of over $900 after checking the car. She had Rich's car at home but was still hoping that she could just drop her Eclipse off, come to work and possibly get the car back that night if they were finished with the work. But now she was going to have to withdraw more money from her savings than she had planned. Much more. All of this was going through her mind as she sat down at her desk.

The work day went by pretty smoothly, a typical Friday. Most of her co-workers had left at 3pm but since she was waiting for word on her car, Jacy remained. Her boss, Caitlin, had been in a closed door meeting for the most part of the day, and most of the consultants were on vacation so it was easy going.

At about 3:40pm Caitlin came out of her office. She came over to Jacy's cubicle.

"Jacy, could I see you in my office please?" she asked in an almost happy tone.

At 3:40pm on a Friday? Jacy thought. "Sure, I'll be right there," she said skeptically. She grabbed a pen and pad in case she needed to take notes and headed for Caitlin's office.

When she got there, Sharon from HR was seated in the office looking up at her. Caitlin closed the door behind Jacy and asked her to have a seat as she took hers. Jacy's heart started beating faster as she planted herself in the seat and sat with her back completely stiff. Sharon, the HR lady, spoke first.

"Ms. Thomas, we've brought you in here to tell you that you're being put on final notice due to a continued pattern of lateness and your inability to meet a work-related commitment a few weeks ago. Caitlin has notified me of these problems and has compiled a record of your log in times over the past two weeks." Sharon pushed two sheets of paper towards Jacy on the small circular table. "As you can see on five out of the last ten days, including this morning, you have been late. And there was also an occasion where Caitlin requested that you stay late to complete a project and you refused. We understand that you have personal commitments but you should be willing and able to make arrangements to satisfy your requirements here as well. This behavior will become a part of your permanent record on file with HR and any further infractions will result in immediate termination. Do you have any questions?"

"But…" Jacy started to say as she looked down at the papers. "It says here that I was only late at the most ten minutes on those days! You can't seriously be on the verge of firing me over that? And I *did* make other arrangements to satisfy my responsibilities here on that day. The Unified project was done in time—Marsha Collins even personally called me to thank me for the great work I did!"

"Ms. Thomas your revised job description and schedule requires you to be here at 8:30am sharp. Not 8:31, not 8:42, but 8:30 or earlier. We have every right to terminate an employee based on being late, even if it's just a few minutes, especially if there is a pattern."

Jacy thought for a moment about all of the other employees in her department that regularly arrived after her. "You would have to let everyone in this department go in that case. I can't believe I'm being singled out like this," she exclaimed shaking her head as she glared at Sharon and then to Caitlin and then back to Sharon, thinking that at any moment they would smile and say 'You just got Punk'd!' with candid cameras and all.

"Jacy, you aren't being singled out. We just feel you have some major areas of improvement," Caitlin piped up with her most professional voice.

"Improvement? Who doesn't? I am commended regularly for my work, I'm usually the first person in the office despite the 'chronic lateness' you cite and I've never missed a deadline. I'm one of the last people in the office right now while most everyone else has left early for the day. How can that result in my being on warning not once but twice and now in danger of being terminated?" Jacy asked incredulously with her heart beating so fast it felt like it was traveling up to her throat.

Sharon and Caitlin looked at each other for a moment with expressions that said they were both considering what she had said and worried about whether Jacy was going to get 'ghetto' and make a scene. Caitlin spoke next after they broke their glance.

"Jacy, we have given you the reasons for this action on our part and have the proof to back it up. I'm sorry but this is a final decision."

Jacy shook her head in disbelief as she looked down at the table. She was learning an important lesson of the corporate world first hand—it doesn't matter how good a worker you are, politics rule and they are almost always premised on personal issues. She knew that the only reason why this was happening was because she resisted Caitlin's unreasonable request the night she had Rich's car. She also believed it was because of Caitlin's insecurities about Jacy's advanced talent in a field that Caitlin had been a part of for over 20 years. And Jacy was right.

When Caitlin heard the glowing references from Jacy's former boss in the New Jersey office, she knew she had to have her on the team, and didn't even require Jacy to come in for a face-to-face interview. She had just talked with her over the phone, explained some of her duties and a few details about the Philadelphia office and Jacy's transfer went through within the week. From the day Jacy came to work in the Philadelphia office a few weeks after their first conversation, Caitlin instantly developed resentment towards her. She hated to see a black girl, young and beautiful at that, with such an advanced and complete knowledge of her field. So she had begun to give Jacy more and more projects resembling busy work that diminished Jacy's intelligence and held her back from the types of high profile projects that would have placed her in a prime position for a promotion. But little did Caitlin know that even on the small projects where she was only expected to proofread documents, Jacy excelled and impressed the consultants with her own custom-tailored changes and additions to the copy, which Caitlin assumed was the work of the consultants themselves.

Jacy looked back up at the two women before her and sighed deeply. This was the destiny of a young black woman with her intelligence and resolution in the corporate world, the all too famous "glass ceiling" that they rambled about in black business journals and magazines. What could she do? She said all that she could say at that moment.

"Alright. Are we finished here?" Jacy said standing up to go.

Caitlin smiled looking relieved. "Yes. Thank you very much Jacy."

Jacy turned and left the office without another word. When she got back to her desk it was 4:05pm. She plopped herself into her chair and stared at the screen for what seemed like hours. But it was only a matter of minutes.

Then suddenly, Jacy stood up decisively and headed back to Caitlin's office.

When she got there Sharon was standing in the doorway with a tote bag on her shoulder engaged in some final light conversation with Caitlin about her plans for the weekend. Jacy stepped up to the doorway behind her and cleared her throat.

Sharon stopped what she was saying and moved to the side to give Jacy room. Jacy continued to stand where she was.

"Caitlin, Sharon I've reconsidered. And this is most definitely not alright with me. I feel that I have been handled unfairly ever since I stepped foot in this office, and I refuse to accept this type of treatment any longer. Please consider this my two weeks notice. I will have a formal letter prepared on Monday," Jacy said staring intently at Caitlin, who was staring back with her mouth slightly open in disbelief, before stepping back and heading over to her cubicle to pack up for the night. Sharon just looked back at Caitlin with a look of concern on her face and couldn't find any words to say. Caitlin had just wanted to scare Jacy a bit, she wasn't actually planning on firing her. She couldn't afford to lose an employee of Jacy's skill level and efficiency at a time when a plethora of important assignments were piling into the office.

Jacy went back to her desk with a huge smile on her face. She had never had a moment of so much satisfaction in her entire life. She felt as if a huge burden had been lifted, but at the same time was very anxious about her spur of the moment decision. She had had it—she would no longer let Caitlin or anyone else dig their boot into her neck. She was going to be a free woman and control her own destiny. From that point forward.

At her desk Jacy noticed that the message light on her work phone was lit. She picked up the receiver and dialed into her voicemail. It was the mechanics saying that her car would not be ready until the next day at 5pm. Jacy looked up to the ceiling and slumped her shoulders. She would have to take the train and then wait for the bus to take her home that day, and the convenience of having the mechanics right down the street from her job was lost. What a waste. But then her thoughts quickly returned to what she had just done and another koolaid smile grew. She put down the phone and started closing up for the night. What did it matter now if she stayed or not? Hell I might even show up at 10am on Monday! she laughed to herself as she grabbed her purse.

* * * * *

As she was riding the train to the bus stop, Jacy's phone started vibrating in her purse. She took it out and saw Timbo's number flashing on the screen. She flipped the top and greeted him.

"Hey Timbo," she smiled.

"Sup," he made a sound like he was stretching and grunted. He must have just woke up, Jacy thought. Her and Timbo had grown a lot closer since the trial. He developed a new respect for her after seeing her on the stand defending Rich so passionately and persuasively. They had gone together to pay Rich's fines after he was taken away. "You need something?"

"Yea, I called to see if you had time to come down with me to a mechanic—I've been having problems with my car. It was pulling and making strange noises. But I decided to bring it in today to a mechanic down the street from my job. They said I need my transmission fixed, new belts and brakes."

"Oh yea? And how much did they say it would cost?" Timbo inquired.

"Like $900."

"Nine bills!" Timbo laughed. "For the transmission and some brakes? You can get new brakes for $20 and ain't no transmission problem that needs to be fixed for $900 unless they have to rebuild the shit! Which I seriously doubt. They fucking with you, where's the car now? It's still there? You didn't pay for nothin' did you?"

"Not yet. They said the car would be ready tomorrow at 5pm. What about the belts? How much is that usually?"

"Jacy, I could have got the crackhead from down the street to fix all that shit for $100, not even." he laughed. "I wish you would have waited. But look, Imma go up there with you first thing in the morning before they do anything else. Where you at now?"

"I'm on the train. I have to take the bus home because they still   have   my   car."

"Alright, where you getting off. I'll come scoop you."

"At 52nd, that's where I would have to get the bus. It's the next stop."

"Aiight just sit tight I'll be there," he clicked off the phone before she could say anything else.

Jacy stepped down the stairs from the subway platform and looked around. She tried to find a place where she could wait without getting harassed, but that was nearly impossible on 52nd and Market Street. She finally decided to just stand on the side where the hacks were soliciting.

"Hack cab, hack. You need a ride miss?" a man asked her with a deep African accent.

"No that's alright," she half-smiled and folded her arms across her chest to demonstrate that she didn't want to be bothered.

"Wooooooooohoooooo. Damn. Do you see *that*!" a brotha yelled at the top of his lungs from across the street at a storefront. He was there with about 3 or 4 other men, one that looked like he could be pushing 50.

"Chocolate!" another in his crew started shouting. "Chocolate!! Come on now. What, you can't speak?"

Lord, Jacy thought, *please come on Timbo.* She sighed and pretended she didn't hear them, something she hated doing. But she knew that if she even showed the slightest interest or response they would be all over her like white on rice. Hopefully if she ignored them enough they'd just leave her alone.

"Man she don't wanna speak to your broke sorry ass." another joked.

"Chocolate, I know you hear me!" he ignored his friend and said again. Jacy turned completely away from them to look down 52nd for Timbo.

"Whoa. Look at that ass. Look like she smugglin two nerf balls!" another in the crew yelled out crudely and all his boys started snickering. It was starting to get embarrassing as others, men and women, were now watching her from different areas of the four cornered intersection. One of the more bold and ugly guys from across the street got restless and jogged across the street towards her with change jiggling in his jean shorts. Jacy rolled her eyes up into her head and thought about walking down the block to Chestnut and waiting for Timbo there. The brotha came up on her and got right in her face. Jacy didn't even look at him.

"So what's up shawty. Can I get the math?" he requested.

"No I'm waiting for my man," Jacy fibbed, hoping it would scare him away. But it didn't. It took more than that to ward off men like him.

"That ain't got a damn thing to do with me. Come on now I'm tryna see you tonight. Maybe we can catch a flick or get some dinner," he said all of a sudden trying to sound sweet, flipping his fingers on her left arm, which was still in a folded position. It was time to start making her move to Chestnut. Just as she was about to act, Timbo pulled up and hopped out of the car Ninja-style. He walked towards them without a word and gripped Jacy by the arm, pulling her towards his car.

"Oh hey, Timbo!" the persistent brother changed his tune in a flash. "What's up, that's you?"

Timbo opened the passenger side car and guided Jacy in before answering. He came back around to the other side, gave a pound and said a few words to the brother, who he obviously knew, and then came back to the car and got in.

On the way home Jacy told Timbo about what had happened only an hour before.

"You quit? For real? Haha I know them white bitches was probably type. You know whitey don't like it when *you* quit, they wanna be the ones to control every damn thing—hiring and firing yo' ass."

"Yea I know that's why it felt so good! Cause I know she wasn't expecting it, at all. She thought she was just gonna string me along until she felt fit to let me go. I'm not having that. I'd rather be broke than to deal with that shit." Jacy glanced over at Timbo. He was definitely not a good looking guy, but he had redeeming qualities about him.

"Well you know you don't even need to worry about that happening. I wouldn't be surprised if Roo was spending his time locked up ordering invitations and a preacher for ya'll wedding," he laughed for a minute at his joke, then started coughing. Timbo was an all day everyday kind of blunt smoker. Jacy just smiled politely. Timbo looked over at her.

"What's wrong? You wouldn't wanna marry my boy if he asked?" Timbo asked.

"Aaahh. I really don't even want to talk about that!" she chuckled. "I'm too young to be thinking about marriage."

Timbo was quiet for a while.

"Well, just to let you know he didn't say anything to me about it. I just seen the way ya'll act together and how he's always talking about you. He really digs you, you know."

Jacy nodded her head and looked out of the window. "I dig him too."

"And I know Roo gotta temper on him. That's why we call him Roo—cause his bark is just as bad as his bite. But I've never known him to hit on a female. And I know for a fact he wouldn't never do nothin' to hurt you. I never thought I'd say it, but that nigga's in love."

"He told you that?" Jacy jerked her neck to look at Timbo.

"No, but I know. I been knowing Roo since elementary. That's like my flesh and blood," Rich explained. Jacy looked down at her hands and played with the blue topaz ring on her finger.

Timbo pulled up to Jacy's apartment building.

"Alright, so I'm going to pick you up tomorrow morning at 9:30am so we can go down and get your car. Don't worry 'bout nothing, it will be handled," Timbo assured.

"Thank you Timbo."

Jacy climbed out of the car and then up the stairs to her apartment. She flopped her weary body on the comfy couch and flipped on the TV, not even bothering to take off her shoes. In a few minutes she had drifted off to sleep.

Briiiiiiiiiiiing. Briiiiiiiiiiiiing! The phone rang startling her out of her dream. She picked up the cordless from the coffee table and spoke.

"Hello?"

"Heyyy." Then silence.

"Who's this?" Jacy asked in a slightly annoyed tone.

"You don't recognize my voice? It's Jason," he said in his best 'sexy' voice.

"Oh," is all Jacy said straightening herself on the couch slightly as she remembered that she had left her home *and* cellphone number on her first message to Jason.

"So what's up. I haven't heard back from you since I called that night we met at Ms. Tootsies."

"Yea, I know, I've been real busy. And things are just gonna get busier."

"How is the house search going?"

"Good. I went by and looked at a few houses with the realtors last week. They look very workable. I'd say about $3 or 4,000 in improvements needed. I'm seriously thinking about closing a deal on one in the next couple of weeks."

"Great! Well don't sit on your hands too long, those fixer upper houses go fast. Call me when you get ready to close and I'll come down to the realtor's office with you. Okay?"

"Alright. Thanks."

"So what are you doing tonight, I'd like to take you out to dinner if at all possible."

"That sounds nice Jason, but I have something to do early in the morning. And like I told you, I'm seeing someone so that probably wouldn't be appropriate."

"Ohhh no no nothing like that Jacy. It would be totally innocent. I just wanted to take a friend out, maybe discuss a few details about your plans and then take you home. I promise, totally innocent."

Skeptical, but figuring there couldn't be much of anything that would come out of a dinner, and not wanting to burn any bridges, Jacy relectantly agreed. She hadn't eaten since breakfast.

"Yea, ok. I guess that would be alright. But I'm going to be a few hours. I'll meet you."

"I could just come pick you up, just give me the directions," Jason pressed.

"No, it's alright, I'd rather meet. How about Houlihan's?"

"Actually, I was thinking of something a little more upscale. Like Ruth Chris Steakhouse?"

"Oh. Okay. Then I'll meet you down on Broad Street. Let's see, it's 5:30 now, I'll meet you down there around 8 okay?"

"Sounds good. See you then."

JACY AND Jason laughed easily and talked fluently throughout their meal. The two glasses of Chardonnay Jacy consumed certainly helped. She looked at it as a celebration of her earlier decision to leave her job and had told Jason all about what had happened at work. To Jacy's surprise Jason actually had brought some very helpful information about the real estate business with him as he had promised they would discuss details about her impending venture. At the end of dinner, Jason pulled out his platinum Mastercard and paid for the $150 meal.

Tipsy and satisfied with her meal, Jacy sauntered towards her car which was parked on a nearby side street with Jason holding her by the small of her back.

"So what do you want to do now?" Jason asked. He looked down at her with his soft hazel eyes and mouth full of pretty white teeth and Jacy became slightly aroused. The man was fine. But she knew better.

"I'm about to head home. I really had a good time, thank you so much Jason."

"Can I come with you? Maybe we could rent some movies or something?"

"Uhh. No, I think I'm gonna call it a night."

"You sure? I really would like to spend more time with you tonight. I'm really enjoying myself," Jason said turning Jacy to face him. "Jacy, you are a gorgeous woman. Inside and out. You're intelligent, ambitious, kind. Everything I like. There's something about you. I just don't want to have to end our time together right now. Please."

"Jason I'm flattered." Jacy wondered for a moment if she had led him on by going out to dinner with him this time. "But

I'm involved with someone, and I really don't want to cross that line. We'll catch up next week okay?"

Jason looked at the brick wall behind them and sighed, exhaling long and hard. "Okay. I can respect that. Are you sure you're alright getting home?" he asked as they resumed walking.

"Yes I'm fine."

They reached Jacy's car and said their goodbyes. Jason waved from the sidewalk with a sideways awkward smile as Jacy pulled off with a screech. The smile was replaced with a pensive grimace as he headed back towards his car.

THE NEXT day at 9:42am, Timbo called Jacy's phone to tell her that he was downstairs. She grabbed her purse off her dresser and made her way down the stairs.

Timbo was waiting in his car with Peedi Crack blasting at full volume, with no regard to the fact that it was 9 o'clock on a Saturday morning and people were sleeping. She slid into the passenger seat and greeted him.

"Could you turn that down a little?" she asked. He did. "You trying to bust my eardrums?" she said joking, once the music was at a normal volume.

"My bad, I needed to wake the fuck up. This is mad early for me." He rolled down the window as he pulled off, hocked and spit outside. Jacy scrunched up her nose. Timbo turned to her. "So where is this—what I can't spit?" he asked seeing her expression. She just smiled, shaking her head, and looked out the window.

"Where's this place?" he continued.

"It's down on 13th and SpringGarden," Jacy answered as he made a right turn out of the complex and headed for the highway. She was a little anxious about this trip to the mechanics, because they may have already been working on the car. Her cellphone rang. Timbo looked at her out of the corner of his eye.

Jacy read the caller ID, it was Jason. She clicked the button to send him to voicemail and continued to hold the phone in her hands. She knew Timbo was wondering what that was about in the back of his mind.

When they arrived at the auto repair shop, a thin rusty looking Italian man was outside looking under the hood of a black Monte Carlo. Jacy looked around the lot for her car, and finally spotted her Eclipse sitting in front of a silver Maxima. Timbo pulled up right in front of the Monte Carlo. As he did another younger man came out of the shop and jumped into their company tow truck.

"Is either of these the guy you spoke to yesterday?" Timbo asked as he put the car in park.

Jacy studied the two men. "Uhhh, no. The guy I spoke to was a lot huskier, bald. I think his name was Joe, or John."

Timbo got out of the car and made his way to the shop door. Jacy sat for a minute wondering if she should just stay put, but figured since it was her car under her name, they would probably need her information.

"Hey buddy, you gotta move your car over to the side," the thin Italian guy said leaning up and pointing with his rag at an area where there was room to park, as Timbo approached.

"I'm looking for Joe, he here?" Timbo asked ignoring his request.

"Joe? There's no Joe here."

"Or John. I need to speak to him about that Eclipse over there. My girl brought it in yesterday," Timbo said pointing over at Jacy and the car in the lot.

"Yea, what about it?" the Italian guy asked, wiping his hands on the rag.

"We're picking it up. Where's the keys." Timbo demanded.

"Oh whoa, whoa. We're not done with it though."

"Yea you are, I'm gonna take it from here."

The guy looked Timbo over for a minute. He didn't look like the type you would really want to mess with. "Hold on a moment," the mechanic said as he walked in through the open garage doors and into the shop. He came back out a few minutes later with another mechanic, presumably John.

"Yes, can I help you," John asked as he walked outside with his sidekick in tow.

"I just want the key to the Eclipse over there, we don't need ya'll services no more."

"Is there a reason why?"

Timbo was visibly becoming annoying. "Listen man. I don't have time for all this back and forth shit. I just want the keys to my girl's jawn so we can be out."

"Well we already started on it, that's why I asked. You're gonna have to pay the balance," John said.

Timbo made a scoffing noise. "And what is that."

"I don't know, we did the brakes and the belt already. That's probably gonna run you about $200, $250."

Timbo chuckled and shook his head 'no.' He stepped closer to John, about a couple of feet from his face. "Listen man, I see you were tryin' to run somethin' on my girl yesterday, but it's me now. You and I both know I ain't paying that much for no damn brake job. And if I go home and look at that car and something don't look right it's gonna be problems from *here on* between me and you and your shop. You feel me?" Timbo said in a threatening tone, looking John dead in the eye. John looked away temporarily at his sidekick.

"You threatening me buddy?" John asked finally getting the courage to look him back in the eye.

"More like warning you. You don't want no problems over here on 13th and SpringGarden over no $70 brake job. Where's the keys." Timbo said reaching for his ringing cell phone and walking towards the shop door. He was about ready to just take the keys off the wall.

"Alright, alright," John reasoned, putting his hands up. He quickly stepped in front of Timbo and led him into the shop. From there Jacy couldn't hear what was going on.

The other mechanic eyed Jacy with a mixture of annoyance and curiosity. She wrinkled up her nose at him and turned to go check on her car.

Timbo and John came out about ten minutes later. They turned to each other and shook hands, then Timbo shoved his left hand in his pocket and dialed back the person who had just called him with the other. When he got back over to Jacy, who was standing at her car, she asked him if everything was okay.

"Yea, everything's fine," he said holding out the keys to her. "Follow me, Imma see if we can get it fixed this afternoon."

"Thank you so much Timbo!" Jacy smiled and took the keys. She leaned over and kissed him on the cheek.

Timbo made his way back to his car and jumped in. As he got in he heard an unfamiliar cellphone ring. He looked over and saw Jacy's phone flashing on the seat. She must have left it by accident, he thought. He picked up the phone and saw 'Jason' flashing on the screen. Without thinking, he flipped it up.

"Who dis?" Timbo demanded in an irate tone. The caller hesitated, and then just hung up.

"What the—" Timbo said to himself, looking at the phone like a dead rat. He finally pressed end to clear the missed call and flipped down the cover.

Part Two

chapter 10
Alone and Very Lonely

I T WAS INDEPENDENCE DAY, a warm Friday afternoon and Jacy felt alone. Rich was locked up until noon the next day. She had only spoken to him twice on the telephone since her first and last visit to the prison. He had still been pissed at her for walking out and she at him for his outburst, but in spite of everything they made plans for Jacy to pick him up from the prison on Saturday, the 5th, with his car. Jacy had yet to tell Rich that she had quit her job, even though the day before Independence day was her last at Summit Financial. Everyone had known of Jacy's resignation as soon as the day after she confronted her boss Caitlin, thanks to Patty the office gossip, who had still been at work that night, listening in on the whole conversation while hidden behind a large white beam near Caitlin's office. The day Jacy had left Caitlin had not even said goodbye, or wished her good luck. Robin, her friend Mike and a few other people she got along with in the office held a happy hour in her honor to send her off. Jacy and Robin were hitting it off and a good friendship was beginning to bud. Jacy gave her contact information and Robin promised to stay in touch to update her on the happenings in the department.

Since her cousin Tammy hadn't heard anything from Jacy about July 4th, she had made plans in Miami for the holiday weekend, and Jacy and Rachelle weren't speaking. Rachelle was still mad with Jacy about the whole thing with Steven, the loser who she had met at Club Chemistry. She was still chasing after

Steven, calling him constantly but never receiving an original call from his side, making herself fully available whenever it was convenient for him, and the last thing she wanted was to hear Jacy's opinion about it. Jacy's two flaky friends back home were both doing their own things with their boyfriends that day. Jacy thought about going home herself and hanging out with her family, but she wasn't up to the drive, and her family didn't have anything planned for the the 4th anyway. She didn't dare call either Jason or Terrell, that would be just opening up a can of worms for no good reason. Her friend Mike was in Chicago for the Taste. She didn't know Timbo enough to hang out with him and Rich's other boys, besides how would that look? she thought.

Jacy hated times like these, when it seemed as if there was nobody in the world she could call on. Outside of her own family of course. *But sometimes you need more than your momma to talk to or hang out with*, she thought. The thought of herself, a young single woman living in Philly, having no one to call on was scary to say the least. Jacy picked up her cellphone and called her Mom despite her reluctance.

"Hey sweetie! How are you doing?" her mom sang through the phone, putting her at ease. Samantha Thomas was obviously happy to hear from her daughter. They hadn't spoken since Jacy called to tell her that she had quit her job. Mrs. Thomas wasn't too happy about it, and warned Jacy that she should have thought things over a while longer, before giving up a constant income, but really could not do or say much more since the deed had been done.

Ever since Jacy's father came down with cancer of the throat from his 40 years of smoking Newports, Mrs. Thomas had all but taken control over the family. Mr. Thomas could only speak through a recorder and was very weak from the chemotherapy. They were able to get rid of the cancer, but his weary condition remained. In the meanwhile Mrs. Thomas had renewed her relationship with God and handled all of the family's affairs with an iron fist. Despite his treatment of Jacy's mother throughout the years, Mrs. Thomas refused to send her husband to a home to be cared for, but instead stayed by his side throughout his illness, reflecting her noble character to no end. Jacy didn't know for sure if she could ever take care of a man like her father, who had caused so much stress in their family life, as her mother did, but she saw that in a way, her mother was finally getting justice. She didn't take any lip from Jacy's father and she was the final say in all decisions to be made with the good money Mr. Thomas earned from his union pension. Though they got along a lot better than when Mr. Thomas was healthy, they still argued. Mr. Thomas would protest but it would get him nowhere as Mrs. Thomas would quickly put him in his place. It was perfect retribution for all of the years of strife he had caused her to suffer through.

"Hey Ma," Jacy said trying to sound enthusiastic.

"What's wrong you don't sound like yourself," Mrs. Thomas had not six, but seven senses, and could immediately tell when something was wrong with one of her children.

"Nothing, I'm good," Jacy fibbed, trying to sound light hearted.

"Well, don't sound good. What you up to today?"

"Just relaxing, how are you and Daddy doing?"

"Oh we're just fine. You know I'm over here watching my stories. Your father was trying to get on my nerves this morning about cutting down a tree in the backyard. Because it drops so much of that red fruit in the summer, but I told him no, I love that tree it's been there since we moved in and it's staying. I came in and locked myself in my room because he's not gonna get my pressure up today. He was out there complaining for a while and then finally left. I just leave him in God's hands, because he's not gonna stress me out today…"

Jacy's mom could talk up a storm. You could hardly get a word in edgewise in a phone conversation with her. Sometimes when Jacy and her mom would get disconnected by accident or the call would drop on Jacy's cellphone, her mom would still be talking for three or four minutes before realizing Jacy wasn't on the other end. But the sound of her mother's cheerful banter was a comfort for Jacy, especially at that time.

"...you know he gets upset over the littlest things, but nobody is trying to go outside right now and chop a tree. Does he really I'm going to go out there with an axe? We don't even own an axe. And I'm not hiring someone to do it either. Besides the landscapers already came out yesterday. He tried to bother your sister about it but you know Camille, she just left the house, didn't say anything. Your brother is off at his summer baseball lessons. Do you know those people upped the price by $20 per session? I just gave him a check for the rest of the season so I don't have to keep writing one every week. Oh! I knew I forgot to tell you something. I saw your old teacher Mrs. Jamison the other day at Shoprite! She asked about you."

"Oh you did? How is she doing?"

"She's just fine. Her son Barry just graduated from Howard University and moved back to the area. She showed me a picture from his graduation, that is one fine looking boy. Maybe you should give him a call Jacy," her mother suggested.

"Maaa," Jacy whined. Her mother was always trying to set her up with some 'nice young man.' But all of the men she suggested were either spineless, chronic complainers or even worse, in-the-closet homosexuals.

"No really sweetie, he seems to be a very well rounded young man. Just give it a chance! Please? For Mommy?"

"Mom," Jacy laughed. "Even if I wanted to how am I supposed to call him. He's a stranger I don't know even know where he lives or what he's about!"

"Oh, hold on I got his number from his mother," Mrs. Thomas put down the phone before Jacy could say anything in response. She couldn't believe her mother actually expected her to just call up this man she knew nothing about and say "Hi."

"Okay. You have a pen?"

"Mom, I'm not going to call him."

"Why not? Jacy at least give him a call and talk."

"Mom, I don't know him! He doesn't know me! I'm not just going to call him up out of nowhere. Besides, I'm seeing someone right now."

"Are you married to this someone?" her mother asked.

"Nooo," Jacy smiled.

"Okay then. So at least keep your mind open to meeting him next time you come home to visit. She told me he works at one of the branches of our bank. He's one of those financial advisors, for investments or something she said. Isn't that nice?"

"Yes ma, very nice."

"So what's really going on with you Jacy?"

"What do you mean?"

"Don't play stupid with me Jacilyn. I'm your momma. Something is wrong, so spill it."

"It's nothing mom. I'm just thinking about stuff," Jacy said preparing to let it all out.

"Like what?"

"Like stuff. I don't know, I feel like I have nobody to depend on Ma. Except you of course, but I mean good friends to lean on out here."

"Hmmm. I understand what you're going through sweetie. When I first came out here to New Jersey with your father, I didn't know anyone. All I had was my brother and my cousins back in Queens, but they were all doing their own things. Thankfully I was pregnant with your sister at the time so it didn't take long for me to be totally busy with her once she was born, and of course I had your father when he wasn't out actin' a fool with his construction buddies. I think what you need to do is occupy yourself with something. Get a hobby or why don't you take up more of your time with that business idea of yours? The houses. What's going on with that?"

"Yea I've been working on that. It's coming along, I think I've found the house I want to buy. I'm supposed to meet with the lady on Monday, and if everything works out I think I'm going to put a down payment to buy the property. But besides that Mom, it's Independence Day on a Friday night, and I'm sitting up in the house. That's not right. There's something wrong with that!" Jacy chuckled and then sighed into the phone.

"What's Rachelle doing?"

"She's mad at me for telling her about herself. She's letting some guy she met at the club dog her out again."

"Oh. Well you know Jacy, you just gotta let some women make their own mistakes with men. That's the only way they'll learn."

Jacy thought about her mom's own relationship mishaps. "But Ma she's made mistake after mistake and still hasn't learned much," Jacy said getting agitated. "She's 24, older than me, and still hasn't learned sh—, hasn't learned anything about men."

"Look at you about to curse at your mother. Jacy you gotta learn to let people live their own lives. You might be strong, but not everyone is sweetheart. You have to accept that and let God take care of the rest."

"I hear you Ma."

"So about Mrs. Jamison's son…" Jacy's mom went on and on about tentative plans for Jacy to meet up with Barry Jamison, what Jacy's sisters and brother had been up to and other news from home with no interruptions from Jacy except an occasional "Mhmm," and "Yes." While Mrs. Thomas was just getting into some recent purchases she had made at Ethan Allen, Jacy's other line on her cellphone beeped with a private caller.

"Hold on Mom, it's my other line."

"Oh, go ahead and take it sweetie, I have to go and pick up some groceries for tonight's dinner," her mom answered. "Love you! Take care."

"I love you too Ma! Tell everyone I said hi."

"Okay. Make sure you lock up!"

"I will. Talk to you later Ma," Jacy clicked over. "Hello?"

"What's up baby?" It was Terrell. Jacy grimaced, but was happy to at least hear from someone on the holiday. She really didn't want to have to spend it sitting on the couch.

"Hey."

"You can't answer your phone no more huh?"

"I answered it just now right? What's up."

"Yea, when I call from another phone. What you doing today."

"Nothing at this point. I'm probably just gonna end up staying in the house and chilling with some wine."

"Oh yea, I heard the boy Roo still locked up. You can't stay in the house on the 4th Jacy. Come out with me to this barbecue my aunt is having down her way."

"Uh. I don't know if that's a good idea Terrell. Rich was really upset when he found out you were over here that time, I don't wanna cause no drama," Jacy hesitated. Part of her was saying it probably wasn't a good move. Still, another part was already pushing her out the door.

"What? Girl, get on your clothes and come on out. You too young to be sitting up in the house all the time. This is Terrell remember? We still friends right?"

Jacy sighed for a long while and then was silent as she considered the pros and cons of going out on the 4th with Terrell. It was being thrown by his Aunt, who lived out in Darby so it was a slim chance she would be spotted by anyone who knew Rich. Besides, even if they did it was completely innocent. They were just old friends, like Terrell said. Right.

"Alright Terrell. But just for a little while. And you. Don't try nothing this time. I mean it."

"Ain't nobody gonna try nothing. Imma come scoop you in a half hour so be ready."

"No I'll just meet you at your Aunt's house. It's off of Main Street in Darby right?"

Terrell sucked his teeth. "Why do you always have to be so difficult? Yea it's off of Main on 9th Street. I'll be there, give me a call if you can't find it." They hung up.

* * * * *

Jacy could hear the music before she even turned a right onto 9th Street. There were people in the front of the quaint house relaxing with drinks, while others were leaning on cars talking. Jacy got out of the car and yanked up her low-rider jeans before heading towards the back where the music was coming from.

About 50 or 60 people were in the back talking, laughing and eating barbecued ribs, chicken, burgers, franks and homemade potato salad. Jacy immediately spotted Terrell leaning over talking to one of his female cousins who was there with a couple of her friends. One of the friends looked awfully familiar to Jacy, but she couldn't quite place the face. She strolled up to Terrell, who was looking good in fresh cornrows a white wifebeater and blue basketball shorts, and grabbed him by the arm.

"Oh hey what's up stranger! I didn't think you were comin' for a minute. Jacy you know my little cuz Takisha. You remember Jacy Kish?"

"Yea. What's up," Takisha said never breaking as much as a smile before slightly rolling her eyes and turning back to her friends.

"What's up," Jacy answered with the same level of disinterest, looking around and trying to be concerned with the crowd.

"You found it alright?"

"Yea I came up here with you before, remember?" she said focusing on Terrell's soup cooler lips again.

"Oh yea," Terrell said while undressing her with his eyes and licking his lips. Jacy had a quick flashback to the night he took her on the couch and shivered. She quickly pushed it to the back of her mind. NO, she told herself.

"It's a good turnout. Your aunt sure know how to throw a party. Where is she? I want to say hi."

"She's in the house somewhere, she'll come back out later. You want somethin' to eat?"

Jacy followed Terrell to the refreshment area, and piled barbecued chicken, corn on the cob and macaroni salad onto a huge plate. They drank Smirnoffs and Coronas and sat out in the yard until it was dark and they were on the verge of being tipsy. To Jacy's surprise Terrell was acting like a perfect gentleman, and didn't get on her nerves even once. The kids set off some firecrackers in the yard and they could hear several others out in the front and down the street popping firecrackers in observance of the holiday. Everything was fine, but one small thing was bothering Jacy. The entire night Jacy was catching the friend of Takisha's who had looked familiar staring at her and Terrell, and then looking away. The girl had toffee colored skin with a light brown micro braids held up in a ponytail. She was on the thick side and was dressed in a very revealing halter top with her belly slightly hanging over a pair of short jean shorts. Jacy finally decided to ask about her.

"Who's that girl that keeps staring over here? Takisha's friend?" Jacy asked leaning over towards Terrell while keeping her eyes on the girl.

"Oh that's Neecey. Don't pay her no mind. She just young, nosy. She fasttt. Fucked with just about every other nigga I know," Terrell sucked something out of his teeth loudly. "The niggas in the neighborhood call her the 'Knob.'"

"The 'Knob?'" Jacy twisted her face up in a question mark before taking a swig of her Corona.

Terrell paused and threw back his head to laugh a little. "Yea you know like a door knob. Eveybody gets they turn with that jawn. I never fucked with her though. Them niggas need to leave those young jawns alone."

"Oh," Jacy said, her stomach turning at the crudeness of what he said, and not believing Terrell's claim to not have messed with Neecey. Why was she grilling them down then?

At the end of the night Terrell begged Jacy to come out with him to a club that was supposed to be having a huge 4th of July bash. While the offer was tempting, she appreciated the fact that he had been there for her and had given her something to do to get out of the house, she decided to call it a night. She thanked his aunt for the hospitality before leaving, and let Terrell walk her out to her car.

THE NEXT morning at 11:48am Jacy sat outside the prison waiting for Rich to be released. She glanced at her watch and pulled out the new book she was reading, *God's Gift to Women* by Michael Baisden. She was taking her mom's advice to get a hobby.

She was at the point in the book when the radio announcer first moves out to Houston and gets a surprise call from his one night stand. She was slightly thrown by the trickery of the desperate woman, who had asked to use his cellphone at the club where they met to make a call and then called her home phone in order to get his phone number. Jacy thought about how easy it would be for any of the guys she met herself at nightclubs to pull that trick.

Just as she was really getting into the book, she heard a tap on her window. She looked up and saw Rich smiling at her so wide she thought his face might crack. His hair was in a wild brillo-like fro and he was in dire need of a shape up of his facial hair. Jacy smiled back and opened the door.

"Hey sweetie!" she said throwing her arms around his neck like a little girl. Rich didn't say anything in response just hugged her back and enjoyed the moment. Jacy pulled back and gave him a long passionate kiss on his lips which lasted for almost five minutes. When they broke free Rich's eyes remained closed as he pulled in his lips to taste her strawberry flavored lip gloss.

"Damn I missed you baby," he said finally looking at her again.

"I missed you too. You look good, but you need a cut *bad*," she teased him. She tossed her hair to the side and reached down to open the car door. "Come on let's get home, I have some things to tell you."

On the drive home Jacy gave Rich back his cellphone and let him check his messages and call his boys. He was on the phone the entire time so she didn't have a chance to tell him about her job or her new business venture. She pulled up to her apartment building and they both got out, Rich still holding the phone to his ear barking out commands. He paused, put his free hand behind her neck lovingly and kissed her on the cheek.

"Imma call you a little bit later. I'm gonna go home, take a shower and shit, then I gotta handle some business. You ain't goin' nowhere right?"

"I don't know. Why don't you just call me when you're done doing what you gotta do." Jacy replied, a little disappointed that the first thing on his mind coming home was business.

"Aiight. Keep your phone close though cause I wanna see you in a couple hours."

"Alright," Jacy said, pecking him on the cheek. She clutched her book and headed upstairs while Rich continued his phone conversation. When she got upstairs, Jacy read some more of the book for a couple of hours while sitting up in bed and eventually ended up drifting off to sleep.

chapter 11
Home......Coming

W HEN RICH PULLED UP to his house he was greeted warmly by his block, Miss Claudette and Miss Janie across the street waved and welcomed him back from across the street, Tracey and his crew from a few houses down on the other side came over to give him a pound, and he stood outside with the guys from right next door to his house for a few minutes to talk.

"Man its been a lotta shit since you went up. You know Ray-Ray and Quinn? Got shot up on 48th, some niggas robbed 'em and then shot Quinn in the head. Ray-Ray tried to make a run for it and got shot in the shoulder. He survived but Quinn was DOA. I think that shit was on some revenge shit, cuz they didn't have to kill the nigga. They got what they wanted. Oh yea, and you ain't never gonna believe who showed up. The nigga Jimmy—he was up here like a week ago. I told him you was looking for him, I swear I turned my back to go in the house and that nigga was gone. AGAIN. Yo, dude was lookin' horrible too..."

Rich's boy Goat briefed him on everything that was going on in the neighborhood and they finally gave each other pounds.

"Aiight nigga," Rich said getting ready to leave.

"Oh wait. I meant to tell you something else. Let me holla at you for a minute Roo," the brotha pulled Rich aside, obviously needing to tell him something in private.

"What's up?" Rich asked with a puzzled look on his face.

"Yo. You know that jawn you brought by here that time? Dark skinned?" Goat said in a hushed tone.

"Yea?" Rich said raising his voice, getting defensive.

"Well I ain't tryin' to start shit, but I thought you should know. My sister saw her with that nigga Terrell at some barbecue, all up in each other faces."

Rich was silent as he grit his teeth. But in his head he was thinking, "What??!?"

"And from what I heard that nigga Terrell going around telling people they back together and shit. Ever since a week before you went up."

Rich laughed a nervous angry laugh and shook his head. "Nigga you betta be lying."

"I'm just tellin' you what I heard. Cause you my boy. I don't know if it's true or not, but that's for you to find out. I ain't gonna just let you be ignorant of the fact."

Rich shuffled around anxiously for a minute before the explosion. "FUCK!!" he suddenly yelled out, flexing his arms like the Hulk to release tension. Everybody turned to look at him and Goat.

"Yo, calm down man. It might not even be true. I'm just goin' by what Neecey told me. Just call your girl and straighten that shit out," Goat said suddenly feeling as if maybe he should have kept the information to himself.

"JUST left the jail and 'bout to have to go back and shit," Rich said talking more to himself than anybody else as he rubbed his hand back and forth over the back of his neck furiously, looking at the ground. "These niggas tryin' have me locked up for life man!"

"Roo, like I said—"

"Man, just shut the fuck up," Rich stared at his stoop for what seemed like ages to Goat, and tried to calm himself down. He had taken a few anger management classes while locked up, but he wasn't sure if they had done him justice. He finally looked up again. "Look, my bad Goat. Good look," he said and then turned to jog up the stairs to his front door.

Before he even made it inside he was finding Jacy's number in his phone and calling it. The phone just kept ringing and ringing. He called it four more times before throwing it across the floor, causing the battery to separate from the phone.

He sat in his living room for a minute calming himself down. There's no way Jacy would do this to him, he was thinking. No way. He would get to the bottom of this. With that thought he calmed himself down enough to head upstairs and get in the shower.

Showered, shaved and dressed an hour later, Rich heard the door downstairs open and close and Timbo's voice boom through the house.

"Yo ROO. Where you at?"

"Upstairs. Hold on a minute."

When Rich came downstairs, he appeared calmer but still had a disturbed look on his face.

"Yo, your bul. That nigga Terrell. He been fucking with my girl?"

"What? Naw I ain't heard that shit. Who told you that?"

"Goat! He said Neecey saw that nigga with Jacy at some barbecue party. Terrell talkin' about they back together now and shit."

"How Neecey know who Jacy is?"

"Man I don't fucking know. Maybe she seen her when she was over here last. All I know is…yo where do your cuz be at Bo?"

"Why? I know you ain't thinkin' about doin' nothing to my cuz off no rumor. That's some bitch shit Roo, he said she said shit. Plus yo ass just got outta jail talkin' about where somebody at. You need to stay yo ass outta trouble and keep a low profile." Suddenly Timbo had a flashback to the day at the mechanic's when he saw a 'Jason' calling and picked up Jacy's phone. He decided now was not a good time to bring that up, it might be just the thing that would cause Rich to snap, lose focus and do something stupid.

"I just want to talk to the nigga. I know that's your blood, but I got to get some things straight."

"How about this, cuz we gotta get the fuck outta here. Imma talk to him. But somethin' don't sound right, and knowin' my cuz he just trippin' right now. Besides, Jacy cool, I don't think she'd fuck up that good thing ya'll got."

Rich walked over to the leather couch and plopped down, putting his head in both hands. "Yea you right dawg. I know Jacy, she wouldn't do no shit like that. She just dropped me off earlier...naw she wouldn't do that to me, she know how I am."

"Exactly. Listen. Forget about that shit right now. I need you to come wit me right quick to this nigga house. One of my boys just spotted 'im chillin out front."

"Aiight," Rich said, reluctantly getting back up from his seat and walking towards the door with Timbo. "Oh wait, where my phone at?" he turned back around patting his pockets and then looking around at the floor.

"Don't worry 'bout that shit right now, this is urgent. I wanna get over there before this nigga try to dip. We'll do that other shit we talked about later."

"Damn!" Rich exclaimed still looking around. He looked at his watch. "Alright, it's only gonna be a couple hours."

Rich followed Timbo out the door and they headed off for their destination. When they were in the car Timbo reached under the seat and kept his hand low as he passed Rich a small black bag holding the two guns that he had been keeping for Rich.

* * * * *

Timbo screeched up in front of the run down rowhouse in North Philly and jumped out of the car with Rich in perfect sync. The brothas standing in front of the house slumped their shoulders in defeat and looked around at the ground as they considered making a run for it, but they knew better.

"YeeeOOO! Sup Rob? Why you been dodgin' me nigga?" Timbo inquired as he walked around his car towards the group.

"Awww man I ain't tryna dodge you dawg," Rob responded throwing his cigarette down on the ground and using his sneaker to put it out. Timbo came up to him and grasped his hand in a soul handshake.

"Let me see you for a minute." Timbo held onto Rob's hand, putting his other arm over Rob's shoulder and leading him to the small alley side of the double rowhouse. Rich lounged back on a nearby wall, holding his shirt up with part of his Beretta showing from inside his pants. He started a conversation with the rest of the young boys that were standing outside. They, on their Ps and Qs, looked towards the street and the ground avoiding eye contact with Rich. They could faintly hear Timbo and Rob talking.

"So why is it two weeks, and I ain't seen nor heard from you 'bout my dough? No phone call, no visit, no nothin', huh? You ain't even try to give me my shit back, where's my shit?" Timbo asked a few inches from Rob's face.

"Timbo look man Imma be honest. I only got a portion of that. Imma get the rest to you next week. I'm sorry man but you know I'm good for it."

"Do I? *Do* I? You was 'good for it' two weeks ago wasn't you? Nigga let me find out you using," Timbo stopped talking abruptly and bit down on his lower lip. He was getting increasingly angry. He took a look around. Rich looked back and then took a look around the block himself. Timbo discreetly pulled out a small handgun with his left hand and held it to Rob's neck. He slammed Rob up against the brick wall causing Rob's head to bang against the brick. He held out his right hand. "Empty your pockets nigga."

"Awww, Timbo come on man, I gotta pay some bills with—" Rob hesitated.

"Nigga I AM your bills!! Now pass that shit!" Timbo demanded taking the safety off. Rob knew that Timbo was not one to play. He reached into his pocket and pulled out a stack of bills. Timbo snatched it away and put the gun back in his pants. He counted off a little over $1,500. Rob was in debt to him for $4,000.

"This it?"

"Yea man, I told you I gotta get the rest to you in a couple weeks."

"I thought it was next week. Man I should just shoot your ass dead right now." Timbo eyed Rob for a while, unnerving him. *Is he gonna do it?* Rob thought to himself. Timbo put the money in his pocket and then brushed his hands together once in a symbol of finality. "Yo, this it. I want the rest of my money by the end of next week. And when I get it you done with me. You can go play these games with some of these other suckas out here. If you *don't* have my shit, all 25 hunned, by next Saturday at midnight you won't be breathing on Sunday! You got me?" he yelled the last part, incensed, spit hitting Rob's face as he talked.

"I got you Timbo. My bad dawg, I'll have it." Rob wiped his eye.

"And I *will* find you, bet on it," Timbo said adjusting his gun and then walking off.

* * * * *

Timbo and Rich caught up with each other on the ride back and decided to go straight down to New Jersey to get their other business out of the way and make sure everybody knew Rich was back on the block. When they finally finished their runs and pulled up to Rich's house it was near nightfall, 7:25pm and everyone was off the block to start their Saturday night partying rituals. Rich was tired and headed up his steps after he had said his goodbyes to Timbo. His mind was back on Jacy and he knew he needed to talk to her as soon as possible to ease his mind. Next door, Neecey was sitting out on the stoop with her arms crossed.

"Sup Rich! Welcome back baybee," Neecey said in her shrill voice, trying to sound as cute as possible.

"Sup Neece," Rich replied, still in deep thought as he reached for his screen door and pushed through into his house. When he got in he immediately started looking for his cell phone again.

"Fuck! Where did I throw that shit?" he asked himself as he scanned the floors. Just then he heard a rap at the door.

"Who is it?" he growled at the door.

"It's Neecey, I wanted to talk to you about something."

Rich wondered what the hell Neecey the Knob could possibly have to tell him. Then he remembered she was the one who had spotted Jacy and Terrell at the barbecue.

"Hold on," he said making a quick decision. He looked around for his phone once more and then went to the door to open it. "What you want?"

"I just wanted to come by and welcome you back," she said as she sauntered her way past Rich and stood in his foyer.

"I didn't ask you in."

"Oh stop playin' boy, why you gotta be so mean all the time?" she said and walked over to his couch to sit down.

"What you got to tell me?"

"Didn't my brother tell you?"

"What about my girl? What the hell is that to you anyway?"

"Hold on nigga, I'm just trying to look out for you. We friends ain't we? Wouldn't you *want* me to tell you if I saw your girl hugged up on some other nigga?" Neecey replied with an attitude, rolled her eyes back into her head and crossed her arms.

"You musta seen wrong, cuz I know my girl Jacy and she know better," Rich said sitting next to Neecey on the couch and looking over the back to check for his phone.

"Oh does she? Is that why she was up under Terrell the entire time having drinks, laughing and holding hands and shit? They was talking all intimate and shit like lovers. While you sitting in jail? That ain't no way for a girl of yours to act in public is it?" Neecey drawled out, embellishing her story. Rich stared her down and gritted his teeth.

Neecey continued. "Then I think they even left together, cuz I saw Terrell pull off right after her going in the same direction."

Rich dropped his head into both hands trying to quell the ball of anger rising from his stomach. Even if Neecey was lying, he didn't want those images running through his mind. Neecey scooted over and rubbed him on the back and shoulder.

"I'm sorry Rich, I didn't want to have to break it to you like that but you made me mad. Nobody never believing me when I tell them something. But this the truth, I know what I saw," she said resolutely. Rich snatched back his shoulder and shooed Neecey away from him with his head still in one hand. But Neecey wasn't giving up that easy.

"I care about you Rich, I always have. And I don't want to see you get played out like that," she reached her right hand down between his legs and rubbed his right inner thigh. "That girl don't know how to treat a nigga like you. I seen the way she be yellin' at you and shit, on the street…that ain't right. You need a woman that play her position and you know I'm down for you one hundred and *ten* percent."

Neecey kissed him on the cheek, and then on the chin. Then on the neck. She then moved her hand up to the bulge that was forming in his pants and lightly rubbed it at first, increasing the pressure. Rich's mind was racing, his fury was turning into pure lust and thoughts of doing the complete opposite of what he should. Revenge flirted and nipped at his heart as he struggled to accept that the woman he loved could have been fucking another dude, behind his back. While he was in jail.

"You just got outta jail and where's she?" Neecey hissed into his ear which was now wet with her saliva. "Haven't had no pussy in over a month and she ain't nowhere to be found? She should be right here right now pleasing you, but she off doing her own thing. She seem like a Miss Goody Two-shoes. I bet she never even sucked your dick. Does she ever suck it real good like I can do it?" Neecey said batting her eyes. She started unbuckling Rich's pants.

"Neecey you betta leave," Rich said weakly attempting to get up, but Neecey used all of her strength to push him back down on the couch and got on her knees in the same motion. She quickly finished unbuckling, pulled out Rich's solid manhood and wrapped her lips around him. Rich moaned at the sensation. He burrowed his eyebrows and tried to think about Jacy, to get the power to resist this act, but he could only think of her hugged up on Terrell. Neecey was quickening her motions and Rich became lost in the moment.

IT WAS 6:40pm and Jacy had just woken from her nap. She stretched and reached over to look at the clock.

"I wonder why Rich didn't call yet?" Jacy thought aloud.

She pulled herself up out of bed and jumped in some cool shower water to wash some of the moisture off her skin from the humidity of the hot summer day. When she got out she lotioned and pulled on some fresh panties and a matching strapless bra since she would probably be spending the night with Rich on his first day back. Once she was dressed in her tan khaki skirt, tight white halter top with a bow at the back of her neck, hair unwrapped and combed out, she started a search for her cellphone.

She looked in her purse, near the alarm clock, in the crevices of the couch and in the kitchen where she usually threw her keys, but couldn't find it anywhere. She picked up her landline and dialed her cellphone number but didn't hear it ringing.

"Must have left it in the car," she said to herself and picked up her keys after sliding into some flip flops, but then she remembered that she hadn't been in her car all day. She must have left it in Rich's car when she picked him up earlier. She had been so preoccupied with the fact that the first thing on Rich's mind was business that she neglected to find her cellphone which she had left in the open compartment between the seats.

Luckily, she knew Rich's number by heart since it was so simple to remember. She dialed his number from her landline but it immediately went to voicemail. She left a message with her home number, then sighed and stood in her living room for a while thinking of what to do. Rich didn't know her landline number so he wouldn't be able to get in touch with her until he checked his messages, but there was no telling when he would check them and she needed her phone ASAP. God forbid Terrell or Jason try to call and Rich pick up her phone. She quivered at the thought.

She would have to drive over to Rich's house to get her phone, and if he wasn't there she would leave a note on his door. "Damn," she said going back into her room to take off her flip flops, put on some tan sandals and switch the items from her denim purse into her Louis Vuitton bag. Jacy headed out the door, locked up and went down the stairs to her car.

When she pulled up on Rich's block it was 7:42pm. She had to drive around a couple of times because she made a wrong turn and had to manuever in order to get onto Rich's small one-way street. When she pulled up she saw Rich's car out front, and a light on in the living room window, which was covered by drapes that were partially open.

Oh good, he's home, she thought. Jacy pulled her car into an available spot a couple of houses down, got out and beeped her alarm. She walked down the street in her tall tan sandals as a few people remaining on the block stopped what they were doing and watched from their stoops. She wondered why some were looking at her so closely; their eyes lingered even after the initial sight of her leaving her car. They had seen her on this block before. She brushed it off and walked up Rich's steps to his front door.

She knocked on the door a couple times but didn't hear a response. She knew someone was in there, because she could see the light on in the living room and could hear and see slight movements inside through the drapes. She looked around her at the people on the block, who were still looking in her direction, then turned around and knocked again plus rang the doorbell.

"Come back later dawg!" she finally heard Rich's voice yell out from inside. Then she definitely heard a female's voice giggling. She was sure. So sure that her woman's instinct, which had been going wild since she pulled up to Rich's block surged through her, down her arm and to her hand which opened the screen door, turned the doorknob and pushed open the front door.

When she stepped in and beheld the sight before her Jacy felt as if she was in the twilight zone. Some bad late night movie, but definitely not reality. The man she had waited for while he was in jail, given herself to, comforted and stood by in his time of need was leaned back on the couch in the mouth of some skank. The female looked sloppy in a pink tube top that was pulled down revealing her D cup breasts. Rich's eyes were closed as he received the fellatio, saliva dripping down the sides of her mouth.

"Oh FUCK naw!?" Jacy screamed at the top of her lungs in stunned amazement and stood in place as if her feet were stuck in cement. Rich jumped up from the couch, hitting the girl on the chin with his knee as he struggled to his feet and fastened his pants at the same time.

"Oh shit, Jacy." he said frantic and flustered. He had obviously been on the verge of an orgasm. He struggled to calm himself as Jacy stood with her mouth wide open, almost in a smile, and he tried to reason with her in a more normal voice. "Baby it's really not what you think…"

But Jacy wasn't hearing anything that was coming out of his mouth. She stood stationary and was lost in her thoughts trying to grasp onto the reality of the situation. She looked at Rich as if she were seeing him for the very first time. She recognized the female from the barbecue and finally remembered that she was the girl from next door. She had noticed her a couple of times standing in the doorway while her brother and his friends sat outside. *Scandalous bitch*, Jacy thought. She finally came to and realized that it *was* in fact Rich who was just sitting there getting slobbered down by this skank, who was standing there holding her breasts up with her arm and hand, with a slight smirk on her face that she was trying to cover with her other hand. Jacy's body and mind shifted back into a familiar zone. Her heart was hardening at the speed of lightening. Her blood pressure went back down and a grin spread across her face. She laughed a little and looked around. Both Rich and the girl Neecey looked on in amazement. They figured she might have lost her mind.

"Baby? You alright?" Rich asked taking a few reserved steps towards her.

"Oh yea, I'm alright Rich. I'm fine, just great!" she said grinning. She grasped her LV bag which was hanging on her right shoulder with her left hand tightly. She looked over at Neecey who had finally pulled her top up and was standing with her arms crossed and weight shifted to one side.

Rich smiled uneasily and began moving towards Jacy again, this time with quicker movements, but her smile quickly faded and she stopped him in his tracks by sticking the palm of her hand up at his face. Her voice came cold and harsh. "I am DONE with you."

She turned and walked out the door just as quickly as she came. Rich went after her like a bat out of hell. Neecey trailed behind.

"Jacy. Please would you just hear me out?" he said walking directly behind her, grabbing her up but each time she just shook free and moved faster towards her car.

"Jacy," Rich's voice started to break up as desperation crept in. "Jacy please listen to me. Don't you know by now I'm in love with you? That triflin' ass bitch don't mean *shit* to me. She was scheming!"

"Oooo, I should have *known*," Jacy began, alternating between talking to herself and to Rich. "Not to trust a nigga. You're no different from any other nigga out here on the street. Why would he be different Jacy? Why?" Jacy said shaking her head as she finally made it to her car. Jacy had come across a lot of idiots in her lifetime, but it was the first time she had actually caught someone cheating on her. And to think, she was worried about being unfaithful to him by hanging out with Terrell. She fought back tears. *Uh uh*, she thought, *I'm not gonna let even ONE tear drop for this nigga.*

"Jacy don't say that. Baby," Rich sighed and threw his hands down in defeat searching for something to say as Jacy searched through her bag for her keys while he stood right behind her. "Baby I'll make this up to you. Anything you want you got it! I promise you this will never happen again. And it's never happened before, I promise! She had this all planned. Come on Jacy!?"

Jacy had found her keys and opened her car door sliding in. Rich caught the door before she had a chance to close it. Suddenly they heard Neecey's shrill voice in the background.

"I ain't had nothin' planned nigga. You know you been wanting me," the nineteen year old Neecey said from a few feet behind them getting ghetto and throwing her finger up in the air to make her point. "You just wayyy too stuck on this bitch to realize."

"Oh THIS bitch?" Jacy asked. She stood back up out of the car and snaked her neck in Neecey's direction. "Trick, I'll be a BITCH over a dumb ass ho any day of the week. Believe that!" She gave Neecey a slow look up and down like she was lower than dirt, then leaned over and spit in her direction. Rich looked shocked. Neecey's face screwed up at the insult.

"Don't be mad at me cause you can't please your nigga..." Neeceys words were dripping with bitterness. She went on trying to find more words to incite Jacy, but Jacy wasn't concerned with Neecey. Or Rich for that matter.

"Whatever ho," Jacy dismissed her with a wave of her hand and then returned her disinterested glare to Rich, who was still holding the door open and looked at her with one of the sorriest looks she'd ever seen on a man.

"Move your hand before I slam the door on it," she quickly snatched the door back from his grip and stepped back inside.

"Jacy you can't be serious, you not just gonna leave me like this right? Over a bitch?" Rich said as Jacy slammed the car door with much force. She put on the power locks quickly and put the keys in the ignition.

"Oh it's like that then? I thought we had something more than this dumb shit Jacy." Rich smacked her driver's side window with his hand. "Leave then, I don't fucking care," he yelled as Jacy manuevered out of her spot and out towards the main street.

chapter 12
Impulse

"I DIDN'T EVEN GET MY PHONE BACK! That's what's pissing me off the most!" Jacy laughed. She was on the phone with her cousin Tammy, who fresh back from Miami, had been briefed on the entire occurrence of that past weekend. It was a blazing hot Monday afternoon and Jacy was sitting at her home desk checking her email. She had an appointment at 1:30pm with Mary from the real estate company which held the property she was looking to purchase. Jason had called and asked to come down with her to inspect the house one more time, so she was meeting him downtown first and then going to the agent's office which was only a few blocks away from the meeting place they decided on.

"Well look at it this way. At least he won't be able to call you right?" Tammy joked.

"Yea, I wish. I left a message on his voicemail with my fucking home number before I went over to his house! Dammit. Why did I just have to leave a message? He hasn't tried to call yet, but it's just a matter of time. I'd rather get harassed on my cellphone than on my damn home number," Jacy pondered as her nails clicked across the keyboard.

"Yea I know what you mean. But listen cuz. And don't get mad at me for saying this, but don't you think you're being just a little hard on the brother? I mean, at least hear him out. You know how trifling females can be, she probably did set him up for that somehow."

Jacy's hands dropped down on the computer keys. "That's no excuse Tammy! He's a grown ass man. He should have been thinking. He should have resisted."

"Ahem miss. But didn't you let Terrell go down on you that time?" Tammy inquired.

"I didn't *let* him do it, he forced me. You met Terrell, you've seen how strong he is. I couldn't have resisted even if I tried," Jacy reasoned. "That was different, and I wasn't even serious about Rich then," Jacy resumed typing.

"If you say so," Tammy relented.

Jacy sighed and then chuckled. "You're hopeless. Anyway, Rich is old news, sorry you'll never get to meet him. But let me go, I gotta go meet this lady with Jason in an hour."

"Jason. How are things going with him? He hasn't tried nothin' with you has he?"

"No. Well not really, I mean he has taken me out to dinner and tried to sweet talk me but that's about it. Why, is he a convicted rapist or something? Let me find out you hooked me up with a rapist," Jacy kidded.

Tammy laughed. "No, nothing like that. He's just a major playa, and he has a temper on him. He doesn't like rejection. I turned him down several times in college and he flipped on me one day. I mean flipped out like made a big scene on the yard, yelling about why I never give him any play in spite of all the things he did for me. We made up, but I always kept one eye on him after that."

"Ya'll went to college together? You didn't tell me that."

"Yea, we had most of the same classes together, and he would help me out with my homework, bring study snacks to my dorm room at night—he even got someone to fix my car for me when it broke down. I guess he thought that gave him a free coochie coupon or something. But he was sadly mistaken. He likes a challenge, and while he can get just about any girl out there with his looks, he wants what he wants and will go the extra mile to get it. Just be careful alright?"

"Tam you know me, I knew he was a dog from the moment I met him. I'll give you a call tomorrow to let you know how everything went."

"Alright cuz. Love you!"

"Love you too."

Jacy hung up the phone then gathered up her purse, keys, grabbed her checkbook and headed out the door.

JASON STEPPED out of his car which had been idling on the corner of 18th and Chestnut looking like he had just left a fashion shoot for GQ magazine. He was sporting a sharp taupe-colored tailored suit with a light cranberry checkered silk necktie. He began walking towards Jacy who had pulled up across the street a few moments ago and had been peeking out of her car for Jason. She had never seen his car, until now.

She had tried to hold her jaw in place as her eyes fell upon Jason closing the car door of a tan 2003 Mercedes Benz S500 which was sitting on 20 inch chrome rims. The windows had a slight tint and the headlights gleamed in the afternoon sun making every corner and curve of the car seem every bit more luminous. Jacy had a keen eye for luxury cars, and powerful cars in general ever since her father took her on a high speed joyride in his then brand new BMW when she was just ten years old. He had taught Jacy about all types of cars from a very young age because she had always shown an interest. When Jacy came home that day screaming excitedly to her mother about her father's new BMW, her mother railed into Jacy's dad about endangering her child and getting her excited about such a superficial and dangerous thing. They fought that entire night and Jacy's dad ended up sleeping on the couch. But their fighting was in vain because the damage had been done. From that point on Jacy was enthralled with fast luxury cars—she just couldn't help herself. The lure of fresh buttery leather seats, glimmery exteriors and powerful purring engines was just too much.

"What's up beautiful?" Jason asked as he looked down the one-way street before he crossed, letting a car pass and then proceeding to Jacy's car.

"Hey how are you?" Jacy said with a wide smile. "You're looking sharp. Aren't you hot in that suit though?"

Jason chuckled. "Well yea, now I am! That's why I was trying to sit in my car with the AC on. I had a very important meeting this morning with some real estate investors."

"Oh I see," Jacy looked around at the sidewalk. There were a few people on the street shopping but not many. "Did you want to just walk over there?"

"No you can park where you're at and we'll drive over in my car. I have to park Sasha in a garage anyway, I don't trust her on the street."

Jacy didn't argue. She smiled instead. "Sasha huh?" Jason nodded, cocking his head to the side with a smile. "Okay, just let me put some quarters in," she said closing her car door and heading around to the meter.

When she finished Jason led her back across the street carefully and opened the passenger side door. She slid in and took in the intoxicating new car scent. Jason came in on his side, put the car in drive and pulled off.

"So what's Sasha's 0-60?" Jacy asked mischeviously looking at Jason out of the corner of her eye.

"Huh? Oh, 6.1 seconds. I'm in love with this car. She's amazing."

"And the horsepower?"

"302, it's a 24 valve V-8 engine. What do you know about that?"

Jacy chuckled. "I know a *lil'* somethin' about that. How long have you had her?"

"About three months. It's a lease of course. I get a new baby every two or three years but now I'm starting to wish I would have bought this one. It moves perfectly with me. It's like it anticipates my next turn before I make it. It even has that Parktronic system that warns me when I'm getting too close to another car."

"Mmmm. That sounds sooo nice. You have to let me drive it sometime," Jacy said as she daydreamed. She was half-kidding, because she knew there was no way a man she had just met was gonna let her drive his brand new Benz.

"Alright. Let's go for a ride down Kelly drive after this then?" Jason said much to Jacy's surprise. She turned to him with her mouth half open trying her best to play off the shock.

"Are you serious? You're gonna let me drive it?"

"Sure, I trust you. You think you can handle a car like this?"

"Do I!" Jacy said just a little too excitedly. She couldn't believe that he was actually going to let her drive Sasha. She thought back to what her cousin Tammy told her about how accomodating Jason was in his quest for her affection. But her need for speed was outweighing all sensible thought.

Jason pulled into the garage and parked taking up two empty spots in a corner. They got out and walked out of the garage crossing the street as they headed for the front door of Sweet Home Real Estate, a storefront office located beneath several apartments. When they walked in a tiny blonde receptionist looked up and smiled.

"Hi. How may I help you?" she asked.

"We have an appointment with Mary Bronson about a property," Jacy answered politely.

"Okay. Just have a seat and I'll call her out."

Jacy and Jason had a seat in the small foyer area of the office. Jacy took a look over the items on the coffee table and saw an interesting looking little book called *Chocolate Princesses*, right on top of an old *Cosmo* magazine. She grabbed it immediately and flipped through the pages. It was a book focused on darker skinned models trying to break into the industry. *I could be in this,* she thought to herself, *but then again just about every pretty dark skinned girl probably would think so.* Just as she was pulling a pen out of her purse to take down the number, Mary stepped out into the lobby and waved Jacy and her companion into her office. They both stood up at the same time, followed her in and then settled into the two chairs in front of her desk as Mary closed the door behind them.

"So are you just about ready to set a closing date?" Mary asked as she made her way to her seat.

"Just about. But like I told you over the phone we want to go take a look at the property one more time before I put a deposit down."

"No problem. Let me just go get the key and we can take a drive over in the van." Mary flashed her phony realtor smile and got up from her seat again to go ask the receptionist to get her the key.

* * * * *

When they pulled up at the house there were a few girls playing double dutch in front. The place definitely needed some major improvements but it wasn't completely run down. The only difference between it and the houses to its left and right was that all of their windows were intact and the paint on the railings wasn't as badly chipped.

When they walked inside, Jason noticed that there were several planks missing from the floors and the railing of the staircase was slightly bent. The kitchen was missing too many floor panels to count and the countertops were worn and broken up. Upstairs, doors were missing from the bathroom and one of the bedrooms, the carpet needed to be replaced in all rooms as well as the hallway, the sink was missing its faucet and the bathtub was cracked in the middle. They went downstairs to the basement which was extremely dirty and full of items abandoned by the previous owner, old bicycles, broken tvs, boxes, and wood planks. There was a musty smell throughout the house.

"What is that smell? Did something—or some*one*—die in here?" he asked.

"I believe that smell is just from the old carpets," Mary answered quickly. The blue carpet had several large dark unidentifiable spots.

"So other than that, what do you think?" Jacy asked Jason as they re-entered the living room area.

"I think it needs a lot of work. New paint job, new wallpaper in the kitchen, new floors, the staircase fixed... Just about every room in this house needs some work, but it's nothing that's out of reach. It's probably going to be a little out of your budget in terms of fixing it up."

"Well the good thing is that most of the damage in the house just needs repairing, not replacing. That should keep your improvement costs down," Mary defended the house, getting slightly worried that Jason could blow her whole deal.

"And that junk in the basement, will all of that be removed before the closing?" Jason asked turning to Mary after pivoting and giving the room another good look.

"Yes, we will take care of the trash removal. I'm not really sure why that all is still down there but it will be gone by next week," Mary responded.

"And how much are you asking for this place again?"

"$8,400," Jacy answered instead of Mary. "Does it look like it's worth that?"

"Yea I guess that's about right. It's up to you Jacy. The exterior isn't too bad, your major work is going to be right in here," Jason said pointing down towards the floor. "I'll estimate that you'll probably have to do about $5-6,000 in repair costs. But if you can hook this place up right I'm sure you'd be able to fetch at least $18,000 for it. Maybe even more if you put that Jacuzzi in the bathroom like you planned."

"Yea, but I still have to find out whether its feasible to have a Jacuzzi in a rowhouse like this. I can swing up to $5,000 in costs, that's close to the limit of my budget but that's a worst case scenario. It might be even less," Jacy turned to Mary. "I think I'd like to take it."

Mary smiled. "Great! Then let's get you back to the office and set up your details. You said that you wanted to pay cash for the house at closing right?"

"Yes, I'll give you a check right now for the 10% deposit and bring the balance in cash or a cashier's check," Jacy glanced back at Jason who smiled at her like a proud dad. They all then headed out the door and went back to the office to set a closing date.

WHEN THEY finally left the office after setting a closing for that very next Monday, Jason held true to his promise. He handed Jacy the keys to his car and let her drive it out of the garage towards Kelly Drive.

Once she had made her way around the museum and entered the Drive, Jacy was overcome with thrill and emotion. The car drove like a dream, smooth and controlled. The pickup was so quick that Jacy barely had to touch the peddle before she hit 40, then 50, then 60. It happened so quick that before she knew it she was doing 70 MPH on the extremely tight winding road. Kelly Drive was pretty empty because it was only around 2:30pm and everyone was still at work, but it was still a difficult road to navigate. She dove around the corners of the road leaning ever so slightly forward in her seat, her graceful legs extending to the gas pedal, and dodged between a white van and a slow moving Ford Taurus.

"Whoa baby, you better slow down this road has a lot of hidden curves and turns," Jason laughed nervously as Jacy ignored him and continued driving with precise agility as she sped around the corners. He smiled and held onto the door as his heart beat with a mixture of fear and delight at the way Jacy was handling the car.

In the meanwhile, Jacy was loving every minute of the drive. She knew she could whip the hell out of a car, was familiar with Kelly Drive, and didn't doubt her skills for one moment. When she finally neared the end, she made a U-turn at a gas station on the corner and headed back towards the city in the same fashion.

As she was picking up her speed again, she saw a police car dip out from a stop-off on the road next to the water behind her. She slowed down a bit and prayed that he hadn't clocked her.

The police car started flashing its lights and began pulling out of the stop-off.

"Shit," Jacy said, more upset that he was messing with her speed high than anything. Her heart fell to her stomach. Jason lifted his head toward the ceiling of the car and sighed. The cop car pulled out, and headed in Jacy's direction at full speed. By then she was doing the limit of 40 MPH next to a couple of other cars on the road but it was too late. The cop came right up on Jacy's tail flashing and beeping his police horn. Jacy got into the right lane and prepared to pull over, but to her surprise and pleasure the police car continued on in the left lane and passed them at full speed towards another destination.

"Whew!" Jacy exclaimed and then got back into the left lane. Her heart slowly returned to its normal position and rate.

"You are hella lucky!" Jason laughed with Jacy as she started to pick up speed again.

As Jacy sped up, she was so caught up in her emotions that she didn't notice she had passed a familiar rust colored Pontiac Bonneville in the next lane whose driver was staring right into their car.

* * * * *

When Jacy came in the door four hours later she was floating on cloud nine. She had just pushed a 500 through Philly! It was by far the best car she had ever driven, or even been in for that matter. She had been in Lexuses, Acuras, one BMW and one Audi but never a Benz, never one that new and never one of that caliber. She felt like a crackhead that had just gotten a fix. Jason had been terrified at some of Jacy's maneuvers but was thoroughly impressed by her skills and knowledge of cars. She had given him a rush he hadn't felt in a long time. It made him want her even more than ever. Afterwards they had gone to the Fridays on JFK

Boulevard for drinks and a meal, and then finally Jason drove Jacy back to her Eclipse.

When she got home, Jacy was in a silly drunk mood. She sauntered into her bedroom, stripped down to her underwear and came back into her living room half-naked to sit down and watch TV. After sitting down she forgot that her blinds were still open and there was a strong possibility that someone was watching her naked behind through the window. She laughed and went over to the blinds and shut them. *Someone just got a nice show,* she thought. On her way back she noticed that the caller ID was flashing. She grabbed the phone off the hook and plopped back down on the couch. She heard the stuttered tone when she picked up indicating that she had voicemail messages. When she dialed in, she found six new voicemail messages waiting for her.

Received at 1:15pm. *Jacy. This is Rich. I need to speak to you, now. Call my cell.*

Received at 1:53pm. *Look Jacy. I know you're not working anymore. Timbo told me. So I know your ass is in the house. You need to CALL ME so we can squash this shit, today. You know and I know that chick don't mean a damn thing to me. Why don't you just talk to me? Come on now you know me, I wouldn't never do anything to hurt you on purpose. Just call me so we can talk. I have your cellphone you know.*

Received at 2:11pm. *I'm not gonna be calling you all day. You need to pick up the fucking phone so we can talk and stop this childish shit. Jacy. I need to talk to you, you just don't understand...<long silence> I have to go out and handle some business right now, but I have my cell phone on me. In case you don't have it, it's 267-660-6000.*

Received at 2:25pm. *Hi Jacy, It's Mary Bronson from Sweet Home. I'm just calling you and leaving a message as promised to remind you of your closing date of next Monday and the address of the title company, which is at 7005 City Line Avenue. Their number if you need to contact them is 215-675-8323. Thank you and give me a call if you need anything else. Good luck!*

Received at 2:42pm. *Who the hell was that nigga I just saw you riding with on Kelly Drive? Jacy you KNOW I don't play that shit. Why do* *you keep doing this to me? You didn't even give me a chance to talk to your ass before you already out here fuckin' with other niggas. I can't believe you! You are one heartless female you know that? Jacy I don't give a fuck if you talkin' to me or not if I see your ass on the street with another nigga he getting fucked up. Early. <click>*

Received at 4:40pm. Oh you still ain't home from your lil' date huh? If I don't hear from you soon I'm coming up there. And you bet' not have nobody with you. We gonna talk about this whether you like it or not, because I just ain't letting you go that easy.

Jacy slowly pressed three to delete the last message and then clicked off the phone. She stared out into space for awhile. Her high was almost gone.

The phone ringing broke her out of her trance. She hesitated, but then boldly picked it up and answered, already knowing who it was.

"Hello," she said dryly.

"So you avoiding my calls? I've been trying to call you all day. You was out with some nigga? Already?"

"Rich! Dammit! I'm sick of this shit! There's nothing for us to talk about because I *saw* you with that trick. I saw it with my *own two eyes*—" Jacy said with hurt clearly in her voice, before getting interrupted.

"Forget what you saw 'with your own two eyes!' You know me better than that, it was just a fucked up situation! Besides what about you? I heard you was messing around with Terrell while I was locked up? And you got the nerve to be mad at me for this?"

"What? Oh hell no. Who told you that, that scheming ass bitch? I bet. And you just believed her over me right? But you want me to believe *you* after what I saw? You're a trip. I'll tell you what I believe. I believe you are just a trifling ass nigga, no different from the rest, that's what I believe," Jacy said, her words cutting into Rich like a ginsu knife.

Rich pulled in air, absorbing the blow and then continued, calmer. "Jacy listen. I don't care about what you did or didn't do with Terrell. I just want us to put it all behind us and start over. We'll call it even. You and I both know that we're good together."

"Rich," Jacy sighed and lowered her forehead into her free hand. "It's just not going to happen. That's some shit that never happened to me before! I never caught anyone cheating on me like that. The only reason why I answered the phone right now is because I wanted you to speak your peace so that you could stop calling this number and leaving messages. Let it go. It's over. If you keep calling this number I'm gonna get it changed," she paused and let her words sink in as Rich remained quiet for several moments.

"It's not over," Rich said more to himself than he did to her. Jacy sighed in response. "Goodbye Rich."

chapter 13
Need Some Time to Get Away

"CUZZZZZZ!" Tammy exclaimed as Jacy lugged her bag up the stairs to the door of her tudor style house.

"Hey girl!!!!" Jacy yelled back as she dropped her bag and ran up to hug her favorite cousin. "I missed you so much. You don't even know."

"I missed you too! Ray, Jacy's here come get her bag!" she turned back into the house and called for her boyfriend and then threw her arm around Jacy leading her into the house. "I'm so glad you're finally here! Man we got so much to do this week! I got us tickets to that new play called *Be a Man About it*, or something, for tonight, Lisa wants us all to go to this hot new club her fiance is throwing parties at on Saturday, and you know Daniel wants to take you and I out on a double date while you're here…" Jacy listened as Tammy ran off their weekend. It was late August, nearing the end of the summer and she had finally made the drive down to visit her cousin in Baltimore for a few days. The events of the past couple months had drained her, especially the work she had been doing on the house she had bought which had commenced at the beginning of August. The contractors Jason had referred her to were difficult to work with at times and had repeatedly tried to get over on Jacy due to the fact that she was a woman, just as she had feared. They bought supplies that they told her cost a lot more than what they were actually worth and were taking a much longer time to do simple tasks than was necessary. It seemed to her that the workers relaxed and busted up on the front stoop more than they worked. Of course, Jacy wasn't having it so she and the lead carpenter were constantly arguing and didn't have the best of relationships. She was nervous about leaving the city to go visit her cousin for these few days because she wouldn't be able to check on their progress.

"...I need to run by the mall and pick up a new outfit for this play tonight, it's supposed to be a lot of people there since it's the opening show. You gonna come right?"

"Yea of course, maybe I'll pick something up myself," Jacy said but knew damned well that she shouldn't be spending any money at the mall. She was basically living off of credit cards at that point and paying a hefty sum of money on her monthly credit card bills. Her last check from her old job had come and gone as she used it to pay her most important bills while saving the rest of the money Rich had given her before they broke up to pay for the home repairs. Speaking of Rich, he had continued to call Jacy on a regular basis despite her request that he give it up. Jacy knew how easy it was after a little time had passed to forget a man's trifling behavior and take him back as if nothing had ever happened, especially when he was being as persistent as Rich, so she had no choice but to hold true to her promise and change her home phone number. She had since disconnected her service to the cell phone she left in Rich's car and used her cell phone insurance to order a brand new one. She kept her old cell phone number for a while so that the people whose phone numbers she didn't know off hand could call. She even called Rachelle to let her know of the new home number despite the fact that they still weren't talking. But after a few weeks, with Rich's sudden realization that she had switched over her service to a new phone, and after a slew of phone calls and messages from him on her new cellphone, Jacy switched that number too, notifying everyone, except Rich of course, of the change. So he had no way of contacting her other than simply showing up to her apartment building. Jacy wasn't worried about that so much because she was rarely home those days, and you had to get past a security door in order to get to the apartments in her building. She had spoken to

Rich once before she changed her cell phone number and the conversation was brief and very heated, she had been very nasty to him being that she was realizing that Rich might have had stalker tendencies.

"Rich what the fuck?" Jacy had picked up finally and asked, incensed. It was one o'clock in the morning.

"How many times do I have to call your ass before you pick up the fucking phone?" Rich asked in an even more annoyed tone.

"How many times do you need to get my voicemail to learn that I don't want to talk to your ass?? I told you I'm done with you!"

"Naw FUCK that Jacy. You AIN'T done with me. That's some bullshit you talking and you the one that's gonna have to learn something."

"And just what are you going to do? Force me to be with you? You gonna stalk me? Rape me? Get the fuck outta here Rich," Jacy said leaning back on her pillow and waving her hand back in the air.

"Would you stop playing? You know I would never do no shit like that..." There was a pause as Rich's voice got calmer. "But Jacy, on the real you got a nigga messed up. I swear I ain't never been this way over no bi—, over no female—"

"Rich I know exactly what you're about to say, but your words don't mean anything to me anymore. Absolutely nothing. Don't call this number again, and I mean it." Jacy hung up in his face and then turned the phone off. When she turned it back on the next day and heard that she had two messages, both from Rich, one in which Rich threatened to come down to her apartment that night, she knew she would have to change that number also. She didn't know if he had actually come or not, but being that he probably didn't remember her apartment number to ring the buzzer, and probably didn't even remember her last name, she would never know.

"I know you're tired from all that driving, come on upstairs to the guest room, I fixed everything up for you," Tammy snapped Jacy out of her reverie as she motioned for her 'little' cousin to follow her up the stairs. Tammy was a tall petite chocolate complexioned beauty. People were constantly mistaking her and Jacy for sisters, though they were only cousins. Other than her large cornrowed braids that reached her lower back, height and thinner frame, Tammy could have been Jacy's taller twin. But her frame and style reminded people of the actress Taral Hicks while Jacy's reminded people more of a Tweet. She was wearing a short tight white baby tee and a red pair of the soccer shorts Christina Aguilera wore in her video to the song *Can't Hold us Down*.

"Ray did you hear me?!" Tammy yelled again for her boyfriend Ray. Ray was a tall, tan, smooth brotha from Atlanta that Tammy had met and fell in love with on one of her regular trips to his city a few years prior. They had met on a Thursday and had fallen in love by Monday, when Tammy had to leave. It was a true love story in the beginning, as her and Ray maintained a long distance relationship for almost a year before he requested a transfer from his job to be closer to Tammy. Tammy was just getting settled in Baltimore at her new job when they met making it impossible for her to move to him. She also had a four year old little girl to take care of who was enrolled in pre-school. When Tammy and Ray moved in together everything seemed perfect. He treated her like a queen, cooked, cleaned and took care of a majority of the household bills with his generous salary as one of the most senior graphics designers at his firm. But as Jacy had learned over the years, all that glitters ain't gold. Several months after he moved to Baltimore, Ray was caught cheating with a woman from his job. Ray had no idea, but Tammy knew a couple of people at his new office, namely gossiping secretaries, who tipped her off to the fact that he was spending one too many lunches a week with Sandra, another graphics designer in his department. Tammy of course had to see for herself, so she sat outside his office building one day around lunch time and to her disappointment she saw Ray and the woman leave the building together. She followed them to a nearby apartment building, which she assumed was Sandra's, and watched them go in. Shock turned to angry tears, so she sat in the parking lot for almost an hour, her eyes red with rage, before seeing them come back out. She quickly hopped out of the car and charged at them, immediately punching and slapping at Ray who, in total shock, defended himself the best he could while Sandra backed up and looked around as if she were expecting camera crews from the show *Cheaters* to come rushing out.

After that episode the whole dynamic of Ray and Tammy's relationship changed from lovey dovey to harsh reality. They loved each other, it was a fact that even Jacy couldn't deny, but as they say, the honeymoon was over, and they were now mainly just co-existing and staying connected through their love for each other. Tammy seemed to wear the pants in that household, bossing Ray around and keeping him on a short leash. Ray just took it, probably out of guilt. Tammy considered leaving him after he was caught cheating, but since her feelings were so deep for the man, something that even she couldn't control, they lived together, and her daughter was so attached to Ray, she decided it was much easier to look past the deed and simply do one of her own. She had never made it known to Ray, but several weeks after they had gotten back together, Tammy cheated on Ray with not one, but two men. One, a brother from her fitness club and the other one of her old boyfriends. The way Tammy figured it, if she was going to take him back, she would at least even the scoreboard.

"Hey Jacy," Ray said smiling as he descended the stairs slowly, meeting Jacy halfway down the stairs and giving her a big hug. Jacy and Ray had bumped heads after the whole cheating incident, but Jacy understood the love they had for each other, accepting Tammy's decision to take him back and write the incident off as a big mistake. Jacy thought Ray was a good guy, but he was just like most men who were led by their penises and did dumb things. Jacy honestly didn't know if she could ever forgive a man who did what Ray did to Tammy, but then again she had never been in love so she really couldn't say.

"What's up Ray?" Jacy said hugging him back warmly.

"Your bags outside?" he said as he started going down the rest of the steps towards the door.

"Yea, its just one bag Ray, thanks. What you been up to?" she asked Ray as she and Tammy slowly continued up the stairs.

"Nothing, just work work work," he turned back and said as he reached for the knob of the front door to go get her bag.

"Where's Tanasia?" Jacy asked of Tammy's daughter when they had reached the top of the stairs.

"She's at her Daddy's house this weekend. He's keeping her until Tuesday so that we can hang out. He's being less of an ass and a lot more of a help these days."

Tammy took Jacy to the guest room and they sat in there talking until Ray brought up her bag, after which Tammy left Jacy in the room to take a nap before the play they were scheduled to see at 7:30pm that night.

WHEN THEY arrived at the theater the ticket purchasing line was wrapped around the corner. Jacy was eternally grateful to Tammy for getting the tickets in advance so that they were able to walk right in. She was still a little beat from her drive down. It was just her and Tammy that night since Tammy wanted it to be a girl's night for the two of them to catch up. They had been tripping out in the car beforehand talking about things that had happened to each of them since the last time they saw each other, as they sipped on Coronas and puffed on a nice sized blunt that Tammy had rolled before they left the house. High and giddy they walked into the theater, took their seats towards the middle of the theater and continued their conversation as they waited for the first act to begin.

During the intermission Jacy and Tammy were in rare form. They strutted around the lobby after making a bet for fun in the theater on how many men would approach them total during the break. Jacy bet four and Tammy bet six. They were definitely standing out; Tammy in the fitted off the shoulder sexy turqoise dress she had bought at the mall earlier that day, and Jacy in a pale pink tight dress with spaghetti straps that she had gotten on one of her shopping sprees with Rich, and matching strappy sandals she had bought that day at the mall with Tammy. She knew she shouldn't use her credit card for something so frivolous, but her unhealthy shopping habits got the best of her. Both women were stunning in their bright cheerful colors, and were definitely carrying themselves with that confident air about them that men seemed to love.

Ever since she had left Rich alone, Jacy was on player mode. The only other time she had been that way was in college. But after this last incident Jacy was beginning to think of and treat men as tools again. They were only good for adding a little spice to her life. She had dated over eight men since she broke up with Rich, five of which she was still receiving calls from here and there, and was sleeping with one who was currently leading the list of candidates. One of her strictest rules was never to sleep with more than one man at once, and she was holding true to that requirement despite the temptations. None of the men really held her interest though.

Upon hearing that Rich and Jacy had broken up, Terrell made a serious attempt at getting Jacy back. But by then Jacy was beginning to remember again why she had dumped him in the first place. He was *always* late. Lying over little things. Making empty promises. She knew it wasn't worth it, so she sent him on his way for good. Nothing could ever come out of a relationship with a man like that, she thought.

Because the work on the house had started, Jacy talked to Jason on a regular basis. He was adamant about staying up on what was happening with the house, and had even talked to the contractors working on the house himself a few times when there were conflicts. Though he tried to make it seem as if everything was totally about business, Jason made it painfully obvious that he was interested in a relationship beyond business. Knowing his type though, Jacy was careful to keep her distance and keep things as professional as possible. But it was getting harder and harder to ward off Jason's advances.

"Excuse me?" Jacy turned around to the muscular chest of a brown skinned adonis with a huge diamond cross hanging around his neck. He was wearing a clean dark brown tank and dark blue jeans. His muscles were bulging from every direction and both of his arms were tatted up, as well as his chest from what Jacy could see. Everything about him exuded confidence and he looked awfully familiar. Jacy noticed several other brothers behind him, some looking just as clean as him, and others looking more on the rough side. One of them was a huge, bodyguard type.

"Yes?" Jacy said keeping a straight face and looking at him inquisitively as she held her drink in the air. For all she knew he could have been about to tell her that she had toilet paper on her heel.

"I had to come over and say something. You are looking good in that pink girl. You're not from around here are you?"

"No, why do you say that?" Jacy said slowly starting to realize where she had seen him from. He was a rapper, not that well known yet, but he had a fairly popular video they were showing on MTV.

"Because you got a different way about you. The way you move, the way you're dressed and carry yourself. Plus I see you got a New York accent."

"I do?" Jacy asked. This always made Jacy wonder because despite the fact that she was born and raised in New Jersey, she had been told she had a New York accent on many occasions. She figured since both her mom and dad were born and raised in NY, their accents had rubbed off on their children. Also, as children they spent 60% of their time visiting family in New York City.

"Yea, like a caribbean feel to it or something. You from New York right?"

"No, I'm from New Jersey, my people are from New York."

"See? New 'Yawk,'" he mocked her speech and then laughed. "I figured. I'm out in New York City almost every weekend."

"Oh for real? Why?"

"I need to go out there to record in the studio."

"Oh yea. I thought I knew you. You have that new video out with Ludacris, 'Stuntin' right? Is it D-4?"

"Yup. So you know about that huh," he said flashing a sexy smile again.

"Yea I like that song, it's hot," Jacy said as she began to see why she was getting several jealous and pissed stares from women in the lobby of the theater.

"So what's up with you. Where you and your girl going after this?"

"Probably to the bed," she responded, having an idea of what was going to come out of his mouth next. She was almost praying he wouldn't go there.

"Well, me and my boys got a suite at the Holiday Inn for the night, we having a few people over to party at our room after this show. Drinks, music, movies we gonna do it up."

"Oh yea? That sounds cool. But I think we'll pass. We're not groupie types so, thanks but no thanks," Jacy said with a hint of attitude in her voice as she turned to look where Tammy had gone. She had actually thought he was coming at her with some respect, but all he wanted was to invite her and Tammy back to the hotel to get them liquored up and in the bed. She was sick of men thinking they could just treat every woman they met like some type of a ho. Jacy was definitely not most women. She wasn't impressed by his little bit of fame, this D-4 cat could keep stepping for all she cared.

"What do you mean? It ain't nothing like that ma."

"Come on now," Jacy said and then turned back at D-4, looking directly in his eyes. "You can be real with me, I know how things go down. For one, my girl already has a man and for two I'm not tryin' to get run through by you and your boys, okay?" Jacy said cocking her head to the side.

"Whoa, whoa, whoa!" D-4 said holding his palms up in defense. "Damn you fiesty as shit! I like that! Okay, you got me, I guess there's no getting nothing past you, damn!"

"Not really," Jacy said crossing her arms and finally finding Tammy standing over by the bar area talking to a nice looking young white man in a suit. "But look I'm gonna go find my girl. It was nice chatting."

"Damn you just gonna leave like that? Alright," D-4 backed off and watched Jacy walk off towards the bar.

When Jacy neared Tammy she decided to get another drink from the bar. Tammy looked at her and smiled as Jacy rounded her and called for the bartender.

"So how many you got so far?" Tammy asked with her back still turned to Jacy after excusing herself from the white gentleman.

"Just one. That rapper dude over there, do you recognize him?"

"Yea! That's D-4. He's pretty big out here in B-more! Did you get the digits?"

"No that nigga was actually expecting us to come down to the Holiday Inn with him and his boys!" Jacy started laughing at the thought as she paid for the $4 shot of Hennessy the bartender had just placed in front of her. She laid down a five dollar bill and turned around to look in the direction Tammy was facing. There was still a few minutes left in intermission.

"Oh really? Well, niggas," Tammy replied as she sipped on her own drink. Jacy counted off five seconds and then took the shot straight to the neck. She put the glass down and asked the bartender for a coke, which he promptly served up.

"There are some cuties in here though, how many you got?" Jacy asked.

"Including that white dude, two now. You better get ready to wash some dishes tomorrow, cuz we bound to get more than one more at this point," as Jacy looked out at the crowd she knew Tammy was right. There were more than a few men staring shamelessly in their direction.

"Now you can dip or dive all you want, but remember the rules is that all they have to say is one word to you and it's considered approaching. Imma be watching your ass," Tammy continued as she flashed a smile at one of the more good looking fellows that was looking their way.

Jacy looked out at the crowd and smiled. This was why she loved hanging out with her cousin Tammy; there was always excitement in the air when the two of them were together. She would have to devise a plan to get by the crowd and back into the theater without having anyone say a word to her. Then hopefully, even if Tammy was able to get two more men she would have overbid and Jacy would win the bet.

"Alright then. Okay," Jacy said in a challenging tone. "Bye bitch, I'll see you in the theater.'"

She walked back off and took the route closest to the bathroom feeling that it was the safest being that there were mostly women around that area. She looked back to see Tammy already getting talked to by the brother she had smiled at just a second ago.

When she turned back around a slender yet busty muscular spanish looking woman rocking a short boyish style and wearing a white wife beater and jeans walked up to Jacy and grabbed her hand delicately. Jacy stepped back in shock and withdrew her hand.

"What's up ma, how you doin'?" the woman asked. She had very masculine movements and reminded her of a female John Leguizamo.

"Uh...nothing," Jacy said almost stuttering. She looked back in Tammy's direction and saw that her cousin was looking right back at her.

"Is that your girlfriend?" the Leguizamo look-alike asked glancing over at Tammy.

"No! I mean no, that's my cousin," Jacy replied getting her cool back. "We're about to go back into the theater, she's trying to get my attention I guess."

"Oh, good. So what's up with you then, you got somebody in your life?"

"Well yea, nothing serious. I date men."

"Oh. Have you ever been with a female before?" the girl asked getting a little too personal for Jacy's taste at this point in the conversation. To be honest the question made her uncomfortable moreso because she *had* actually considered trying out women while she was in college. It never happened, but it was always something that Jacy had been slightly curious about.

"Uh, no. I think I'm cool with the guy I'm seeing now."

The girl whipped out a business card and wrote something on the back. "Well, my name is Tarren, my friends just call me Ren. If you change your mind give me a call aiight?"

Jacy took the card reluctantly. The girl must have read her thoughts, sensing she was bi-curious or something. "Thanks," Jacy replied, shocked at her own willingness to stand and talk to the girl past an initial hello. To be honest, the girl wasn't so bad looking. She was about the same height as Jacy even with the heels Jacy was wearing, and definitely reminded her more of a man than a woman. Jacy had never really been into spanish guys, but she liked the way the girl carried herself and how she wasn't scared one bit to walk up and say what she had to say.

The girl smiled at Jacy and then turned back towards her friends who were standing by the water fountain. Jacy went into the bathroom where she touched up her makeup for a few minutes, and then headed back out towards the theater hoping most of the people there had gone in already. Luckily they had, and Jacy was able to maneuver her way near the entrance of the theater, but before she could step inside, a brother grabbed her arm and turned her in his direction catching her by surprise.

"Hey, what's up?" he asked. He was a short older-looking light skinned guy with baby dreads in his hair. Jacy couldn't stand men that wore baby dreads. She pulled away from him without saying a word, pissed that she had allowed the brother to speak. She continued on into the theater where she almost collided with Tammy who was standing right near the door in the darkness.

"That's six! I win!" she exclaimed happily and did a little dance.

"How many did you get just now?"

"Just one, but you got two, haha!" Tammy taunted as they started heading down the aisle and back to their seats.

"No I didn't, I just had one! That short dude you just saw me with!" Jacy said defending herself.

"Um, excuse me but I think you forgot Consuela over there in the wife beater! That's six!" Tammy said as they took their seats.

"Huh? Girl please you can't count that. She's a woman, the bet was on men!"

"We never said that, we just said how many times we got 'approached' not by whom," Tammy whispered as the music began playing and the curtain opened.

"Oh no you *don't.*" Jacy hissed back. "It was for guys, girls don't count!"

Tammy shook her head and they got quiet as the first actor came out on stage saying his opening lines.

* * * * *

"You're gonna be scrubbing the shit out of some dishes tomorrowww." Tammy pretended to scrub something in the air continuing to tease Jacy as they left the theater after the show. They were both tipsy from the strong drinks the bartender had prepared for them in the lobby.

"The only thing Imma be scrubbing tomorrow is the crack of my ass in the shower. You know damned well that women don't count." Jacy laughed and almost took a big fat L as she walked down the three steps that separated the expansive lobby from the foyer entrance of the theater.

"See look at you, about to bust your ass in front of all these people. You know you lost!"

"We only did five bitch! You overbid. I won, you lost, too bad for you and your delicate hands. But it's alright, cause I know you got Palmolive," Jacy taunted back as they pushed open the glass doors and walked out. Tammy was saying some more choice words as Jacy looked back at her big cousin and laughed like she hadn't laughed in months.

"Chocolate," the familiar voice said calmly as Jacy looked back from Tammy to the street. D-4 was standing right at the entrance of the theater leaning on the side of an electric blue 2003 H2 Hummer flanked by his boys. At first when she heard someone say "chocolate" she was gonna look up and say something smart, but when she saw the shiny new Hummer her chin almost dropped to the sidewalk. Tammy nudged her to bring her back to reality.

"Yea, hey," Jacy replied making as if she wasn't impressed after all, and started walking again. D-4 stepped up off of his truck.

"What's your name?" he demanded more than asked as he leaned forward and grasped her arm pulling her back towards him.

"Negro, you do not know me like that. Ease up," Jacy said shaking free from his grip and turning around to look him over.

"My bad ma. You definitely ain't the nicest girl in the world huh?" he said happy that he had at least finally gained her full attention.

"Look, if you're trying to ask again if we wanna come—"

"Chocolate, damn. Can I catch a break? Naw I wasn't even gonna ask you to come back to the hotel. I can tell ya'll ain't those type of chicks. I just wanted to get your name and number if possible? I might wanna holla at you sometime."

"Oh. And if you were to holla at me, what would we do?" Jacy inquired as she studied him again, folding her hands across her chest and trying to stay steady despite her half-drunk condition. He was definitely fine, but Jacy was sure women sweated him all day because of that and his hometown fame, so she sure wasn't letting on to the fact that she was attracted to him. Besides, what could ever come of talking to a rapper? He'd never want to go out for fear that someone would recognize him, always busy or on the road, and there wouldn't be much to discuss except his career. They would only have three letters in common: S E X.

"We'll figure that out. Get something to eat or whatever? Let me call you."

"I'm only in town for a couple days, I don't even know if that would make sense," Jacy watched as a couple of D-4's boys approached Tammy and they started an animated conversation.

"I told you I come up to New York all the time."

"I don't live in New York, I live in Philly right now."

"So? Philly is on the way ain't it? I can stop by and see you or whatever."

"Whoa. See now you're getting way ahead of yourself," Jacy laughed. "I never even said I was giving you my number."

D-4 frowned as if his pride were hurt for a moment, but his swagger quickly returned and he tried a disinterested attitude. "So listen, you gonna give me your number or not? Me and my boys gotta get out of here."

"How about not. If you're in such a rush, then please don't let me hold you," Jacy said turning and dropping her hands to her side, then clasping them behind her back as she looked towards Tammy and the other guys from D-4's crew.

"Wait, wait. Come on I'm just trying to get to know you alright? Can you cut me a break and at least let me show you the town one of these days?"

Jacy sighed, satisfied that her bluffing had worked. She was actually very attracted to D-4, but was just trying to feel him out to see just how interested he was in her. She knew that a man with as much attention on him as a rapper would usually be stuck up or just looking to get some quick pretty ass from whoever was offering it. But the fact that he seemed to be sweating her a bit instead of giving up so easily was a good thing.

"Alright," Jacy said pulling out her cellphone. "What's your number?"

"You ain't gonna give me yours? What's that about?"

"I will call you. What is it so that me and my girl can go?"

This time D-4 sighed, and looked back at his boys as if he wanted to see if they were hearing or witnessing any of this.

"484......445......8080" he said quietly watching her put the number in as he ran it off. "What's your name?"

Jacy finished putting his information in the phone as she spoke. "It's Jacy."

"Jacy, let me see that for a minute?" he asked as she finished up, and took the phone out of her hands before she could resist. He pressed a few buttons and then handed it back to her.

"What did you do?" Jacy asked as she looked down at the screen on her phone. There was a call in progress.

"You dick!" she said a level higher than normal speaking tone and slapped his arm, but couldn't maintain a straight face. She had to laugh at his little trick, even though she thought it was dirty. She thought back to the Michael Baisden book she had read. D-4 winked at her and turned around to head back to the driver's side of his Hummer, yelling to his boys to "quit bullshitting and get in." Jacy just laughed and shook her head after ending the call. She watched as Tammy wrapped up her conversation after getting one of the guys' number herself. *Hmm,* Jacy thought, *me and Tammy gonna have to have a talk.* They then headed down the street laughing, tipsy and carrying on, mainly about the fact that they had no idea where they had parked the car.

chapter 14
Things are Not Always How they Seem

JACY WOKE UP the day after the play, Friday at 12 noon to the sound of her cellphone ringing. She was on her stomach with her face plastered against the yellow flowered pillow. Her head was pounding and her neck was hurting from the way she had been sleeping. She looked down and noticed that she was still dressed in the pink dress she had been wearing the night before. She and Tammy apparently didn't think they had enough to drink after the play, so they went to a bar in downtown Baltimore afterwards and got toasted.

"Ohhhhhh," she moaned as she lifted herself up slightly to grab her phone. She pressed the talk button without even looking at the screen. She whispered a strained "hello" into the phone.

"Hey. It's Rachelle."

"Rachelle? What's up," Jacy said trying to perk up a little, but it didn't work.

"Were you sleep?"

"Yea. I'm a little hung over. But what's up," Jacy responded closing her eyes and trying to ignore the pounding in her temples.

"I was just calling to see how you're doing."

"I'm alright, how are you?" Jacy said before sighing sleepily into the phone.

"Alright I guess. What you been up to?"

"Just trying to get myself together girl. I'm down in Baltimore visiting Tammy."

"Oh yea? How's she doing?"

"She's fine. Her and Ray. Matter of fact I *know* they're fine. They were shaking the whole house last night." Jacy said laughing with Rachelle and getting more comfortable with the conversation. She finally tried to sit up, but quickly realized that was a bad idea as she started to feel queasy. She sat on the edge of the bed and dropped her head in her free hand.

"Oh really! Damn it must be nice!" Rachelle said laughing along with her. "So how are you and Rich doin?"

"Oh Lord. I wish everyone would stop asking me about that man," Jacy chuckled while rubbing the side of her head. "I'm not seeing him anymore, I caught him with his pants down. Literally!" she laughed.

"What? You caught him cheating?"

"Well yea somewhat, he was getting his knob slobbed by some skank ass bitch." Jacy replied angrily, suddenly feeling like she was about to throw up any minute.

"No!!!"

"Yes!! And it's over so please don't ask for details. I'll tell you about it sometime. Listen I gotta go throw up okay."

"Damn, OK. Just give me a call when you feel better I got some stuff I wanna tell you too."

"Alright then. Bye," Jacy clicked end on the phone and ran out the room to the bathroom holding back the urge to hurl right in the hallway as best she could.

IT WAS 3:45 Friday afternoon and Jacy had finally wound down a little from her hang over. Her and Tammy were sitting side by side in the living room watching Judge Mablean lay into a couple on *Divorce Court*. They had decided to chill in the house that night and go out Saturday night. Tammy had taken the day off from work that Friday as well as on Monday. Ray had gone in to work, but promised he would get off on Monday too so that they could all enjoy a long weekend.

"So what you wanna do today," Tammy asked and then leaned over to grab some chips from the bowl on the glass coffee table.

"I don't know. I'm just glad I finally feel better. How come you didn't get a hangover?"

"Cuz I drank water throughout the night and went in the kitchen and got a big glass before going to bed last night. I told you about that before but your ass don't listen."

"Yea. I bet it was more than water that got you hopping out of bed this morning. Ray musta had a *special* 'injection' for yo' ass!"

"Shut up heffa," Tammy said laughing and hitting Jacy in the head with a pillow. "You coulda had that special treatment this morning too if you wanted. With that fine muscular D-4. Why were you being so mean to him?"

"Cuz he's one of those guys. You know, they think they are God's gift the way women throw the pussy at them all day. But I don't know, I guess he's cool. He ain't adding these panties to his collection though," Jacy said snapping her blue cotton underwear under the white robe Tammy had lent her.

Tammy chuckled. "Don't speak so soon. Ain't no telling really."

"Oh yes there is, I'm telling. I have a lot of will power. Besides I already have a warm body at home. I'm not messing that up by fucking around down here."

"OH YOU DO HUH?" Tammy yelled in her ear. "You didn't tell me nothing about that!"

Jacy sighed and smiled. "I told you I was seeing some people."

"Yea but you didn't tell me you was fuckin' any of them!"

"My bad. I'm seeing this guy Eric. He's got it goin' on, but I just don't see myself with him... I mean I just don't see us in a *real* relationship. You know?"

"No."

Jacy sighed again. "It's hard to explain Tam. I guess I just don't like men right now. To tell you the truth I'm actually considering calling that Puerto Rican girl that tried to talk to me!" Jacy laughed.

"WHAT??? Damn girl! Did Rich really fuck you up that bad?" Tammy said eyeing Jacy sideways with a look of incredulous disbelief. "I gotta meet this nigga."

"Nooo. It's not even that, not really. I'm just tired of the bullshyt. I'm about ready to try something new."

"Well date a white man or something then. Don't go muff-diving!" Tammy exclaimed.

"Tammy, you are ridiculous." Jacy shook her head and laughed. "Do you ever not say what's on your mind? Damn. Don't tell me you never thought about it."

"Well I have *thought* about it, but I would never actually do it. Not with all of this marvelous dick available in the world," Tammy said with a daydreamy look on her face as she looked off into space. *Probably remembering last night,* Jacy thought.

"Well I'm about to take some action. Maybe not with a female, but something's gotta give. Something's not right, and I actually feel bad about the way I've been treating men lately. Maybe I just need to be alone for a while."

"Maybe. But we both know that's not going to happen. Just have fun, be safe and don't get serious with anyone if you feel like that."

"Yea, I don't want to bring anyone else into my mess. But I swear it's like everybody's trying to get serious these days. Maybe cause it's about to get cold," Jacy said chuckling.

"Yea you know niggas scramble to find a girl when it's starting to get cold and when football season rolls around. Cause all they wanna do is sit at home, watch the game, and then get their nut off later. But soon as the giving season comes around, Christmas and the holidays, they decide they want some 'space' again," Tammy said shaking her head and laughing to herself.

"Well you don't have to worry about that no more. You found someone you can at least tolerate."

"Yea," Tammy paused to think. "Jacy I just had to learn that nobody's perfect, including me. So we can't sit around and judge each other all the time. I love Ray, and I know he loves me. It's not that fake love that women are always talking about, it's real. He's done his dirt, I've done mine, we both still do stupid things and annoy the hell out of each other sometimes. But love conquers all. I just have to think of what it would be like without him, and that usually makes things a lot clearer at times when he pisses me off."

"That's deep Tammy."

Tammy looked over at Jacy. "Hush," she replied hitting her with the pillow she was clutching again.

"No for real, I wasn't saying that to be funny. That's good to know."

Just then Jacy heard her cellphone going off in the kitchen where she left it last.

"Must be Rachelle. She called me this morning," Jacy said getting up and heading to the kitchen.

"Oh really? Ya'll talking again?"

"Yea I guess," Jacy replied as she looked at the caller ID on her phone. It came up unavailable. She looked back at Tammy who was watching what was on TV intently by then and picked up.

"Hello?"

"Sup," a deep voice said.

"Who's this?" Jacy said sitting down at the island in Tammy's kitchen.

"Take a guess."

"I don't feel like playing a game, who is this?" she said getting annoyed, still not recognizing the voice. She had an idea of who it was but wasn't for sure. With all the guys she was dating at the time it would have been very foolish of her to take a guess.

"Damn, do you always have an attitude?" the male voice asked as she heard some commotion in the background on his end.

"Only when people call playin on my phone," Jacy said still standing, now with her hand on her hip, about to go off on the person on the other line.

"Calm down ma. This D, from last night."

"D? Oh, D-4. What's up." Good thing she didn't guess. She looked back at Tammy again, who was now looking right back at her. She rolled her eyes and sat down again.

"Tryin' to see what's up with you. What you got going on for today?"

"Um. I don't know yet, I'll probably be hanging out with my cousin tonight."

"Oh alright. Is that gonna be the case this whole weekend?"

"Probably," Jacy said, getting ready to be hung up on or something. It had happened before when she went out of town and met someone who suddenly realized he probably would never see her again. He had simply hung up in her face.

Silence for a while. Jacy looked down at the screen and then held the phone back up to her ear. D-4 started talking again. "What about Sunday. We can just chill up here for a couple hours. I have a pool out back if you swim. You can bring your girl if you want, my boy was asking about her."

Jacy thought about it for a moment. What harm could there be in going over there and chilling for a while, her and Tammy would probably just be doing the same exact thing they were doing right now on Sunday. And she didn't have to do anything she didn't want to do with D-4.

"Hold on a sec," Jacy said not waiting for confirmation from him to be put on hold. She walked back in the room where Tammy was. "Tam, you wanna go to D-4's house on Sunday? They having a little pool party or something."

"Uh, yeaaa!" Tammy said looking at Jacy as if she'd asked her if the sky was blue.

Jacy put the phone back to her ear and walked back into the kitchen. "Yea I guess that's cool. What time you want us to come by?"

"Come around noon. Call me before you leave to get the directions aiight."

"Okay. We'll see you then."

SUNDAY MORNING was like De Javu for Jacy. She again woke up, stomach down, head hurting, to her phone ringing, this time it was in her bag on the floor.

The night before, Tammy, Ray, Jacy, Ray's good friend Daniel, Lisa and her fiance had gone clubbing at the place Lisa's fiance was promoting. Jacy was drinking tequila shot for shot with Ray all night, but took Tammy's advice to have water in between drinks. She was still swaying by the time they stepped into the house at 3:30am, but wasn't feeling as bad that Sunday morning as she was before, and she had at least managed to remove her jeans before crashing in the bed this time.

Jacy dragged herself up from the bed and glanced at the clock, which read 12:32pm. She picked up her purse and traced through it looking for her phone. When she found it, it was too late. When she checked missed calls she saw that there were two missed calls. One was unidentified, and the other was a 484 number. Realizing it was after noon she automatically knew who it was. Calling back the 484 number she sat back on the bed, happy that at least she didn't feel as queasy this morning. I guess that water thing really does work, she thought.

"Sup. You still coming over or what?" D-4 asked impatiently.

"Ahhhhhh," Jacy moaned. "Damn my head is hurting. Yea we'll be over but it's gonna be a little later."

"How later?"

"I guess a couple hours. I gotta pull myself together real quick."

"Well call me before you about to leave. I got shit to do later."

"Yea ok—" Jacy started, but D-4 had hung up before she could even say those two words.

"No this nigga didn't?" Jacy said looking at the phone as if *it* had done something wrong. Her face got hot, and she dialed back the number. He picked up on the first ring with a "Yea."

"Don't be hanging the fucking phone up in my face. If you don't want me to come by than just say so, I got shit I could be doing myself!" Jacy exclaimed knowing damn well she didn't have anything to do that Sunday except act stupid with Tammy.

"I didn't say all that. My bad, come by around 2:30 aiight? I'll be here."

"Alright then. Byyye," Jacy said with a hint of attitude.

"Bye," he said and they hung up. Jacy laid back down for a half an hour to get herself grounded. When her cellphone alarm went off nudging her out of a light sleep, she pulled herself together and went to wake Tammy so that they could both start getting ready to go over D-4's house.

When she and Tammy were finally ready they went downstairs to get a bite to eat. Ray had gotten up earlier and cooked them a big breakfast of bacon, eggs, sausage, toast and grits. Jacy picked up a forkful of food and placed it in her mouth but as soon as she did she regretted it. She was still a little hungover. Knowing she wouldn't be able to eat a meal that large just yet she apologized to Ray, and sipped on her glass of orange juice, nibbling on a piece of toast. As Tammy and Ray ate, talking about their decision to make bi-monthly mortgage payments to reduce their interest, Jacy pulled out her pocketbook and counted up the money she had left under the table.

"20, 40, 60…two," she counted off almost in a whisper. That should get me home alright, she thought to herself folding the bills in half and then stuffing the money back into the special compartment in her bag. She zipped it up and then set it aside for when they were ready to go.

* * * * *

It was 2:35pm and Jacy and Tammy were finally stepping out the door. Jacy had called and got the directions to D-4's house, which was located in a pretty ritzy area outside of Baltimore according to Tammy. She had told Ray they were going out to run some errands for the afternoon and visit a friend, which Ray was fine with since he had planned on watching a game on TV with his boys that day.

They pulled up at D-4's house a little after 3pm. There were six cars in the driveway and lining the street, D-4's hummer, a black jaguar, blue Mazda, a black Expedition and a cherry red Nissan Altima. The house was absolutely beautiful. It was a modern white stucco house, not quite a mansion, with room sized windows upstairs and a grand double door entrance. Jacy wondered how a rapper of his limited notoriety would be able to afford a house like that, but then as if the 'duh' fairy had hit her upside the head she realized exactly how.

After parking Tammy's Nissan Maxima, they walked up the driveway to the front door dressed to kill. Jacy in a cute pair of short jean shorts with flower designs on the front and a light blue see-through shirt that fell off her shoulders with a white tube top underneath. She wore her LV bag and the matching mules that Rich had bought her. Tammy was wearing an airy light tan dress that came to her mid thigh with an even lighter tan belt and shoes to match it. Tammy had on some Gucci shades, while Jacy wore her favorite Express sunglasses. D-4 came to the door all smiles with one of his boys not far behind.

"Well it took ya'll long enough!" he said half-jokingly and stepped aside to let them in as he held the door. He was looking very good, with no shirt on revealing his perfectly sculpted chest, and a pair of white swim trunks. They had obviously just got out of the pool. Jacy and Tammy's shoes click clacked across the white tiled floor as they followed D-4 back to the pool area. A few people were in the kitchen drinking and talking, and they could hear music getting louder as they neared the backyard. When they arrived back there it was about 12 people chilling in and around the inground pool.

"Ya'll need to change or something?" D-4 asked as he let his boy and the two girls out, and shut the door to the backyard after walking out with them.

"No, we're not getting in the pool," Jacy said as she and Tammy walked closer to where everyone else was at.

"Ohh. Ya'll too cute to get in the pool huh," he chuckled along with his friend.

"Yup," Tammy answered for the both of them with a pleased grin on her face as she took in the sights.

"Well excuse me."

"Hey Tammy!!!" a brotha yelled as he jumped out of the pool leaving a screw face on the female companion he had been splashing and playing with. It was the guy who's number she had taken.

"What's up Chuck?" Tammy said as if they were old friends and gave him a hug after he had finished drying off his chest. Jacy watched them closely with one eyebrow raised. I definitely gotta talk to this chick, she thought.

D-4 grabbed Jacy's arm gently and pulled her to the side. "So what's up shawty," he asked as he draped his beautifully cut up arms around her shoulders and hugged her to him. The man was a work of art. He was about a head taller than her so he lightly put his chin on top of her head and rested it there for a minute before letting go and taking a good look at her.

"You look damn good," he said biting his lower lip. "You feel like a drink?"

"Ooo no. Not right now," Jacy said remembering the night before and her Tequila run with Ray. Even the smell of alcohol would make her head hurt right now. "I think I need to eat something before I drink anything again."

"Oh alright. We got some chicken in the kitchen, come on."

He grabbed Jacy's hand and they went back into the house as Chuck led Tammy over to a pair of chairs near the pool and they continued their very involved conversation.

"This is a beautiful house," Jacy commented as they rounded the corner towards the kitchen again where the guests were still standing around eating.

"I guess it takes one to know one," D-4 said turning around and pushing Jacy back against the kitchen counter, placing his hands on either side of the counter behind her and looking her straight in the eye. Jacy kind of liked his forcefulness. He spoke in a low tone. "Girl you are a *brick*house."

Jacy laughed a little at his attempt at wit. He probably used that line a lot. "Thanks."

"Pretty face, bangin' ass body. Sexy personality. What do they call that?" he said turning his head off to think.

"Stop trying to flatter me," Jacy said fighting a smile. She looked around. "Is it yours?"

"What?"

"The house?"

"Oh, yea, me and a couple of my boys stay here. A triple threat!. That's what they call it," he said going back to his original train of thought.

They chit chatted a little more, Jacy got some KFC chicken for herself, and then they headed back out to the pool. Jacy had deduced from their short conversations that D-4, who's real name she found out was Derrick, was definitely out for the drawers. Why wouldn't he be, she thought, he's about to blow up on the music scene and has girls practically throwing it at him all day. She noticed the nasty stares she was getting from the two girls that were in the kitchen with them.

The get together turned out to be a lot of fun. Jacy felt better after eating something and had a few drinks. Tammy had been toasting ever since she had taken a seat by the pool with Chuck. They got to know a few of the other people who were at the party and they all seemed to be real cool, even some of the females. It was around 6:30pm when guests started leaving. Everyone was feeling tipsy and happy under the now dimming sun—Jacy was sitting sideways in D-4's lap out by the pool chatting it up about one of his latest music projects, right next to Tammy sitting up straight in her lawnchair talking to Chuck and another one of his friends. They were still enjoying themselves but knew it was probably about that time for them as well.

"Well," Jacy said putting down her drink and searching her bag for her cellphone. "I guess it's about time we get going huh Tam?"

"Yea, it's starting to get late," she answered from her lounge chair, arm thrown over her head, squinting from what was left of the sunlight at Jacy. Jacy had found her cellphone and glanced at the time, then tried to get up from D-4's lap.

"Why ya'll gotta go? You got something urgent to do?" D-4 said pulling Jacy back onto his lap.

"Nothing in particular, but we ain't gonna be chillin here all night," Jacy chuckled regaining her balance in his hands. "We gotta get into something!" she said lowering her head, putting one hand up and one hand on her head like she was about to do a Jamaican dance as she moved in his lap a few times. She felt something hard develop on the back of her thigh. She shot D-4 a knowing glance. He smirked back.

"What's wrong with staying here?" his boy Chuck piped in. "We can have a party right here in the house tonight, maybe invite a few people over." Chuck wasn't too bad looking himself in a pair of red trunks.

Jacy and Tammy gave each other 'the look.'

"Naw I think we gonna get going in a while," Tammy said.

"Yea but I know you don't have to be out this very second. It's only 6:30, damn!" D-4 said getting animated. He was cute.

"Okay! We'll stay for a few. But then we out!" Jacy said making the hand motion with her thumb.

"Well let's go on inside because it's getting dark out here," Chuck said getting up and lending a hand to Tammy. They all followed and went into the house to relax on the sectional sofa.

They all chilled for another couple of hours and before they knew it, it was completely dark outside. They had all been talking and laughing like old buddies, losing all track of time. D-4 asked Jacy to come upstairs a minute so that they could talk. He led her up the stairs and into a large bedroom with a balcony and king sized bed.

"So what's up with you and me?" he asked sitting down on the bed and motioning her to him. Jacy was laughing at him in her head. He really thinks he's slick or something, she thought. She plopped her Louis Vuitton bag down on the dresser and went over to sit next him on the bed.

"You already know."

"No I don't, you gotta let me know," D-4 said leaning over and trying to kiss her on the mouth. Jacy dodged him and it landed on her cheek. No telling where those lips have been, she thought.

"Derrick!" Jacy said playfully shoving D-4 to the side. "I already told you I'm not down for that groupie shit. I know you got groupies coming out the woodworks now that you're getting famous. I think you're a cool guy though." Jacy nodded her head in short motions. D-4 looked at her with a smile in his eyes.

"Well, I can respect that. Any other chick would have been pullin' back on her draws already," he threw his head back and laughed devilishly. "But girl, you are fine as shit, so if you ever change your mind holla at a nigga."

"Don't hold your breath!" Jacy laughed as she stood up to go to the bathroom. "Where's the bathroom at?"

"There's one right in here through that door," D-4 pointed to a closed white door.

"Alright, I'll be right back," she said walking over to door and letting herself in. Once inside she took a look at herself in the mirror and saw that her hair was out of place. "Damn! How long was it like that? Why didn't Tammy tell me?" She combed it down with her fingers wishing she had brought her bag in with her, then went to relieve herself. She walked out and saw D-4 lounging on the bed.

"You're cold Jacy, but I like you. Give me a call before you leave B-more so I can show you around or something," D-4 requested, standing up. Jacy nodded her head, grabbing her bag off the dresser and followed him downstairs.

An hour later, Jacy and Tammy finally managed to resist the niggeritis and pull themselves away from the guys and out of the house. D-4 and his friends were disappointed, but decided to go clubbing for the night.

* * * * *

That night, the only fireworks coming out of Tammy and Ray's room was yelling and hollering. Ray was upset with Tammy for coming in so late smelling like a man's cologne, and had found two numbers in the purse she had worn to the theater on Thursday night.

"You are always making a big fucking deal about everything! I told you those are friends of mine!" Jacy heard Tammy's voice high and clear.

"Don't lie to me Tammy!!! I know you're fucking with these dudes. I just know it! You are trying to play me for a damned fool!" Ray yelled.

"Would you just shut the fuck up? Shit I get so tired of even hearing your voice sometimes. Just close your mouth and think it instead! You'll get the same result." Tammy tried to brush him off.

"Oh you wanna be funny? It won't be funny when I pack my shit and head back to the ATL."

"Then go!!! Go!!! I don't fucking care! You are always threatening with that shit, but you don't never *do* it."

"Strutting around here looking like a fucking ho, acting like a trifling ass ho. I should have said something when I saw you walking out the door in that little dress today."

"Oh now I'm a ho right?"

"Yes." Ray said definitively. "Only a ho would go out to some dude's house when she already got a good man at home. It's Jacy, I swear it is. She's a bad influence on you."

"Oh no you didn't! I know you're not trying to bring my family in this!" Tammy asked incredulously.

"Well it needs to be said. She's cold, she uses men and throws them away, and you're trying to follow right in her footsteps!"

"Let me tell you something nigger." Jacy could imagine Tammy standing sideways with her hand on her hip and the other pointed at Ray. "In case you didn't know, I would drop you in an instant before I drop Jacy. That's my blood. Don't you ever talk bad about my family."

"Fuck you Tammy. I swear I've had enough of this." Ray said in a tone that said he was drained and giving up.

"Had enough of what?" Tammy egged him on.

"Had enough of you, cheating on me and acting like it's cool. I know your ass is creeping out on me!"

"Creeping out on you? Oh now you want to get all moral about the wrongs of cheating? You fucking bum." Tammy dismissed him again and Jacy heard her walk out of their bedroom.

"Woman don't you dare walk away from me when I'm talking to you!!! Admit it! Admit that you've been fucking around on me!" Ray yelled, his voice resonated throughout the house like a madman's.

"Alright, you want to hear it?" Tammy said from the hallway. "I'll say it. Yes, I fuck a new man every night, while you're sleeping I creep out and see my Sunday, Monday, Tuesday, Wednesday, Thursday, Friday and Saturday man. One for every fucking day of the week! And all of their dicks are bigger than yours! They *always* give me *exactly* what I need." Tammy screamed back. In their rage, they must have completely forgotten that they had a guest. "Are you happy now!?"

There was silence.

"I said are you happy to hear the truth?" Tammy asked again sarcastically.

"I fucking hate you Tammy." Ray said, and Jacy heard him slam the bedroom door.

chapter 15
Back to Reality

I T WAS MONDAY AFTERNOON and Jacy was getting packed up to head for home. The night before had drained her. Tammy and Ray had argued into the wee hours of the morning, even after Ray had slammed the door shut. Tammy had gone back in their room a half hour later and it all started right back up again.

Jacy was dead tired and didn't want to drive, but she had to get back and supervise over her house in Philly. Wednesday was supposed to be the last day of repairs on the house. Tammy came in the guest room and they talked and talked and talked about their weekend, when they would see each other again, D-4's pool party, and some news about the family. Jacy struggled with herself on whether she should bring up Tammy's fight with Ray the night before, but decided against it. She knew that they would resolve it the way they always did. No point in peeling sour apples. But several questions tugged at Jacy's mind the whole night listening to Tammy and Ray argue: Is that what I want? Is that what love is about? Is it really worth it, to me?

Tammy and Jacy went downstairs and hugged for what seemed like forever before Jacy stepped outside and slid into the driver's seat of her Eclipse. Waving, she pulled off and headed in the direction of Route 95.

About an hour into the ride home, Jacy received a call on her cellphone. Watching the road and searching her pocketbook for her phone, she finally found it and saw that it was D-4 calling. She clicked the 'talk' button right before it became a missed call.

"What's up?" she said keeping her eye on the road. A silver PT Cruiser had just cut her off and she could see some traffic starting to form up ahead. Jacy figured it was just because the toll plaza was coming up.

"Where you at?" he asked ignoring her question.

"Uh. I'm on the road, heading back to Philly."

"Why didn't you call me? I thought you was supposed to come through before you left?"

"My bad. I had to do something with Tammy earlier today and I forgot to tell you I was leaving on Monday," she replied and then there was silence on the phone for a few seconds. She checked the screen and then put the phone back to her ear.

"Aiight," he finally said. "Well have a safe trip home."

"I will. Give me a call next time you up this way, in New York of whatever."

"Aiight. I'll definitely do that. Lata."

They hung up and Jacy continued home, she sucked her teeth at the long lines at the toll booth. As she inched forward waiting her turn, she reached over and opened her LV bag to get her toll money ready. She looked in the compartment but only saw $2 folded up in there. She looked up squinting her face in confusion. She looked back down again and pulled out all of the contents of the compartment, credit cards and all. She looked through everything but all she saw was $2.

"What!" she started looking through her bag furiously for the missing $60 as people started to honk their horn behind her at the toll plaza. She moved up a few feet and then continued her search. When it came up fruitless again she threw the bag and all of its contents on the floor.

"I can't believe this!!!" she reached her hands out and then put them both on top of her head as she picked her brain and inched again forward in the line. She thought back to the last time she had counted her money in Tammy's kitchen. She was getting closer and closer to the booth as she remembered going over D-

4's house right after that. Between then and now she hadn't even opened her bag to take money out. Something was fishy.

She was finally up to the toll booth lady. Luckily, the toll was $2 so she gave the lady the last of what she had in her purse. But she had at least one more toll coming up before she reached Philly. She tried to remember how much it was. Then she remembered that she had left her bag alone in the room with D-4 for at least five minutes. That was the only time her bag had left her shoulder or her sight during the party.

"That nigga stole my money!" she came to the realization as she drove off from the booth. She tried to calm herself and think hard if she had gone in her purse to buy *anything* since her visit to D-4's house. She didn't want to bear false witness on the brother, but all of the evidence was starting to point in his direction.

She picked up the phone and went to her incoming calls list. She dialed the first one on the list trying to figure out what she was going to say. She didn't want to outright accuse him, but what the hell else was she gonna do? She decided to go with the calm, reasonable approach at first. It didn't matter, because either way he was going to deny it. But she just had to call...

"Sup," he said as if everything was just great.

"Question for you," Jacy said trying to hold her rage. "Did you find $60 laying around your house yesterday?" She knew damn well there was no way the $60 could have just dropped out of her special compartment, especially without bringing the other $2 it was wrapped up in, and especially since the bag was zipped closed.

D-4 was silent for a moment. "No."

"You sure? Cause I'm missing $60 and the last place I had it was over your house." Her bag had always been in her sight, throughout the entire trip, except for that one moment with D-4. Tammy was her blood cousin, she used to help change Jacy's diapers, there was no way she would take money out of her purse like that without telling her. That was out of the question. Besides, Jacy had gone right up to her room Sunday night and put her bag on the bed before coming back down to chill with Tammy. Ray had been gone somewhere with his buddies for most of the night, despite his promise to spend time before Jacy left. Jacy had gone to bed, her purse and all, before Ray even got in the door and started arguing with Tammy. So Tammy and Ray were not even options. No, it was D-4, Jacy told herself, *That fool is probably broke as shit, driving around in a Hummer and stealing from people.*

"I told you no, I know you're not trying to imply what I think you're trying to imply?"

"All I know is that $60 is missing from my purse, the money I needed to get home, and you were the only person I left alone with my purse *Derrick*. How the fuck could you just take my money like that?" Jacy said raising her voice.

"I don't believe this. You're actually gonna sit there and accuse me of stealing 60 measly dollars? Girl I don't need your fucking money! You probably dropped it somewhere," he said getting defensive.

Jacy wasn't buying it. She had dealt with pathological liars before. "How the hell am I gonna drop $60, and not notice, out of a bag that was closed? And then I still got the $2 it was wrapped up in? You know you took my fucking money, and left that $2 to throw me off and make me think I spent the rest. You trifling *ass*!" Jacy threw her hand up and slammed it on the steering wheel. She was through with the formalities.

"You probably did spend it. And sitting here accusing me of shit."

"Look, I know my money. I track my shit and I *always* know how much money I have in my purse. I don't got it like that to be 'losing' or giving away 60 bucks nigga."

"How many times do I have to tell you I didn't take your money!! Look I got $2,000 sitting right here in my room, I don't need to be taking your little $60," he scoffed.

"Are you some kind of clepto? Stealing people's money for fun?"

"Oh now you way out of line. Calling me a clepto. How you gonna accuse me of this shit?"

"You know what? Fuck you, cause I know you took the money." There was much emotion and inflection in Jacy's voice by then.

"I can't believe this shit, I invited you into my home and everything."

"You know what, if I magically find the $60 I'll call and apologize and you can hang up in my fucking face. But right now as far as I'm concerned, you took that shit." Jacy was past reasonable and was knee deep into believing that this man had actually opened her bag and took three twenty dollar bills. Now she would have to put her gas on her credit card, which was already near maxed out. And she would have to somehow scrape up change to make her next toll. She couldn't believe she had actually allowed herself to get taken like that.

"You want $60? Shit, I'll give you $60."

"I want MY $60 nigga."

"Yea, whatever. I'll give you YOUR $60. Just come on back and I'll give you the shit. Cause I got money. I don't need to be stealing shit from nobody. I'll *give* you $60 if it's that serious, damn," D-4 mocked Jacy.

"Forget it Derrick, cause you obviously need it more than me," she flipped down the phone to end the call. He must have thought she was BoBo the Fool to believe his story. She started talking to herself to figure out her plan of action now that she had absolutely no money in her purse and no idea where one of her ATMs were. To be honest, she didn't even really have money in her accounts to be withdrawing at that moment. She was coming up on the next toll booth which was for $1. Her phone rang and she saw that it was D-4 calling. She pressed 'end' and reached down retrieving her bag. She rustled down to the bottom looking for change. She found 65 cents. Opening the change holder in her car she found a whole lot of pennies and another quarter. The toll people didn't accept pennies. She reached underneath her seat and then the passenger's seat tracing the carpet for change and finally came up on 85 cents in quarters, dimes and nickels. Jackpot. She drove up and paid the toll lady, asking her if there were any other tolls further up to Philadelphia.

"Umm. Yea I think you got one more coming up for $4."

"$4? Ohhh. What happens if I don't have any cash on me? Do they take credit card?"

"No I don't think they accept credit card Ma'am. If you don't have the money to pay the toll they'll tell you to drive on and take a picture of your plate. You'll get a ticket in the mail."

Jacy sighed, defeated. "Thanks."

"Great," Jacy said to herself as she pulled off. Her phone rang again, it was D-4 calling. His ass *knows* he's guilty, she thought, that's why he's trying to call and clean up. "Shit, if somebody accused *me* of stealing from them I'd say 'Fuck you' and hang up the phone. I wouldn't be trying to call and argue," she said to herself.

Her phone rang three more times before she finally snatched it up.

"What!?"

"Jacy, listen I'm serious, I did not take your money. I don't have no reason to take that shit."

"Derrick. I'll give you one more chance. If you admit it now, I'll forget it. I'll let it slide this time, just as long as you promise not to do it again. Okay?" Jacy said in her most reassuring voice possible. Of course she wasn't serious, but she figured she'd try one more time to get it out of him.

There was silence for about five seconds before D-4 answered. "Naw, I know I wouldn't forgive someone that admitted to stealing from *me*. I promise you, I didn't take it," he said sticking to his original story.

Jacy just hung up the phone.

chapter 16
Niggas Tryin' to Get Over

"$EVEN THOUSAND DOLLARS!!??" Jacy exclaimed as she looked over the invoice the gruff-looking carpenter had handed her. "You said it wouldn't be more than $5,500 *including* the whirlpool!" she yelled as she flipped furiously through the pages of supplies he had used to repair the house. The house looked great, clean, all the windows in tact, new paint throughout the inside and outside of the house, but not $7,000 worth.

"What is this? $400 for floor planks? $350 for paint? What did you get Gucci paint??" she said looking up at him with disgust.

"Ma'am all the supplies you see there were needed to complete the work. That's the price, I don't know what to tell ya."

"Tell me this is a joke!" she flipped through the paper again. "The Jacuzzi was $1,500? We discussed this, there are Jacuzzi's available for $800. I can't believe this."

"We couldn't find any Jacuzzi's for that price Ma'am. That was the lowest priced version we could find," the carpenter, an older black man in his 50's wearing a pair of dirty overalls and a white t-shirt, said looking as if he could care less about the situation.

Jacy sighed shaking her head from side to side and looking around the house. She knew she should have just stayed in Philly for the last weekend of work.

"You gave us the $2,000 deposit, so your balance is..." the carpenter pulled out his pen and wrote on his hand as if he really needed to do the math for that. "$4,974.16."

"This is crazy. You told me $5,500. You charged me $1,200 for labor, to 'hook me up' and then you pad the prices of the supplies. If I knew it was going to be this much I would have never hired you for this," Jacy was overcome with a new regret. She hadn't gotten his initial quote of $5,500 in writing since Jason insisted that they keep things informal so that she could take advantage of 'the hook up.' She should have known not to go for that ghetto shit. This was all her fault.

"We did not pad the prices. That was the cost. It is what it is."

"Okay, so where are the receipts?"

The carpenter hesitated for a moment. "You want receipts? I'll get you the damn receipts," he said starting to get upset, a dead giveaway that he realized that he was caught. He turned to head toward the door and call for his son who was in the truck outside. Jacy wasn't moved by his anger. She figured these fools must have thought she was shitting gold bricks to actually believe she wouldn't notice or care about a $1,500 difference in price. Just because she had a designer bag on her shoulder didn't mean she was made of money.

"Junior!" he called. His son, a cocky son of a bitch who had also given Jacy problems throughout the process, got out of the pick up truck and slammed the door.

"What's up Pop."

"You got those receipts from the supplies? The woman wants to see receipts," he said sarcastically. 'The woman,' Jacy thought, and rolled her eyes into her head. She knew she was messing with the 'ghetto protocol,' but she now saw that the 'hook up' she was promised was non-existent. What was the point of going on with the charade?

"What? Man I don't know where all those damn receipts are. What's the problem?" he said looking at Jacy with an annoyed look on his face.

"The *problem* is that this paper says $6,974 when you all told me it wouldn't be more than 5,500 dollars for the whole job!" Jacy said pointing to the paper and staring him down, ready for a full-blown fight. She was fed up with this chauvinistic muthafucka.

"Well that was just an *estimate*. The supplies came out to be a lot more than we thought," he replied, talking to her slowly as if she was a retard.

"See that's why I wanna see the receipts. Cause I ain't never heard of paying $400 for paint."

"Man," Junior took off his hat, ran his hand over his almost bald head and looked at his father who was turning a deep red from frustration. "I don't know where the receipts at. I'm gonna have to find 'em."

"Well you know what. When I see the receipts I'll pay you the full balance. Cause right now you all are trying to pull some shit on me and I don't appreciate it. I thought you were supposed to be 'hookin' a sister up.' Yea right," Jacy said shaking her head again. She was about tired of niggas taking money from her, first D-4 and now this. She was broke as it is, and people were still trying to take her. *You just can't trust niggas*, she concluded. It was a hard but necessary lesson for a young woman like her to learn.

"Ain't nobody tryin' to pull shit on you. And we ain't leaving here till we get paid, so I guess we got a problem," Junior replied shifting his weight to the other foot and shoving his hands in his pockets.

"Like hell you ain't tryin' to pull something! How you call yourself doing work and buying these expensive supplies but then don't keep the receipts? That's some ole ghetto ass *bullshit!*" Jacy banged her fist back on the stair railing to emphasize her point. Her New York accent was in full swing as she cursed the carpenters. She looked at them in disgust.

No response. Jacy continued looking at them incredulously.

"Look," Jacy said, finally pulling out her checkbook. "The house looks good. I'm not denying that. And I appreciate the work. But ya'll are talking about emptying my bank account at this point, and I still got a rent to pay and no job. So for now, I'm going to give you a check for the balance up to $5,500, which is $3,500. When you find the receipts and prove to me that it cost more than that, I'll find a way to get the rest to you. This is honestly all I can afford right now," she said signing her name, ripping the check off her book and handing it to the father.

They hesitated for a moment but seemed to understand where she was coming from at last. Junior took the check from Jacy. "Alright, but when we find those receipts we want the rest," he said fixing his hat back on his head and heading towards the door with his father close behind. They slammed the newly repaired door behind them and soon it was as if they were never there to begin with.

Jacy sighed and plopped herself on the bottom step of the newly carpeted stairs. Her head dropped into her hands and she slowly started to accept her reality. She was broke. She had no income coming in and plenty of bills needing to go out. Not only did she have to pay her regular bills such as rent, car payment, insurance, credit cards and utilities, she also had over $25,000 in student loans that she was still in forebearance for. But that forebearance period was going to expire soon and they were going to start requiring her to make payments. Especially for the private loans she had taken out while in school to fund her partying and bad shopping habits. They only allowed a two year forebearance period and then they wanted their money, no excuses. Regret. That was a word she was becoming more and more familiar with as time went on.

The only thing she didn't regret was quitting her job. Despite her current financial situation, she had never felt more free. She felt as if a huge burden had been lifted from her shoulders after leaving that place. Even if she had to be dead broke, living back with her parents, with D grade credit and no money in her pocket, in her eyes it would still be better than being molded in the tyrannical hands of Corporate America.

Jacy thought long and hard as she sat on the step about how she had been deceived by 'the powers that be.' After getting straight A's and B's, and continuously making the honor roll in high school, it was just a given that Jacy would go to college. There was never a second thought about her future. She fell right into the trap, believing that the only way to go in life was college then on to corporate america. She sincerely regretted spending all that money on college just to get a job that paid her a starting salary of $37,000, no where near enough to pay off her mountain of student loans in a reasonable amount of time, in addition to her regular bills required to live. After paying even her most basic bills she still barely had enough money to buy groceries. So where was this success that everyone had told her about that was supposed to magically appear after you graduate from college and get into a corporate job? Was she supposed to toil in Corporate America until she was 45 years old in order to enjoy a whopping salary of 75 grand? Then, after the prime of her life was gone, treat herself to an extra outfit or two and a trip to Florida?

Jacy got up and headed up the stairs to take another good look at the house. Everything smelled clean and brand new. That made her smile. The bathroom was looking great, with new tiles and faucet, the bedrooms were cleaned out with fresh new carpeting and the hallway and room walls were painted a soft yellow color that had a calming effect. She considered for a moment moving into the house herself before selling it while she got herself together financially. She would seriously have to consider it, but it wasn't the best area, or most secure living arrangement for a young woman on her own. As she was heading back down the stairs she got a call from Jason on her cell. She picked up and said a sad hello.

"Hey Jacy, what's the problem? I just got a call from John. He said you didn't want to pay them the whole balance?"

"Did he tell you how much the balance was?" Jacy asked scrunching her face up again at the mention of the carpenter's name.

"No, but he said he explained to you that the supplies cost more than they estimated."

"They are talking seven grand Jason, $1,500 more than they estimated."

"$1,500 more??" Jason said, genuinely shocked. "Damn."

"Yea. He had the nerve to throw that paper at me like nothing was wrong. I just gave him $3,500 for now because Jason, I honestly don't believe the supplies cost that much. They couldn't even produce receipts! I thought you said those guys were legit, Jason."

"Well yea, they're friends of the family. Look I'm gonna call him back and get all this straightened out, OK?"

"Okay Jason, but seriously, I don't have an extra $1,500 to pay them for this work."

"I know, I know. I'll handle it," Jason said before they said their goodbyes and hung up. Jacy headed out the house and to her car. She sat there for a while looking at the steering wheel, and then finally started her car and drove off.

chapter 17
Cruel Intentions

"**H**ERE IS A LIST of all the repairs that need to be made before this house can be approved for HUD," the home inspector said handing Jacy a sheet of paper from her checklist. The list was half a page long.

"Whoa. New boiler, fix back door, new gas burners…" Jacy said scanning the list. It was a week after the repairs had been completed and she was doing the required inspection to get the house approved for a HUD family. "And the piping may need to be replaced for the Jacuzzi? Why?"

"For one, the structural integrity of the Jacuzzi in the bathroom upstairs is questionable. Not to say it's a done deal, but the whole thing may need to be removed. I'm sending in another inspector next week to get a final word on that. But from what I can see you might at least need brand new piping in the bathroom to reduce any future flooding risks."

"Ma'am," Jacy moaned, starting to think this whole thing was a bad idea. "I've already spent $6,000 on repairs."

"Well," the inspector said as she made her way towards the door. "If you want to get this place HUD approved you'll need to get all of that done as well."

Jacy frowned at the inspector's smug attitude.

"The other inspector will call you later this week. Have a good day Ms. Thomas," she said as she left the house, and Jacy standing there with a look of utter defeat on her face. She looked back down at the sheet of paper and felt tears forming in the corner of her eyes. What was she going to do? Jason had managed to talk the carpenters down to $6,000 even, but it was still $500 more than Jacy had planned on spending. She would now have to turn around and spend $1,000 or more on the repairs to meet the inspection requirements. She felt like she'd been had. Big time.

Picking up the phone, and wiping away the tear that had managed to drop down her face, she called the only person she could.

"Jason," Jacy said in response to his chipper hello trying to keep her voice strong.

"Hey you! What's up."

"Nothing. The inspector just left here, and she had this long list of more repairs that need to be made before I can get the house approved for HUD. It's gonna be at least another $1,000..." Jacy's voice trailed off as she choked up and could no longer stop the tears from flowing.

"Calm down Jacy. Just calm down," Jason said, clearly shaken by the sound of Jacy breaking down. "You still at the house? I have to handle something at work real quick, but why don't you meet me at my house in Mount Airy in 45 minutes and we'll work this out, okay?"

Jason ran off the directions to his house, which Jacy soaked in without having to write them down, and they hung up.

* * * * *

When she arrived at his house half an hour later she had to wait in a spot on the street for a few minutes before he finally pulled up behind her in his Benz. His house was a pretty three story Victorian single family home complete with a porch and swing in the front. She climbed out of her car and met his concerned eyes. Her facial expression was sad, tired, and her eyes were still red from crying. He opened his arms and took her into his chest.

"Come on in," he instructed, letting her go and heading up the short walk to his front door. He let her in and closed the door behind him. He was dressed in a sharp tan oxford shirt and dark trouser pants. She inhaled his Armani cologne. Once in, they had a seat on his soft white leather couch and Jacy showed him the list of items.

"They said you need a new boiler? I saw that thing myself, it didn't look too bad," he scanned the list some more and then passed it back to Jacy sighing. "I know some people down at the HUD office downtown. I'll see what I can do."

Jacy's face brightened a bit at hearing that. He seemed to have endless connections. "Jason. I really don't know how to thank you for all your help. I know I have got to be driving you crazy with all my problems, it's just that I've never—"

"Jacy you don't need to explain. This is your first time doing this stuff, I understand," he said kicking off his shoes and getting more comfortable on the couch as he leaned back and took Jacy in for a moment. She was wearing a pair of stretch jeans that were cuffed at the bottom and a simple orange Express tee.

Jacy smiled graciously. "Thank you Jason," She then looked down at her hands trying to think of something to fill the uncomfortable silence. "I really appreciate it."

"Relax, I don't have to be back at the office until 3 o'clock," Jason said, motioning for Jacy to sit back and relax. It was now 1:30. He reached over and turned on the TV. Jacy sat back and started watching the Outkast video that was now flashing across the screen. Jason kept his hazel eyes on Jacy. She was a little uncomfortable at first but soon got involved in the video and hanging with Jason was helping her to forget about her problems, temporarily.

"Damn, that girl has a body on her. I think that's the ideal female shape." Jacy commented about the woman standing near Dre in front of his car in a black bathing suit. "But they didn't have to put her in that bathing suit to see that."

"Maybe, but she don't have a thing on you," Jason said resting the side of his head on his right knuckle as he leaned back on the side of the couch and glanced at the screen.

"Pssshh," Jacy made a sound of disbelief and bobbed her head a little. "Yea right. I know I got a little ass, but her ass is rotund!" she did a hand movement and laughed with Jason. They laughed and talked for a while longer about that video and then the next video that came on after it.

"Damn. This girl is always crying about wanting to die over some man," Jacy sighed. "She had better be careful before she puts a curse on herself or something."

"She's just doing what she got to do to sell records. Everybody knows she can't really sing that well, so she has to write some catchy ass lyrics," Jason responded.

"I guess. But damn, can't she write some catchy lyrics that don't require giving up her life or being a fool?" Jacy said shaking her head and chuckling.

"You never met a man that made you crazy like that?" Jason asked after a short pause.

"Not in my life. Maybe that's my problem, I've never been in love so I wouldn't know what it's like to want to *kill* yourself because of a man."

"Never been in love?" Jason asked incredulously. "What planet are you from? A woman who's never been in love?"

Jacy peeled her eyes from the screen and looked over at Jason. She just shook her head and looked at him with a serious expression on her face. His hazel eyes sparkled with curiosity.

"Not even a little bit?"

"Nope. I've definitely been in lust though."

"Oh really."

"Yup. Lust."

"Have you ever opened yourself to fall in love?"

"Yea, well no, I don't know," she said thinking about the question. "I thought you couldn't stop love whether you're open to it or not."

"Well, yea. But if you never take a chance to really get to know someone, how can you ever fall in love with them?"

Jacy turned her attention back to the TV screen. "I guess."

Jason got up and went to the kitchen. He came back with two tall glasses of soda, handing one to Jacy before sitting back down on the couch, much closer to her than where he had originally sat.

"Thanks," Jacy said sipping the soda and then placing it down on the table. He did the same, and then put his left arm behind her head on the couch. Jacy took note, and then continued watching TV.

"That soda tastes like Bacardi," she said grinning.

"Yea I spiked it," Jason laughed.

"Well damn you coulda told me, what if I had been on medication or something?" Jacy said half-serious. She smiled and joked, "Shit, I might have to start taking Zantac or something for depression soon. With all this mess going on with the house."

"Why don't you just give me a chance Jacy?" Out of nowhere, Jason turned and whispered, his raspy voice cutting into her right ear.

"What?" Jacy asked trying to turn her head but couldn't since his lips were literally two inches from her ear. Jason began planting kisses on her neck. Jacy felt a rush of fluids run through her at the action. He continued kissing her, moving downward to trace the V-neck of her shirt. He then sat up more and used his left hand to fondle her breast through the shirt.

"Forget about that house. *I* can give you what you want," Jason assured.

"Umm. Jason, I don't think this is a good idea," Jacy said trying her best to resist despite the fact that her body was telling her 'yes.' She was a little hard up. She had stopped dealing with Eric a couple of days after she returned from her trip to see Tammy, because he was starting to get annoying. He was calling all the time and starting to get mad at the fact that Jacy was still seeing other people. He had even called her three times during her time in Baltimore.

"Shhhhhh," Jason shushed Jacy as he lifted her shirt up, pulled her bra down and then grabbed her breasts with either hand, fondling them as if he was testing melons at the supermarket. He looked down at them like a kid seeing his first pair of breasts.

"Jason, come on," Jacy said, even though she was slightly enjoying the feeling. Jason reached up and kissed her full on the mouth like a mad man. His kiss was a little too wet, but the sensation he was causing by rolling her nipples between his fingers was negating the unpleasantness of the kiss.

"Oh Jacy," he moaned as he removed one of his hands and moved it down between her legs.

"Jason, okay, that's enough," Jacy said slowly starting to regain her senses and trying to push him off but he wouldn't budge. "Jason."

Jason was lost in his own world. He rubbed between her legs furiously trying futilely to stimulate her clitoris through her jeans. He reached back and zipped down his trouser pants to release his penis, which was at full attention by then, and then went back to trying to get in her jeans. When Jacy saw that, she had had enough, the turn-on had quickly turned to a turn-off as she realized what was happening here. Jason had probably been planning for this moment for a long time.

"Jason get off me!" she yelled to deaf ears. He continued trying to unbutton her jeans as she pulled, pushed and slapped at his hands.

"Sit still!" he yelled back becoming annoyed at her resistance. "Come on, let me get these pants off so I can really make you feel good." He leaned down and sucked on her nipple trying to get her back into the mood, but it was no use. She tried to push his head back and finally had to push her thumbs into his eyeballs to get him to take his mouth off of her body, a move that she had seen done on a TV show.

"Owww!!! You bitch!" he yelled and jumped up from the couch rubbing his eyes. He probably couldn't see anything at that moment. Jacy took it as her chance to get the hell out of there.

She jumped up pulling down her shirt and grabbing her purse as she headed for the door, but Jason recovered and grabbed her arm before she could make it.

"Where the hell do you think you're going?" he asked blinking rapidly because he still couldn't see very well. "I've been doing a hell of a lot for you Jacy, I think it's about time you paid up don't you??"

"Hell no! Is that why you were helping me? Geez, are you that desperate?" she screamed boldly trying to break free from his hold. Jason got right up in her face and grasped her by both arms.

"Do you really think I would bust my ass talking to people for you, coming to meet with you and using my connections for nothing? What do I look like some type of fool to you?" Jacy just looked up at him with a blank look on her face and swallowed hard. "That's what I thought! Now pay up!" Jason demanded as he roughly pulled down the zipper on her jeans and tried to yank them down but Jacy resisted. As he was looking down Jacy kneed him hard, right between the legs, hitting him square in the balls. He keeled over in pain as Jacy hurriedly made her escape through the front door.

As she was making her way around her car to open the door Jason appeared at the front door and started yelling obscenities.

"You fucking bitch! I hope your whole damn deal falls through! I hope nobody buys that damned house from you, and good luck with the home inspectors! You evil *bitch*—"

Jacy slammed her car door and drove off as Jason continued to angrily yell after her from his porch, seemingly unaware of the fact that he was causing some of his neighbors to look out of their windows.

chapter 18
Can Things Get Any Worse?

I T WAS A CHILLY TUESDAY evening in late September, and Jacy sat in her apartment staring pointlessly at the television screen. She almost felt as if the television was making her dumber or something. It was pretty much all she did those days, sit in front of the screen watching shows that served as mental tranquilizers. Even watching television was becoming useless because she wasn't even aware of what was happening on screen half the time. She was totally engrossed in her thoughts.

Jacy was officially broke, and had no idea of how she was going to pay her bills in the coming month. It had been several weeks since the second home inspector had come out, and while he didn't say she would have to remove the Jacuzzi from the bathroom or even fix the pipes, he did confirm that the rest of the repairs would absolutely need to be made before anything was approved. She had no way of paying for a new boiler, and no one she could trust to do the work. She no longer had Jason to depend on to help her with the project, so she was completely alone. She had called Tammy and told her everything. She threatened to come up and kill Jason with her own two bare hands, but Jacy told her to stay exactly where she was, that she didn't want to make things even worse. Besides, she had hurt him a hell of a lot more than he had hurt her.

After the incident, Jason became Jacy's personal stalker. He would call several times a day, leaving messages explaining how sorry he was and that it would never happen again. He would show up to the newly repaired house at various times to try to catch her coming out or going in and leave flowers at the door. One day he did catch her at a time when she was at the house checking on things, but Jacy refused to open the door. He eventually gave up, going back to his car and driving off, but Jacy was still cautious.

When she finally left the house she got in her car and drove off. Jason had the nerve to be two cars behind her trying to follow her home. *As if I wouldn't be able to recognize a glimmery tan Mercedes Benz driving behind me. He must really not be thinking right,* Jacy thought. She didn't panic, just used a trick her mother had taught her a long time ago and drove right to the nearest police precinct. Jason got the idea, made a U-turn and pulled off towards the highway in the opposite direction as he saw her pull into a space behind the building.

To put it short, Jacy was numb with problems. Nothing was going right for her, and she again felt alone in Philly. She had a stalker. No money. No job. $15,000 *further* in the hole. And her credit card was maxed out. She had sent out for a couple of new credit cards while her credit was still worth something. The house was far from being ready for HUD approval and she had no one to help her with it, and no money to get it done for that matter.

She didn't have anyone to hang with or rely on. Even the several guys she had been talking to one by one stopped calling or caring. She had left a message for Rachelle the week before, but had yet to receive a call back. Maybe she should just give up and move back in with her parents or even down to Baltimore with Tammy. Sell the house at cost to someone who actually *did* have their operation together and cut her losses, dodge her creditors.

A thought ran across Jacy's mind to get something to eat from the fridge, but then she remembered, that she had virtually nothing in the fridge. She hadn't gone grocery shopping in over a month. Money was tight. She leaned her head back into the couch and sighed. It was times like these that caused suicide to actually cross a person's mind. Jacy thought to herself that she would never actually do it, not only because she was taught from a young age that people who committed suicide automatically damned themselves to Hell, but also because it was just plain stupid. But still, the thought managed to fight its way to her conscious mind for a few seconds before quickly getting pushed back. Jacy had been fighting a serious bout of depression which had officially begun several weeks before.

Something had to give.

chapter 19
Silver Lining

IT WAS MID-OCTOBER and Jacy was walking in her door with a bag of groceries. She had received a wire that day from her parents, giving her enough money to pay her rent, which was ten days late, and buy a little food for her house. She had gone to a few restaurants downtown, yet again, to apply for their waitress positions. But they all, like the ten others she had applied to in the past month, required previous restaurant experience. Jacy thought it was so dumb that a restaurant would be so particular about someone who was just going to serve food. She would have to learn how to work a register, carry a tray of food out and take food and drink orders. *Oh so complicated,* she thought. She would have to look in the papers for 'no experience required' waitress positions out of town that night. She figured she would have better luck in the suburbs.

No one was yet interested in the house in Southwest Philly. Jacy figured it was because of it's lack of HUD approval. Most people that looked to buy homes like hers went through HUD or another government program for low-income families. She would either have to come up with an extra $1,000-$1,500 besides her bill money soon, or resign to moving into the bad neighborhood herself. Or try to sell the house for dirt cheap.

When she had finished putting away her groceries, she put on a pot of water to boil so that she could make some tea. She stood in the kitchen, suddenly becoming frozen in thought. What was she doing? Why did she continue to even try? If ever there was a rock bottom, she had reached it. She was lodged *in* the rock. It was time to give up.

Her body became weak as she finally broke down, allowing a cascade of tears and emotion to flow. She fell to the kitchen floor on her knees and banged her right hand on the cabinet door repeatedly.

"Why God???" she screamed, but was answered with a long period of silence. "Why are you letting this happen to me??" She dropped to the side on her behind and leaned against the refrigerator to cry. Muffy came into the kitchen, curious about all the noise. She purred and nuzzled her nose into Jacy's midsection.

"All I wanted was to do something better for myself," her voice trailed off.

Jacy had done the one thing she had never imagined doing in her life. She had failed.

* * * * *

It was 9pm later that night as Jacy laid in bed, in the pitch darkness, her eyes wide open. She had made the final decision that evening to begin moving into the house she had purchased, the very next day. She had no other choice. She would abandon her lease and security deposit and deal with the blow to her credit. She would live in the neighborhood on her own, buy a gun and protect herself the best she could. She knew she was going to have some problems with the females that lived on that block. They had already been giving her dirty looks whenever she went to the house to check on things. Jacy was going to either have to cut her hair or get braided, because the first thing those chickenheads would reach for in a fight was her hair. She heard a loud knock on her front door breaking her thoughts.

She slowly turned her head to the right trying to figure out who could be knocking right on her door when everyone had to get past the security door downstairs first. That had been happening way too often, what was the point of a security door if everyone could get past it? The person knocked again, this time a little more impatiently. Fear turned to curiosity.

Jacy got up from her bed, turned on her bedroom light and tip-toed out towards the front door. She peeked out of the peep-hole and saw nothing. Curious, and knowing she hadn't yet lost her mind, she went back to the bedroom and grabbed a tall glass encased candle from her desk. She went back to the door, where she again heard a knock at the door. This time, she held the candle up in the air, ready to smash it over the head of whoever it was if needed, and slowly unlocked the door. She was praying that it wasn't Jason, but how in the world would he be able to find her? She wasn't listed. She had a fearful thought. Maybe he had found a way to follow her home after all? As she slowly creeked the door open, candle ready, she wondered if she could be writing her death certificate in the process. Maybe this wasn't such a good idea. The candle might hold the person off for a moment but then what? She wasn't about to leave Muffy in there with the killer. She would have to run back, grab Muffy and then bolt out of the door. Maybe she should go grab Muffy now. Then again, someone might as well put her out of her misery, what the hell did she have going on with her life? All of these thoughts ran through her mind as she finally opened the door and froze at the person she saw before her, candle still held high in the air.

Rich hugged Jacy and held onto her for dear life. Jacy felt as if she was about to fall backwards from his strong embrace. She dropped the candle and stood stiff with shock, but relieved that it wasn't a killer after all. Rich continued holding her for what seemed like hours.

"Aaaaaaggghhh. My baby," Rich growled out, smiling. He sniffed Jacy to capture and refamilarize himself with her scent. "I missed you so much. I can't stay away from you no more. I don't care what you say." He still held onto her, the door wide open as Muffy ran out into the outside hallway. Suddenly, without warning, and for no particular reason, Jacy broke down again and started crying. She became weak and fell into Rich's embrace. It was as if at that very moment, all of her problems and emotions came to a head and she just completely snapped. She didn't hold back. She let the tears fall one after the other as she cried in his arms.

Rich held her up, then reached down and swept her up by her legs. He carried her into the bedroom and laid her on the bed. She was still crying profusely by the time she hit the sheets. She cried so hard that her whole body was shaking uncontrollably. Concern wasn't even strong enough a word to describe what he was feeling at the moment, as he sat on the bed next to her stroking her hair. He stopped stroking and kept quiet for a while. He let her cry as he examined her face closely and tried to figure out for himself what was wrong.

An hour and a half later, Jacy finally calmed down, she was all cried out. It was as if she had just suddenly run out of tears. She stared up at the ceiling and was silent. It was only then that Rich spoke up.

"Tell me what's wrong Jacy. You know I'll fix it," he said. Jacy was still silent and continued looking at the ceiling, dried tears on either side of her face.

"Okay. You don't want to talk that's cool. But I'm not leaving." They heard a rap at the front door. Rich leaped up and headed back to the front room. An older black man stood at the still-open door holding Muffy.

"She was out in the hallway, I saw your door open. Here you go," the man said as he handed the cat to Rich.

"Thanks my man. Sorry 'bout that," Rich apologized and then closed the door once the gentleman turned to leave. He brought Muffy to the back where he saw that Jacy was now sitting up on her bed wiping at her eyes.

"I don't know what the hell I'm gonna do." she blurted out. Rich put Muffy down and came back over to the bed sitting down next to her with his ears wide open and eyes fixated on her face. He was looking and smelling good in a tan State Property hoodie and a pair of jeans. Jacy spilled her guts, telling him everything from the problems with the carpenters to the problems with the house to the fact that she didn't know where her next meal or rent payment was coming from. She conveniently left out the part about Jason because she knew Rich would find and kill him. No need for more drama.

"That's it? Jacy why didn't you just call me?..." he reached into his pants pocket without hesitation and pulled out a thick wad of cash. He threw the whole pile on the bed.

"Rich. I can't just take your money like that. I've gotta find a way to do this on my own, I can't keep depending on people—"

"Jacy," Rich cut her off before she could finish. "I'm trying to make you my wife one day. I realize me being here right now doesn't mean that we're back together. I know it's gonna take time. But this money is nothing to me when it comes to you. I don't think you understand that. Whether you're my girl or not, I'm not gonna just let you be broke like that. No food in the house? Uh uh, hell no." He placed her hand over the money. "This money is *yours*. No strings. I owe you that much after the shit I did to you. It's to help you get back on your feet, but it's not to say you belong to me. Even if you tell me to fuck off right now and leave, this is still your dough. Do you understand me?"

Tears were starting to fall down Jacy's eyes as he spoke. Maybe God was finally giving her a sign that her stretch of bad luck was ending by sending Rich over at the lowest of her moments. **He** had always come through for her in the past, why wouldn't he now? She had hit rock bottom and there was definitely no direction she could go but up at this point. The only way things could have gotten worse at that point was if someone blew up her house.

Jacy reached over and hugged Rich to her. Rich hugged her back, glad that he had gotten through to her. She broke the embrace and finally spoke again.

"Friends?" she smiled at him.

Rich cracked a smile, even though he had been secretly hoping she would say she was ready to take him back. "Friends," he managed to say.

They laid in the bed and talked. Rich was so happy to see his Jacy in the flesh, smiling again.

chapter 20
Good Times

"I'M SORRY, could you repeat that?" Jacy asked.

"Uh sure. I said my brother and I are interested in buying the property you have for sale on Wallace Street? We saw the for sale sign as we were driving. Has it been sold already?"

"Oh, no it's still available. When did you want to come see it?"

"Well, we're both off today at noon and we're really kind of in a rush to find a place to live. You see our lease is about to be up at our apartment in Germantown and we're tired of paying rent. Do you think its possible for us to see it later on today?"

"Let's see," Jacy said pretending to look at her imaginary calendar and play this cool. "I have a few things to do between one and three. Would 4pm be good for you?"

"Yea that's great. We'll meet you there at four then?"

"Absolutely, see you then," Jacy hung up the phone and let out a huge sigh. She then got up and danced around her room for a bit before calling her mother and excitedly telling her that someone was actually interested in her house.

* * * * *

It was 4:10pm when the two young brothers pulled up in front of the house. Jacy met them at the door.

"Come on in," she said leading them into the living room.

The brothers seemed to be impressed with the cleanliness and new feel of the house. The carpets still smelled fresh and the off-white color of the paint made the house look even more spacious. Their eyes seemed to go off into space after they saw the beautiful new Jacuzzi tub in the bathroom. They explained that they would need the basement for storage and that the extra bedroom could be used as a joint office for the two of them. At the end of the tour, and to Jacy's great delight, they asked her what the asking price was for the house.

"$19,300," Jacy said confidently. The two brothers looked at each other and then went off to a corner to discuss. Jacy waited patiently by the door, trying to look as if she didn't care either way if they decided to buy or not. The house had appraised for $19,000 but Jacy felt confident charging the extra $300 because the house looked so damn good compared to the other houses on the block. And she had made some changes of her own to the house after the appraisal that would increase its market value.

"We'll take it," the taller, darker brother said resolutely. Jacy couldn't help but smile, but she kept her composure.

"Great. I require a $1,000 deposit to hold the house until we can change the title. The balance is due at closing. I'll just need to get a sales contract drawn up in your names."

"That's fine," the same brother said as he pulled a blue checkbook out of the backpack he had slung over his shoulder. He was obviously the main decision maker.

"Will you be taking out a loan?" Jacy asked as she watched him pull out a pen and start filling in the check.

"No, we're going to pay it in cold hard cash," the other more light-hearted brother said as he took another look around and headed back towards the kitchen.

"Oh. This is going to be a very simple process then."

"Yup, that's how we like it to be!" the man said smiling as he ripped off the check and handed it to Jacy.

"So, when exactly did you want to move in?" Jacy asked as she walked around the house with him once more making small talk.

"As soon as possible. I wrote my cell number on that check, just give me a call when you have the closing date."

"Will do," Jacy answered as she grasped the railing of the staircase and followed them up.

chapter 21
Relax

RACHELLE AND JACY sat at the bar at Copas drinking and toasting to Jacy's success in finally having sold the house. It was the end of the third week in October. It had taken a few months longer than she had planned, but Jacy had finally done it, and without having to do all of the minor repairs the HUD officers had demanded since she wasn't selling the house to a HUD family. As a show of good faith to the new home buyers, who were really great guys and had paid the balance in cash as promised, she bought a new boiler with the money that Rich had given her anyway. Rich also had some of his boys install the boiler, so she didn't have to pay for labor. She had over $19,000 in the bank in savings, and a little under $4,000 in her checking account, the remainder of the money that Rich had given her to help her get back on her feet. She was already making plans to buy her next house. She could finally breathe a little easier and it felt good.

"Here's to a wildly successful real estate business. I'm so proud of you Jacy!" Rachelle beamed as she held her watermelon margarita glass up in the air and they clicked them together.

"Thank you Rachelle. For once, something I planned goes *right*," Jacy laughed and sipped on her glass of raspberry flavored margarita.

"Yea I know. I didn't know you were going through all of that with the repair guys. You know they are always trying to take advantage of women. They think we're stupid," Rachelle said this and then a slightly embarrassed look crossed her face as she realized the irony. Rachelle had finally come to her senses and saw the guy she was 'seeing,' Steven, for what he was: a low down dirty dog. He had been seeing Rachelle off and on for a month, always after midnight, and always at Rachelle's house, before he finally admitted to her that he had a girlfriend to whom he was planning on getting engaged. It took Rachelle several months to recover from the blow, swallow her pride and finally call her best friend up. She had to admit Jacy had been right all along about Steven. She hadn't said so, but she was tired of Jacy being right all the time about the guys she dated. For once she wished she could meet a man that didn't want her just for what was between her legs.

"So what are you going to name your business?" Rachelle continued.

"You know I haven't even decided? I have no idea. Maybe something simple like JT Real Estate. I don't know."

"How about Break Barriers Real Estate. Something to signify the struggles you went through?"

Jacy laughed. "You know that's not a bad idea. I'll think about it. You know, I really think this whole thing was a lesson. God was trying to get me better prepared for life, I think, in a way. My new life. And teaching me that sometimes I have to let go of my resent, think things through before I act, follow my Spirit before I make a decision. And accept help from the *right* people, not assholes like Jason."

Rachelle just mulled over what Jacy said instead of answering.

"I know God is watching over me. Those guys came out of nowhere! And just wanted to buy that house in cold hard cash! That's almost unheard of Rachelle." Jacy said and then began sucking on the lime from her drink.

"So Rich really came through huh?"

"Yea, he did."

"So what's up with you two? Ya'll back together?" Rachelle had since been briefed on the entire Rich and Neecey situation.

"Nope. Just friends."

"And he's cool with that? He don't look like the type to be cool with you just being his 'friend!' Especially after all that cash he gave you, man I wish I could find a brother willing to drop $5,000 just like that," Rachelle said snapping her fingers and then taking another sip of her margarita.

"Well he'll have to be cool with it, because I'm not ready to take him back. To be honest between you and me, probably never will. But he's been a life-saver. I appreciate what he did no matter what happens," Jacy said.

"Jacy, why are you so hard on him?" Rachelle looked at Jacy sideways.

"Oh Lord. Not you too!" Jacy laughed and then leaned back on her stool to dust imaginary dirt from her hands.

"No I'm serious, the man came through for you big time, he's proclaimed his love for you and you can't get over one incident? The man obviously cares about you, I think you should just let it go. It's hard to find guys like that."

"Well everyone is entitled to their own opinion," Jacy said and then looked in the mirror behind the bar to make sure her hair was laying right.

"Damn, okay *bitch*," Rachelle said and chuckled a bit.

"Oh, no," Jacy said realizing the way she had just said that. "I didn't mean it like that. I just don't see things you and Tammy's way, it's hard for me to forget things that easy. *Especially* with men."

"That's an understatement," Rachelle answered and snaked her neck slightly back to the drink she was holding up in the air. Just then Jacy's cell phone started going off. She went in her bag and saw that Rich was calling.

"We talked him up," Jacy said and answered the phone. "Hey...I'm down at Copas chillin with Rachelle...I don't know yet, we might go out or something...What?...I'm not...<sigh>...hold on okay?" Jacy got up from her stool and headed towards the back to talk in private. When she arrived at the small hallway leading to the bathrooms, she stopped and put the phone back to ear.

"What do you mean I'm trying to avoid you?"

"Why every time I ask you what you doing you say you're doin' somethin else?" Rich responded.

"That's not true. I just saw you last week." Jacy said, moving to the side to let someone pass on their way to the bathroom.

"Oh, so what I'm only supposed to see you once a week or something?"

"No, but I have a lot of things going on right now, I can't see you every damned day."

"I ain't ask you to see me every day," Rich said growing impatient with his tone. "I asked you why you're always making an *excuse* not to see me."

Jacy paused for a moment. "I thought we had an understanding Rich, you're acting just like a jealous boyfriend again."

Rich yelled something in the background to someone and it sounded like he was getting into his car. "Well look, I'm not gonna sit here and argue with you, you got somethin' else to do then do it. I'll holla at you later."

"Later," Jacy said shaking her head and clicking the 'end' button on her phone. She sighed and then headed back to the bar area.

"That was him?" Rachelle asked as she watched her friend make her way back to the seat.

"Yea, tripping."

"What did I say?" Rachelle nodded her head confirming what she had predicted earlier.

They continued talking and drinking until they were on their third individual margarita pitcher each.

Rachelle busted out laughing. "He got out of there hella fast huh!" she was talking about how Jason had run off after Jacy led him to the police station. Jacy didn't tell Rachelle or Tammy about her incident with sticky fingers, a.k.a. D-4. She decided to keep it to herself. It was just too embarrassing and delicate a situation.

"Hell yea, hopefully that shows him I mean business," Jacy responded.

"Hopefully. Girl you always getting yourself mixed up with these crazy men." Rachelle leaned over and grabbed a cherry from the bar. "What ever happened to that cute light skinned brotha from Chemistry that you met? I forget his name..." she snapped her fingers trying to recall as she chewed on the cherry.

Jacy thought a minute. "Kevin. Yea I remember him. You know I never even called him," her words slurred a bit and she knew it was time to call it quits on the margaritas.

"Damn, why not? He was fine as shit."

"Rich, that's why. You know what? I'm gonna call him as soon as I get home. He probably won't even remember my ass though," Jacy said grabbing her bag and then putting it back down to pull on her jacket.

"Oh, you ready? Yea me too," Rachelle said and paid for the bill. "This was on me."

"Thanks girl!" Jacy said and reached over to give her best friend a hug. They got up from the bar and walked out into the brisk night breeze to start the 'drunk South Street stroll' to their cars.

JACY DRAGGED herself into the door at 9pm, her head buzzing with liquor, and laden with three new numbers she got while walking to her car from Copas. She threw her purse and a shopping bag from Blondie's on South Street on the couch and headed for the back, but then stopped in her tracks, a thought crossing her mind. She continued on to the back and did a search for the bag she was wearing at Chemistry the night she met Kevin. She was serious about calling him; it was about time she tried out a guy with a college education and a good legit job. She finally found the bag and rummaged through it, pulling out several cards before coming upon the card she was looking for in the front pocket.

She headed back for the living room and picked up her cordless. Dialing the cellphone number, she giggled to herself and waited for him to answer.

"Kevin Trouvant," a deep male voice answered.

"Hi…" Jacy hesitated. "Kevin?" *Duh, he just said his name,* Jacy thought.

"Yes, who is this."

"I don't know if you remember me, this is Jacy, I met you at Chemisty. Months ago."

"Jacy," he was silent for a moment as he tried to remember. "Oh, Jacilyn, yea I remember you, the red dress right?"

"Yea," she answered laughing a bit.

"How could I forget? You were the best looking lady in the club."

Jacy smiled at the compliment. "So… how are you doing?"

"I'm alright, just leaving the office."

"Damn, long day huh?"

"Yea I had to do some serious overtime to get these contracts together. I was behind, but I'm finally caught up. One of the partners was on my ass earlier this week about these…" Kevin continued talking but Jacy just couldn't stay attentive in her drunken stupor. She said a few 'uh huhs' and 'yeas' but really didn't hear much of what he was saying. Damn he's kinda killing my high, she thought and laughed to herself.

"So what about you? What was your day like?" he finally asked.

"It was good. I just got back from hanging out with my girlfriend," she responded.

"Oh yea? What were ya'll doing?"

"Getting drinks at Copas."

"Sounds good. I need to get out more. So what made you call after all this time Jacilyn?" he said sounding like her father. She was kind of surprised that he remembered her full name. Most people just called her Jacy.

"Uh, nothing really. I just came across your number and decided to give you a call."

"Hmmm. Okay," he said almost as if he didn't quite believe her. "So what are you doing this Sunday night?"

"I don't know yet."

"Well if you're free we should go get something to eat, or something to drink. I know of a nice place in the Northeast."

"Alright," she agreed. "Sounds good to me. Just call me the day of to let me know the details."

"Cool. But listen I gotta go, I'm just pulling up to my boy's house. I have to pick something up and then I'm gonna head home. So this is your number?" he ran off the number that showed up on his caller ID in his deep baritone voice.

"Yup, that's my home number. Do you want to take my cell number?"

"Yea, hold on a second," he said. Jacy waited a few seconds while he looked for a pen in his car. He finally came back. "You still there?"

"Yup. You're ready?"

"Yea, what's the number?" Jacy ran off her cell number and Kevin took it down.

"So call me on there, that's the best number to reach me at. I'm not home a whole lot these days." Jacy explained.

"Alright, will do," he answered.

"I'll talk to you later then."

"Alright, take care."

chapter 22
The Start of Something Beautiful

SUNDAY EVENING, Jacy was standing outside on her cellphone guiding Kevin to her building. She had done something new and unprecented: allowed Kevin to come pick her up from her house on the first date. She felt familiar with him, even just over the phone, so it just felt natural having him pick her up. The way an old-fashioned date should go.

He finally pulled up and almost passed where she was standing, but slowed down before it was too late. Jacy came down the stairs as he was backing up the car, a white 2001 Infiniti I20. She was wearing a long off-white wrap dress that she had picked up downtown. It was ribbed with a matching belt tied around the middle and complemented every curve of her figure. Her bra lifted and separated her breast perfectly under the dress and the waist was keenly tapered to give her the full 'hour glass' effect. Kevin nearly ran into a car that had approached from behind as he backed up, watching Jacy make her way to the car. Once the car had passed, he kept his eyes on her as she walked around the front of the car and reached the passenger side.

"Hey," he said, at a loss for words. He sat there for a moment taking her in.

Jacy was doing the same. Kevin was looking distinguished and handsome in a cool blue button down shirt and navy blue slacks. He was a shade darker than Shemar Moore, with a face that put Shemar to shame. He was obviously a brother that took a lot of pride in his appearance. As when they met, he smelled like a wonderful scent of cologne. Jacy couldn't remember the last time she went out with a brother that wore a shirt and slacks on a date. She liked it. *Now this is the type of guy I could see myself getting serious with*, she thought.

"Hey you," Jacy answered and leaned over to kiss his cheek. He smiled and started making a U-turn to head out of the apartment complex.

"So where are we going again?" Jacy asked.

"The restaurant at the Doubletree downtown. It's very classy, good food," he answered.

"Oh, I thought you said something about the Northeast."

"Yea, I called but they're not there anymore, the number is disconnected. I don't know what happened, they had the best chicken breast dinner I've ever tasted."

"Oh, too bad. At least the Doubletree's close. I heard they have good food too," Jacy continued with the small talk as Kevin headed toward Route 76.

20 minutes later they pulled into the garage below the Doubletree. Kevin bleeped his alarm and they headed for the elevator. When the elevator came they stepped in and when the doors closed, Kevin grabbed Jacy by the waist.

"You look sooo good," he said, trembling a bit as he pulled her close and looked into her eyes. "I'm glad you finally decided to call me. I was a little disappointed when you didn't."

"Oh really? I'm sorry, my schedule has just been so crazy over the last few months," Jacy smiled, looking back up into his sparkling brown eyes. He reminded her of the pretty boys she used to know in college, light skinned, impeccably dressed, always smelling good, well-groomed. Except he had an edge to him that those boys simply lacked. Where they were more effeminate in their movements, demeanor, and speech, Kevin was all man. There was no doubt about it.

The elevator dinged and Kevin led Jacy out towards the restaurant. He had made reservations so they were able to be seated immediately.

The conversation progressed well throughout their meal. They somehow got into a deep conversation about the California recall that had occurred in the prior month, leaving the state of California in the hands of Arnold Swartzenegger. They had gotten into the conversation because Kevin had revealed that he was originally from San Francisco.

"She seemed to be completely focused on his past actions with women, instead of challenging him on issues that had to do with how he would be able to run the state. I think that's why no one was really taking her seriously," Jacy said of one of the candidates.

"Yea. And it didn't help that he was making her look like a complete fool at that debate," Kevin answered as he took a bite of his steak.

"I'm curious to see what he can do for California. From what I've read, the other guy Davis, wasn't doing the best of jobs. Sometimes you just have to take a chance on something new because anything's better than the old," Jacy said bringing her own life to mind.

"Very true." Kevin agreed. Smiling, he looked down, his fork poised over his plate. "I know that first hand."

Jacy looked at him curiously as she cut into her Chicken Cordon Bleu. "What do you mean?"

"I mean..." he hesitated and there was a short pause. "Well first of all, I know it's probably a little soon to be saying this, but I think I really like you. I feel very comfortable around you and it's been a long time since I met a woman so classy. My last girlfriend was a real piece of work."

"Oh yea?"

"She was a real nut. She broke into my house through the window one day while I was at work, trying to find proof that I was cheating on her. Which I told her time and again I wasn't."

"Oh no, she didn't."

"Yea. She tripped the alarm and the police picked her up. She actually thought she was going to get away with that. I dropped the charges after she agreed to leave me alone for good. But you know, all that was really my fault."

"Your fault? Why do you say that?" Jacy asked as she took a sip of her Chardonnay.

"Because I'm always choosing women that I have no business dealing with. You know, the lady hoodrats. I get all the warning signs."

"Lady hoodrats?" Jacy chuckled and crossed her legs underneath the table.

"The ones that play like they're perfect ladies in the beginning, but after you hit it the hood comes out," he said boldly. He felt comfortable saying these things around Jacy, because he knew it didn't apply to her.

Jacy laughed a tiny stifled laugh that shook her entire body. She had food in her mouth and had almost spit it across the table. She swallowed. "After you hit it huh?"

"As soon as you hit, they start acting brand new. Calling all the time, letting themselves go. No more please and thank you's when you open the door for them. Getting loud in public. And then they start getting ridiculously jealous and insecure about every little thing. That's what happened with this last girl."

Jacy thought about what he said.

"But with you, I can tell you're the genuine article. Everything about you screams class. Like the way you drink your wine without sticking your pinky out." Kevin looked down at Jacy's half-full glass of white wine. "If I go out with one more woman that orders wine she can't even pronounce, and then flicks her pinky out while she's drinking it, I swear I'll just get up and leave her sitting right there."

Jacy laughed. "I've heard that's considered 'low-class' by uppity folks."

"It is. Not to say I'm uppity or anything, I just don't like it when someone pretends to be something they're not. All I'm saying is if she *is* a hoodrat, she should tell me right away so that I can know," Kevin said matter-of-factly.

"So that you know what?" Jacy asked after swallowing a forkful of crispy string beans.

"So I know we need to hit the two-for-one special at the Rib Joint." he said cutting into his steak.

Jacy laughed. "You are too much."

"What?" he asked smiling. "It's the truth."

They continued talking about issues ranging from politics to music. Jacy couldn't remember when she had last been so intellectually stimulated over a meal. She was really starting to dig Kevin, his looks, the way he carried himself, his humor and his wide knowledge of a variety of subjects. Not to mention the fact that he was still grounded, and could relate with Jacy in talks about everyday life, despite the fact that they had been brought up into two different social classes. Kevin's family was unquestionably upper class with his father making $350,000 a year as a world-renowned surgeon, while Jacy's family was working middle class, her father bringing in $65,000 at his peak in the construction business. She had already learned more from him in their two hours together than she had all year long. It was refreshing and energizing for her mind.

After their meal, Kevin took Jacy to a spot near Penn's Landing to sit and watch the boats sail by on the river. There was a slight chill in the air but being that it was unseasonably warm for the month of October they didn't need jackets. Kevin reached behind Jacy and pulled her closer to him on the bench they were seated on. He started talking about a boat his father used to own that they would go fishing on from time to time. Jacy sighed and listened, enjoying the moment. It just felt—right.

chapter 23
What it is About Him

KEVIN TURNED HIS HEAD. The hairs of his low cut fade bristled against the white cotton pillowcase. Jacy could tell he was about to fall asleep, because he almost always slept on his side. Her eyes traced down his back, his butterscotch skin against a ribbed white wifebeater. She noticed a small dark brown discoloration on his back near his left underarm. He wasn't exactly muscular, but he had definition in his arms and a distinctive shape to his shoulder blades. His scent was always robust and manly, even when he wasn't wearing cologne. Jacy immediately felt at ease after a difficult day when she greeted him with a hug and took in his familiar scent. She looked forward to hearing his rich, deep voice asking how her day had been. He spoke in low tones at times, mostly when he was in engrossed in thought, but Jacy could always hear every word.

Jacy was lying sideways with her right hand holding up the side of her head so that she could have a straight view of the TV screen at the foot of the bed. She took her other hand and ran it down Kevin's back slowly. He smiled and got more comfortable. She leaned over to his ear.

"Are you going to sleep? You're going to miss the movie," she said softly, just above a whisper.

"No, I'm up."

"Yea, right," she teased and swiveled her hips so that her body was straight forward on the bed. She pulled herself up and leaned back on the headboard of Kevin's plush oak bed.

"No seriously, I'm up." Kevin answered, turning back towards Jacy and placing his hand on her stomach. "But baby, I can't watch this dumb ass movie anymore though."

"Awww. You don't like it so far? I think it's alright," she smiled and shifted her weight to lean over and rub the back of Kevin's head. "But I guess if it was good I wouldn't be talking while it's on huh?"

It was the day before Thanksgiving, a Wednesday afternoon, and Jacy and Kevin were relaxing in bed watching rented movies. Kevin was off of work and they were getting mentally prepared for the big day—Kevin had been invited to Jacy's big family Thanksgiving dinner in Somerset. Since his family lived in San Francisco, he didn't have any plans for the holiday other than going to one of his friends' houses. But Jacy offered first. He was not one of those men that was scared to meet a female's family, and for a woman like Jacy making that kind of step was not such a bad idea to him. They were going to take the two hour drive out the following day to avoid traffic and stay over until Friday evening. Some of Jacy's family from New York was going to be there, and even Tammy, Ray and Tanasia were making the trip up, so it would be a pretty big event.

"Let's watch that other movie, *They*," Kevin said. "My boy Greg told me that was one of the best slept-on scary movies he's ever seen."

"Alright. Yea, cause this one isn't making the cut." Jacy got up and sat on the floor in front of the entertainment center. "So, are you going to be okay?"

"For what, the thing tomorrow? Yea yea. I'll be fine. Mothers love me." Kevin said brushing at his stomach with both hands cockily.

"Okay Mr. Smooth, but it ain't just my mom that you'll have to worry about. My family can get a little...uh, rowdy when they're all together."

"Rowdy? How?" he asked sitting up on his elbows.

"Not bad rowdy I guess. Just a little loud, a little animated. And let me tell you right now, my Uncle Pete will be there and he can't hold his tongue. He says exactly what's on his mind."

"Okay, what else should I know?"

"My father probably won't like you. He's never liked *any*one I've brought home. So don't take it personal okay." Jacy said sliding the disc into Kevin's DVD player.

"You never know."

"No, I know," Jacy said smiling and nodding her head. "If tomorrow is a disaster promise me you won't run from the house screaming."

Kevin got up from the bed and eased his way over to where Jacy was sitting; she was still playing with his DVD player. He sat too, straddling her from behind and wrapped his arms around her. Despite their frequent rendezvous at his or her place over the past month, Jacy and Kevin hadn't had sex. He respected her decision to wait awhile before getting intimate.

"Baby, I wouldn't leave you."

Jacy turned her head and gave him a kiss. "Thank you sweetie."

"I would just never go see your family again, that's all," he said, joking. Jacy turned around and pushed him back onto the floor. She smacked at his leg.

"You're not funny," she said and then turned back around to figure out why the DVD still wasn't playing. Kevin leaned up, pressed a button and the movie automatically came up on the screen. He then pulled Jacy up off of the floor, turned her around and bent down to kiss her passionately. Jacy melted inside as she stood on her tippy-toes, held her head up and kissed him back.

"JACY! IS that you?" Mrs. Thomas shouted delightfully from the kitchen as Jacy let herself into the house with her key. Kevin was right behind her holding a vanilla cake that Jacy had baked. Her mother made her way around to the foyer and gave her daughter a big hug.

"Mommy! How are you?" Jacy replied giving her Mom a bright smile that showed all of her teeth. Her mother was a warm, sweet, medium-complexioned woman, with a head full of beautiful silky silvery hair, and a smile that put Jacy's to shame. She was wearing a big red sweater, black stirrup pants and a pair of low heeled black pumps. Mrs. Thomas' style was chic but conservative.

"And this must be Kevin? Right?" she said looking him over with a smile.

"Yes, Mrs. Thomas, very nice to meet you." Kevin answered as he leaned over involuntarily to give her a hug. He handed her the cake.

"Well you look like a very nice young man. Come on in!" Jacy's mother instructed. "Everybody's down in the rec room, your cousin Tammy told me to tell you to go see her as soon as you get in. She has a surprise for you."

After hanging up their coats, Jacy and Kevin made their way downstairs into the rec room, which took up the entire length of the house, a spacious one-story, four bedroom ranch that stood on a near quarter acre of land. The rec room, painted a medium-tan color, was decorated with a Thanksgiving theme in mind. As Jacy came down, she saw Tammy sitting at a table talking to her mother, Jacy's Aunt Breanna. Ray was sitting with Tanasia on his lap watching TV in the loveseat with Uncle Pete, while Jacy's paternal grandmother, Uncle Pete's wife, Aunt Breanna's husband and Jacy's father were sitting on the large sectional couch.

"Hey everyone!" Jacy said as she began making her rounds. Per protocol, she went to her grandmother, the most senior person in the room first, then on to her father and the rest. "Everyone, this is Kevin, Kevin this is..." she said running off everyone's titles. Kevin greeted everyone individually. When she reached her father, a thin darker skinned man, Kevin went over to shake his hand. Her father didn't smile or speak, just lifted his hand to meet Kevin's. Jacy introduced him personally to Tammy as well, who stood up and gave him a big hug.

"It's very nice to meet you all." Kevin said to everyone, smiling confidently.

The family members smiled up at Kevin, some returning the phrase, and then returned to watching their program. They were watching an old episode of *In Living Color* on TV.

"They put *In Living Color* back on TV?" Kevin asked, his eyes becoming glued to the screen as he shoved his hands in his pockets and sat on the arm of the sectional couch.

"They play it on FX now. *Married with Children* comes on now too." Aunt Breanna's husband Jack replied and then took a big chug of his Heineken. "It's about time, I have no idea why they took it off in the first place!"

"Cause all those big wig network people can't stand to see a nigger on TV succeeding that's why. That Keenan Ivy fella, he was doin' the damn thing! Then those crackas wanna go and take him off," Uncle Pete shook his head and complained. Jacy could tell Uncle Pete was well into his drinking ritual.

"Oh Pete hush up," his wife Ethel commanded and waved him off. "Nobody wants to hear all that. That wasn't the reason it was taken off."

"Woman, you don't tell me when to hush!" Uncle Pete sat forward and looked at Aunt Ethel like she had just escaped from the crazy house. "I'd like for your high saddity ass to tell me why they took it off then?"

"Pete give it a rest, alright?" She shook her head.

"No, since you know it all tell me why then?" Uncle Pete persisted.

"I don't know exactly—"

"That's right, exactly. You don't know nothin', and I'm tellin' ya right now why." Uncle Pete sat back and took a long sip of his beer. "Gone be tryin' to 'hush' me and shit. I know what the hell I'm talkin' about."

"Both of ya'll need to shut the hell up. I want to hear the program." Jacy's grandmother spoke up. She turned back to the TV and chuckled at a skit they were doing.

Jacy rolled her eyes over to look at Tammy who had stopped chatting with her mother and was giving her the same look back. She decided to go over and see what the big surprise was with Tammy. It was either that or listen to her aunt and uncle argue over a TV show.

"So cuz." Jacy said as she sat down at another chair at the table with Tammy and her mother. "What's the surprise Mom was talking about."

Tammy held out her left hand and smiled like a two-year old.

"We're doing it," she finally said.

Jacy's mouth hung open.

"Ray and I are getting married!!!" she screamed causing Ray to look over and smile. Tammy and Jacy jumped up at the same time and hugged across the table frenziedly, shrieking and shaking from side to side.

"You're finally getting married!?" Jacy shrieked. "Oh my God!"

"Yes yes! He proposed to me yesterday, can you believe this??"

"Oh my God." Jacy said again and put her hand up to her chest as she gazed at the ring weighing her big cousin's finger down.

Jacy and Tammy continued to laugh, cry and fuss over Tammy's two carat engagement ring. Jacy was genuinely happy for her cousin; Tammy had been hoping for that proposal for at least a year. They might as well be married, they already act like a married couple, Jacy thought. She wasn't even bitter towards Ray for what he had said about her during their argument. To be honest, she was more upset with what he had said about Tammy. But Jacy was not one to judge, and wasn't about to start telling Tammy of all people how to live her life.

"Dinner is ready! Everybody upstairs!" Jacy's mother yelled from the top of the staircase.

* * * * *

Jacy's mother had barely had a chance to say "Amen" after saying Grace before Uncle Pete had snatched up the spoon for the baked macaroni. He put scoop after scoop on his plate until Uncle Jack grew impatient.

"Pete. Stop trying to eat all the damn macaroni. Other's gotta eat too," he said in a genuinely hostile tone.

"Man cool it. I ain't taking all the macaroni, why don't you stop focusin' on me? Huh, how 'bout that," Uncle Pete answered, still piling his plate.

"Pete give someone else the spoon, I only have two pans of macaroni for everybody. And you know everybody wants that the most." Jacy's mother demanded. Uncle Pete finally passed the spoon to his wife. Jacy's little brother and sister had since joined everyone at the table, having come down from their rooms.

There was quiet at the table for the first half an hour of eating after everyone's plate was full with turkey, ham, stuffing, greens, yams, biscuits and baked macaroni and cheese. Jacy's mom broke the silence.

"So, Kevin, I heard you work as a consultant?"

"Yes, in the Mergers and Acquisitions department Mrs. Thomas."

"Merges and who?" Uncle Pete interrupted.

"Mergers and Acquisitions Uncle Pete," Jacy answered.

"Is that when you help companies come together as one?" Jacy's younger sister Tamila inquired. She was a spitting image of her older sister.

"Yes, that's exactly what I do." Kevin confirmed with a smile. "I help consult them on the best way to handle that process."

"I see. That sounds like very interesting work!" Jacy's mother replied happily.

Uncle Pete sighed.

"Did you by chance work with Second Union's merge with Supernovia Bank?" Uncle Jack asked Kevin.

"No, actually we have worked with Second Union in the past, but we didn't handle their merger with Supernovia."

"Oh, good. Cause I don't like that Supernovia Bank, they've been giving me such a hassle. I'm thinking about taking my accounts somewhere else," Aunt Ethel piped in.

"Take your accounts somewhere else then, don't nobody care about your little accounts." Uncle Pete just had to put his two cents in.

"Pete, don't start, please. Let's have a peaceful dinner." Jacy's mother said.

"I swear I don't know where this boy got to be so damned rude." Jacy's grandmother shook her head. "Maybe I didn't beat his ass enough as a child, I don't know."

Jacy sighed and looked up towards the ceiling. Her eyes fell back down on Tammy who was stifling a laugh. Jacy's father, who was Pete's younger brother, was chuckling too.

"Oh, you beat me enough. That's one thing you can be sure of!" Uncle Pete said nodding his head furiously.

"Well maybe I done beat the sense outta you. We got company over here, you don't act this way around company!" Jacy's grandmother replied.

"What I wanna know is why ya'll always ganging up on me? I ain't been doing nothin' but havin' some innocent conversation." Uncle Pete waved everyone off with his hand.

IT WAS 7pm when everyone finished eating and piled downstairs to play cards and watch TV. Kevin, Jacy's father, Aunt Breanna and Uncle Pete were deeply involved in a game of Spades, Jacy's sister and brother had gone to a party at her sister's college, everyone else was relaxing on the couch and watching TV, while Tammy and Jacy were sitting on the loveseat having girl-talk. Jacy intermittently glanced over at the spades table to watch Kevin.

Just as she looked over, Uncle Pete stood and slapped a high card down on the table. He grinned so hard his dentures nearly fell out. Until Jacy's Dad whipped out the big gun, the big joker and cut right through one of Uncle Pete's guaranteed books. The grin turned to a frown as Uncle Pete immediately started blaming his partner, Aunt Breanna, for playing wrong.

As the night drew on people started leaving. The spades game had been played and won, by Jacy's father and Kevin, who of course couldn't leave the table without being accused of cheating by Uncle Pete. Aunt Ethel and Uncle Pete were the first to leave, then Tammy's parents drove Jacy's grandmother home to Queens.

"Jacy, could I see you for a moment," Jacy's mother came over and grabbed her daughter's hand. She led her upstairs to the living room.

"Yes, mother," Jacy said as she had a seat on the white leather couch. Jacy was always expecting the worst.

"Jacy. That Kevin. I really like him."

Jacy's face slowly formed into a smile. "You do?"

"Yes! I mean, I really really like him. I think he's growing on your father too!"

"I know I saw! He actually gave Kevin a pat on the back!"

"You'd better hang on to this one Jacy, he's one of the good ones."

"I think so too Mom."

"And you know, if he can make it through a night with your father's family—"

"He's gotta be a *special* kind of man." Jacy chuckled.

chapter 24
Perfection

SEVEN WEEKS AFTER THEIR FIRST DATE, Jacy and Kevin were official. They were even making plans to go down to the islands on vacation with Tammy and Ray in the new year to escape the cold.

They rarely, if ever, fought and Jacy was starting to fall into a comfortable routine with Kevin. He would go to work while Jacy worked from home, researching and calling people, occasionally checking on the work that was going on at the new fixer upper house she had recently bought in West Philly. She had found new professional and reliable carpenters that she got along with well, so she didn't feel the need to check up on them every minute. When Kevin got off he'd either stop at his condo to pick up something or come straight to Jacy's house to eat whatever meal she had made, take her to dinner, or order out, then they would sit up under each other and watch primetime television, talk to each other about their life and plans, and then get ready for bed. They had become intimate in their ninth week. It had been a mind-blowing experience for both. Kevin did everything imaginable to make sure that Jacy came to climax before penetration. And when he did it was almost as if she and he were floating on a different plane together during the act. She felt no pain, only pleasure when they were together.

Jacy stood behind the shopping cart while Kevin reached up and grabbed a box of Frosted Mini Wheats from the top shelf. It was Sunday afternoon and they were out grocery shopping for

Jacy's house. Since Kevin was staying over Jacy's house most of the time being that his job was closer to her apartment than his condo in Bucks County—he had offered to buy her some groceries for the house. He also insisted on sending her to get her nails done on a regular basis since Jacy had fallen off her normal grooming routine during the time she was having problems. He left a few sets of clothes and two suits at her house so that he wouldn't have to stop home when he got off of work.

"Ewww you like those things?" Jacy said of the Frosted Mini Wheats, playfully screwing up her face. "They're gross!"

"Girl are you kidding me? This is the best cereal in the world!" he responded dropping the box on top of the pile of other items in the cart.

"Nope sorry, *this*," Jacy said grabbing a box of Honey Nut Cheerios. "Is the best cereal," she finished and dropped the box in the cart.

As they were loading their items on the conveyor belt in the checkout line, Jacy's cellphone started going off in her purse. She figured it must be her Mom calling her to find out if she had gone to church that morning, which she had. The number came up as private. Jacy hesitated, but answered the call anyway.

"Hello?" There was no answer, just breathing on the other end. "Hello?" she asked again. The person finally just hung up.

"Who was that?" Kevin asked as he pulled the now-empty cart forward in the line to let the person behind them start loading.

"I don't know, they hung up." Jacy was thinking she hoped it wasn't Jason trying to start up with the harassing phone calls again. But he had never done a hang up, he always ran off his mouth as much as possible before Jacy could hang up on *him*. She didn't want to change her number again after already having gone through that process with Rich before. It was just too much trouble. She put the whole thing to the back of her mind.

When they got home they carried in the packages and when they had finally finished putting the last grocery away, Kevin came up behind Jacy in the kitchen and wrapped his arms around her waist, whispering sweet things in her ear. In a matter of moments the words became racier, and Jacy became slightly weak in the knees. Kevin, sensing this, turned her around and kissed her neck, her chin, her forehead and her ears before picking her up by the thighs and carrying her to the back of the apartment.

chapter 25
Wrong Place, Wrong Time

THE NEXT AFTERNOON, as Jacy sat at her computer typing an email to Rachelle at her job, she heard a buzz indicating that someone was at the front door. She got up and pressed the intercom.

"Who is it?"

"It's Rich. Open up."

Jacy was quiet for a moment. She had seen and talked to Rich a few times since she started seeing Kevin, but did a lot more avoiding of him than anything.

"Hold on a minute, I'll be right down," she answered and unlocked the door to head downstairs.

When she reached the security door and opened it Rich was standing there with an angry look on his face.

"What's up?" Jacy asked smiling. When he didn't answer, she just turned around absent-mindedly and headed upstairs, not thinking much of it. Rich followed her up to her apartment.

Once in her living room, Rich walked over and plopped himself down on the couch. He looked gravely down at the space between his legs on the floor. Jacy came over and sat next to him, now sure that something was wrong.

"What's wrong," she demanded more than asked.

"Who's that nigga you're seeing," he said lifting his eyes to the wall. Rich never hesitated to get straight to the point.

"Uh…what?" Jacy became flustered, like a schoolgirl caught in a lie.

"Don't play dumb with me Jacy. I saw you with my own eyes, out shopping with that light skinned nigga yesterday. Who the hell is he? That same dude I saw you driving with that day isn't it."

"No…" Jacy was looking at the floor now. "No it's not that guy."

"So who is it then?"

"Why does it matter? Who he is? He's just a guy I know," Jacy said getting up and heading for the bathroom to wash her hands, look at herself in the mirror, anything to escape the tension that was forming in the living room. Rich hopped up and followed her, now amped up.

"What the fuck do you mean what does it matter?" his voice boomed throughout the apartment, shaking Jacy down to her slippers. He banged his fist on the open bathroom door which shook in response for a few seconds. "*Fuck* yea it matters! I'm over here sweatin' your ass, trying to make sure you OK, and you out here fucking with other guys in the meanwhile! I thought we was…" Rich's voice trailed away as he looked for the words to complete his sentence.

"You thought what Rich? That we were going to get back together? I *never* told you that was going to happen," Jacy turned to him. The truth was, Jacy did care about Rich. But she didn't know if she could trust him after the incident with Neecey. And she didn't know if he was the type of man she wanted to be with on a long term basis. "Why can't things just stay like they are right now between us?"

"I can't believe this shit!" Rich yelled. But then his voice went down a notch and became monotone as he seemed to be talking to himself. For a split second it sounded as if he wanted to cry, but Jacy had to write it off as just a pitch change in his voice. "You know, Timbo told me I was being a fool, acting like a little bitch calling you all the time and tryin' to be there for you. I'm glad he saw you with that nigga yesterday and came to get me, or else I'd still be acting like a dumb ass. I should have listened to him sooner. When he told me about that Jason nigga!"

Jacy was finally putting two and two together. Rich must have been the prank caller at the supermarket. He must have been watching through the large store windows as Jacy picked up her phone at the cash register, or from somewhere within the store. But how did he know about Jason? Her expression had obviously given her question away.

"Yea, he told me about that Jason muthafucka that called your phone when I was locked up. So you *was* fucking around on me, right?" Rich cocked his head to the side and nodded.

Oh damn, Jacy thought. She was a little confused at how Timbo knew anything about Jason, but things got clearer as she thought about the day she had accidentally left her phone in Timbo's car. "No, no Rich. Jason was the guy that was helping me with the real estate thing. It wasn't anything between us, that was totally professional."

He was quiet for a while as he processed what she had said. Her voice became normal again as she hoped he had gotten over his rant. "Rich, I don't know what to say." She looked down at and held onto the sink. Rich stood at the doorway. He tipped his hat to the side and leaned against the wall nervously. They were both quiet for what seemed like hours.

"Say you'll leave the nigga alone and be with me," Rich finally said.

Jacy let go of the sink and stepped backwards. She looked at Rich for a long while. He looked so vulnerable. But there was nothing she could do about it. "I'm sorry Rich, I can't do it."

Rich looked at Jacy with pain in his eyes. He watched as she slid past him and back into the living room. He stood there for a moment, becoming increasingly furious with each beat of his heart. He finally turned around and walked back into the living room. When he got there he caught Jacy before she had a chance to reach the kitchen and yanked her back by her hand harshly so that she was facing him. She just stood there in shock at the sudden motion as well as the pain in her arm from being pulled, and frozen by the fire she saw in his eyes. Rich still had a very tight grip on her hand.

"What the hell do you mean 'you can't?' What are you in love with the nigga or something?" Rich questioned, yelling directly into her face. His own words, and the possibility that the answer to his question might be 'yes' made his heart do a jump-skip and the blood rush to his head. He was very close to blanking out.

"No, I just...I don't know I'm just...Rich I'm sorry but I don't want to be back with you like that. I can't forget what you did. I don't know if I trust you. I just can't," Jacy said, stumbling over her words. She felt herself about to cry but bit her lip and shook her head.

"YOU don't know if you trust ME. You don't know if you can trust ME huh? You got some fucking nerve Jacy!!! I know for a *fact* you was fucking around with Terrell while we was together!!!" Rich was now leaning down into her face, spitting word after angry word. All of a sudden out of nowhere, he threw her hand away. Before Jacy could even react, Rich violently threw his right fist into her living room wall. He had broken through the hard drywall and straight to the other side with one swift motion.

"RICH!" Jacy screamed as he pulled his fist back out, dusty and almost bleeding, from the now gaping hole in the wall. "What the fuck is wrong with you!" She exclaimed wide-eye-and-mouthed. Concern was in her frightened tone. She watched as his chest heaved in and out from pure frustration.

"Fuck you Jacy. You are so muthafuckin' heartless. Stay fucking with niggas feelings! That's probably another reason why Terrell's ass is sitting up in the hospital right now." Jacy's eyes and mouth got even wider at hearing that bit of news. What had he done to Terrell? "But you know what? Fuck it, Imma grant you your wish and leave you alone for good. I'm done Jacy. Just like you told me 'We done,'" he said throwing his palms down in the air for finality. He strolled towards the door. A small droplet of blood fell from his knuckles.

"Rich—" Jacy tried to say as he unlocked the door and snatched it open.

"No, shut the fuck up," he turned to yell at her. He stood and looked at her for a few more moments before heading down the hallway, not bothering to close the door back.

Jacy stood in the foyer staring out into the hallway with her mouth still slightly open, unable to move or breathe. She heard someone across the hall open their door just enough so that they could peek out. A few seconds later she heard the security door slam downstairs.

chapter 26
*Fairy Tales **Do** Come True...Don't They?*

MONTHS HAD GONE BY, four to be exact, since Jacy had last seen or heard from Rich. She was beginning to see that he was holding true to his promise. She had tried to call him a couple of times but only got his voicemail. So she gave up, and decided to put her full focus on her budding relationship with Kevin. Jacy and Kevin had been seeing each other seriously for almost six solid months by then and things looked very promising. They had gone on a vacation in early January with Tammy and Ray as they planned, on a seven day, six night cruise to the Bahamas, a trip which Kevin paid for with the exception of airfare. He was already spending over $2,000 for the cruise so Jacy insisted on getting their plane tickets to Florida. The cruise was the perfect fairy tale adventure. Jacy had never been to the islands so it was a wonderful experience for her to see that beautiful weather, the crystal clear water and white sand beaches. Things were getting real serious real fast, and Jacy liked it.

For the previous Christmas they compromised that Jacy would spend the holiday with Kevin's family since he had given up time with his family on Thanksgiving. As expected, Kevin's mother and father were a little on the bourgie side, but after the initial unpleasantries and obvious inspection by his mother, Jacy opened his mother up with a question about the beautiful expensive looking large Persian rug in front of their fireplace. Mrs. Trouvant answered that it was an expensive silk rug called a Nourmak worth over $7,000. Jacy's eyes nearly popped out of her head at the figure causing Mrs. Trouvant to become animated in her description and history of the rug, and warm up to Jacy's inquisitiveness. They talked for the rest of the night and seemed to forget that Kevin and his father, a quiet but serious man with an easy smile, were even in the room. By the end of their four day stay in San Francisco, Mrs. Trouvant was asking if Jacy and Kevin could change their flight to the next day so that Jacy could accompany her to her hair appointment and from there on a girl's day out at her favorite spa. But Kevin, who had surprised Jacy with a diamond tennis bracelet on Christmas day, insisted that he needed to get back home to work or else he would be making up work on New Year's Eve. They had reservations at a ritzy hotel in New York City for New Years Eve and New Years Day, which was also Kevin's birthday.

Jacy felt as if she was in some type of fairy tale. This wasn't supposed to be happening to a girl like her. She had never even been in a serious relationship, let alone during the holidays. And to spend that holiday with a man's family was unheard of for her. She had never experienced anything even remotely like it. She couldn't yet say that she was in love with Kevin, but she was as close to it as she had ever gotten. She felt as if this all was too good to be true.

Despite her happiness and the time she was spending with Kevin, Jacy couldn't help but think about the whole situation with Rich, the disappointment she saw on his face when she told him she couldn't leave Kevin alone, the hurt in his eyes before he left. She hoped that he wasn't *too* torn about the whole thing. She had really hoped they could remain friends. But as she originally figured, that would be impossible.

When Rich had left Jacy's apartment that day, he sat in his car for a full hour holding onto his wheel and staring straight ahead at the building. Call him crazy, but he had actually thought Jacy might come running out after him. He couldn't believe this was actually happening to him. He had never been in love with a woman before. Had never felt those feelings, never thought those thoughts. He had always treated the females he came across like crap, like hos and like objects to be used and thrown away. But he had opened his heart and mind to Jacy and what did he get for caring? A knife through his chest. If that was what love was about, he didn't want any part of it. As he finally turned the ignition in his car he decided that he would never allow love to happen to him again.

* * * * *

"If it seems too good to be true, it probably is."—old adage

It was a week after Jacy's birthday, Saturday, March 27th when Kevin broke the bad news.

They were sitting on the couch in his condo, watching Spongebob Squarepants on Nickelodeon. Kevin had his arm around Jacy's shoulder, playing with a lock of her hair. He looked down at her, admiring the contours of her face. She looked back up at him, sensing his gaze, and Kevin got lost in her soft brown eyes for a moment. His expression turned sad. He finally took his arm from around Jacy and looked down at his hands.

"I'm moving to Atlanta."

Jacy continued to look at him with a question mark on her face.

"My company is transferring me to the Atlanta office to head up a new group. It's a promotion, they're raising my salary to $120,000," he looked up at Jacy, hoping she would light up at hearing the figure. But she didn't. He looked back at the TV.

Jacy turned her head back and looked off to her right at the floor, her lips pursed closed. Did he just say he was moving to Atlanta?

"Jacy, come on, say something."

"Well. Hmm. What would you like for me to say?" Jacy snapped as she whipped her head back in his direction to look in his eyes. She was almost tearing by then.

"I...I don't know," Kevin hesitated, slightly shocked at Jacy's sudden reaction.

"When are you leaving?"

"Next month, April 7th."

"April 7th?? That's less than two weeks away! When did you hear about this?" she asked.

Kevin looked back down at his hands. "About a month ago."

"A whole month ago? Why didn't you tell me then?" Jacy demanded. "Never mind. I don't care, the point is you're leaving." She threw her hands up and stood up from the couch to go to the bathroom. She was about to cry and didn't want him to see it.

"Jacy, it's not the end of the world. We can do the long distance thing for a while, and when we're both ready, maybe you can move out to Atlanta and settle there too," he said still seated.

"Move out to Atlanta? Hello? I just started a real estate business out here. Am I supposed to just pick up, leave everything behind, including my family, and move to Atlanta now?" Jacy turned around angrily, with a few tears already running down her face.

"I didn't say that. I...I don't know Jacy," Kevin said leaning forward on the couch and clasping his hands together.

"Yea I don't know either," she said walking back over to the coffee table to pick up her purse. She slung the dark brown leather bag over her shoulder and headed for the door.

"Where are you going?" Kevin demanded, finally getting up from his seat. His legs were a little wobbly.

"Out," she said bluntly and began unlatching the locks.

"Jacy I think you're getting way more bent out of shape about this than necessary," he said swiftly moving to where she was and grabbing her by the arm. "You know I care about you, I think I may even be in love with you. But I have to think about my career right now. I'm 30 years old and this promotion will put me a step from being upper management at my firm. This kind of position for someone under 50 is unheard of!"

"I understand that Kevin," she clutched her bag and sighed. They were both quiet for a while. "Of course I want you to take that promotion." Jacy lifted her head up slightly to keep the tears from falling. She shook her head and spoke to herself. "Things were just going so well for once…"

"It's not like this is it baby. We'll stay in touch and alternate visiting each other every month," Kevin tried to say as assuringly as possible. But Jacy wasn't convinced.

Jacy sighed. "Kevin I've tried long distance relationships before. They don't work. You'll go out there, the long distance thing will get old, and we'll both eventually move on to dating people where we live. We'll grow apart."

Kevin was silent. Jacy looked down and spoke again.

"I guess we should just play it by ear. Like you said, we can stay in contact, and if something happens in the future where we can be close, then…then maybe we'll try this again," she said, still looking down, shaking her head as another tear fell. She was trying to be strong. She looked up after gaining control of her emotions again.

Kevin looked long and soberly into her eyes, trying to read her expression. He studied her keen features, the arch of her eyebrows, the almond shape of her eyes, long lashes, the curvature of her nose and glistening lips. He brought his hand up and caressed the side of her face. He didn't want to leave her. He didn't. But the choice was no longer his; he had already accepted the transfer. His office and apartment were already set up for his arrival in Atlanta. It was not something that he could pass up— that would have been career suicide.

"Okay," he finally said. Jacy forced a quick smile on her face and leaned over to give him a hug and a kiss on the cheek. She then turned the knob behind her and walked through the door. She clutched her jacket as she fought the brisk March breeze.

chapter 27
Back to Square One

"**D**AMN, SO TERRELL *was* in the hospital? What the hell did they do to him?" Rachelle asked, enthralled by the fact that someone had been sent to the hospital over Jacy.

"I don't know, but I finally got in touch with him on Tuesday. He was pretty tight lipped about it. A man and his pride. But he did tell me he had a broken arm and his back was thrown out of alignment. He's gotta see a chiropractor or something."

"So…they just whooped on his ass real good huh?" Tammy chimed in, trying to hold back a laugh.

"It couldn't have been Timbo cuz that's his cousin, but I know it was probably Rich and some of those other knuckleheads he hangs with. But I'll never know for sure. Rich isn't speaking to me or answering my calls." Tammy and Rachelle both said "oh" in response.

"So Kevin leaves today right?" Tammy asked, bringing up a sore subject for Jacy. Jacy sighed. She, Tammy and Rachelle were on a three-way call. Jacy was sitting at a local bar in her neighborhood having a few drinks by herself. It was a little after 2:15pm in the afternoon on the Thursday Kevin's plane was scheduled to leave.

"Yea, he called the day before yesterday to tell me his flight leaves at 2:45pm today," Jacy answered.

"He called huh? Well maybe he was hoping you would stop him," Rachelle commented.

"No I don't think so, there's nothing that could stop him and I don't even think I would want to stop him. This new position means a lot to him. He did want me to come see him off at the airport, but I told him it would just make things harder," Jacy sipped her vodka tonic. It was her second round.

"Yea, I can feel you on that. So ya'll are going to at least try the long distance thing?" Rachelle asked.

"Other than just calling to say what's up, naw I don't think so. Remember Will? I just don't think long distance relationships can work."

"Well me and Ray had a long distance thing going for a while, and we made it," Tammy interjected. Her wedding date had been set in June. She was spending the majority of her time shopping for a wedding dress and searching for a venue. They made plans for Jacy to come back down to Baltimore in the coming month to help Tammy with the arrangements.

"True, but you guys were mutually in love. I seriously don't think he's in love. And you didn't have to drop your life in order to be together."

"But Ray did. He left his job to be with me, the one with the least holding them down in their city has to make the compromise. Why can't you start up a real estate business in Atlanta?"

"Girl, I'm still small beans!" Jacy chuckled to ease the stress building from hearing Kevin's name again. "I doubt they have decent houses that go for less than 100 grand in the ATL. I've gotta start off small and work my way up to the big leagues."

"You could get loans?" Rachelle offered.

"Rachelle, like anybody's giving me a $100,000 or more loan with all of the debt I have," Jacy's blood pressure went up a notch at the thought of her student loan debt. She called to the bartender for another drink. "Besides, he never even asked me to move in with him or anything. He just said I can get myself 'settled' there. I'm not moving all the way out to a city I know nothing about and have to get a new apartment, find a new job, get a new bank, new bills, address changes, and all that shit for a man who I'm not even sure loves me. I won't do it."

"Do you love him?" Rachelle asked.

"I don't know about all that. But I know I care about him a lot, and I got to be so comfortable around him. I felt almost the same about Rich for a while, so maybe it was just a 'thing.'" Jacy said, but wasn't really sure how she felt about Kevin *or* Rich.

"So then how can you want him to love you?" Tammy asked as if they were doing a tagteam.

"It's not that. I don't know. Not being sure of how he feels is enough of a reason for me to not move down there, but the fact that *I* don't even know if I love him is an even bigger reason." Jacy sighed and felt a lump growing in her throat. Nothing had ever gone right for her in the relationship department, why would anything have changed with Kevin. She had to face it, if she ever wanted to settle down and stop playing around with men, she would have to settle for drama in the way that Tammy and her mother had. Again, she had to constantly ask herself: "is it all worth it?"

"This is a tough subject for me right now guys, can we move on to something else?" Jacy asked her friends.

"Alright, alright," Tammy let up.

"Actually, I'd better get off this phone. I have a meeting I need to prepare for in 20 minutes," Rachelle said.

"Yea, maybe I better get back to work too," Tammy agreed. "I have a closing at 3:30."

"Alright then guys. I'll talk to you later," Jacy said and pulled her new drink closer.

"Bye," Rachelle hung up as they heard someone talking to her in the background.

"Later cuz." Tammy hesitated for a moment and then assured, "It'll be okay Jacy, everything happens for a reason. Just take care of yourself."

"I will."

Jacy hung up her cellphone, placed it on the bar and rested her chin in the palm of her hand. Despite the fact that it was the middle of the day, there were several people in the bar drinking and talking. She stared off into space and thought about the fact that Kevin's flight was probably now boarding. They were probably calling for first class and passengers with disabilities right now. She thought about the possibility that her last chance at a normal life was now getting up from the waiting area of the Philadelphia International Airport and heading for the walkway of a plane to Atlanta. In five minutes it would be handing over its one-way boarding ticket. In ten minutes it would be shoving its carry-on bag into an overhead compartment. In fifteen it would already be seated comfortably and settled into its new destiny.

Her cellphone message indicator started beeping loudly. She looked down at the screen and saw it flashing. Someone must have called while she was on her three-way call. She checked the time. It was exactly 2:22pm. She hesitated, but then snatched the phone up from the bar and held down a button to reach her voicemail. There was one voicemail message:

Hey, Jacilyn. They're boarding my plane. I guess I was kinda hoping you'd come see me off anyway. It's alright. But I, um, have something for you. I guess I'll just have to mail it to you...God, I miss you already <nervous chuckling>. You'll probably think I'm crazy but I'm starting to think this wasn't such a good idea. <Long sigh>. But I know it's no longer an option. I wanted to tell you...I...that...<long pause>...aaah you're right I'm just making this harder. I'll call you when I touch down. Take care.

Jacy ended the call and frowned at the phone. She felt a tear trying to make its way to the corner of her eye but fought it, and won. Within a millisecond she was back to her normal self, forgetting what was said in Kevin's message. She shut off the phone and put the back of her right hand back under her chin, her other hand brought her drink up to her lips.

"Excuse me ma, somebody sittin' here?" a male voice asked.

Jacy took her hand off her chin and looked over at the dark chestnut brown face that was looking back at her, pointing at the stool next to hers. He was alright looking, not gorgeous. Bright eyes, a small gap in his white teeth, dressed clean yet rugged in a light grey Sean John t-shirt and jeans. He was definitely a thug.

"No, you can sit there," she said offering a small smile back.

The brother sat down. "So what's a pretty girl like you doin' in here this early."

"Just having a drink. What about you?"

"Same. I need to take my mind off some shit."

"Oh yea, me too."

"Like what? What's wrong with you?" he asked rubbing the side of his nose and making a strange sound.

"Nothing you'd be interested in knowing about." Jacy looked down in her drink.

"How would you know that? What's your name?"

"Jacilyn, but my friends call me Jacy. You?" she said looking back up.

"My fam call me Popi."

"Is that your real name?" Jacy asked dryly as she turned to look back down at the bar.

"No, that's what I go by."

Jacy didn't really even care what his name was, called or given. She didn't know how much longer she could go on with these charades. For her, this whole conversation was just the beginning of another end. The constant filling of a bottomless void.

"So let me get your number. I'll call you and we'll go out, do something." Popi said getting to the point.

Jacy sighed.

Without another word, she pulled a pen out of her purse and wrote her number down on a napkin. She passed it to him. He would be her next temporary distraction. But something would have to give soon. Something. Because as far as she was concerned, thugs were only good for a little fun.

acknowledgements

Thank you to God, and my family —
for believing in and being there for me.

THUGS ARE FOR FUN:
Part Two...

Here are the questions on everyone's mind:

Will Jacy *ever* settle down?

Will she swallow her pride and fly to Atlanta to be with Kevin, or try to reconcile with Rich?

Will Terrell retaliate?

One question can be answered for sure. YES! There will be a sequel to *Thugs are for Fun*. Keep a look out for **the sequel.**

* * *

www.JazoliPublishing.com

Give Your Feedback

Provide your own personal feedback on the story. Your opinions may actually be reflected in the sequel!

www.JazoliPublishing.com/feedback.html

about the author

J.Gail has been writing creatively on and off
for the past decade. *Thugs are for Fun*, the story
of a young black woman's life in the new
American millenium, is her first novel. The
author currently resides near Philadelphia.

Give the gift of the exciting book

THUGS ARE FOR FUN

to Your Family and Friends!

Check your Local Bookstore or Order Here

☐ YES, I want _____ copies of *Thugs are for Fun* at $14.00 each.

☐ YES, I am a bookstore, distributor or wholesaler interested in purchasing *Thugs are for Fun* for our inventory. Please send me more information.

─ ∙ ─ ∙ ─ ∙ ─ ∙ ─ ∙ ─ ∙ ─ ∙ ─ ∙ ─ ∙ ─ ∙ ─ ∙ ─ ∙ ─ ∙ ─ ∙ ─ ∙ ─ ∙ ─ ∙ ─

Please include $2.50 shipping and handling for one book, $1.50 for each additional book. Pennsylvania residents **must** include 6% sales tax. Payment must accompany all orders. Allow 3-10 days for delivery.

My check or money order for $_____ is enclosed.

Please charge my ☐ Visa   ☐ Mastercard   ☐ Discover

Name _____

Organization_____

Address _____

City/State/Zip _____

Phone _____

E-mail _____

Card #_____ Exp. Date_____

Signature _____

(over)

- For my records -

I just ordered _____ copies of

Thugs are for Fun

My book(s) are scheduled to arrive 3-10 days from:

_____
Today's Date

Call or fax 888-715-9599
if you have any questions that can't be answered on our
website: http://www.JazoliPublishing.com.

Make your check or money order payable to
Jazoli and return with this form to:

Jazoli Publishing
P.O. Box 1316
Code B-OF144-1
Brookhaven, PA 19015

www.JazoliPublishing.com
This is real life.
It ain't no fairytale.